OF SILVER BELLS AND CHILLING TALES

Edited by
TIFFANY CURRY, TARA JAZDZEWSKI, SEAMUS
KING, AND ALEXA ROSE

Printed in the United States of America

First Printing, 2020

ISBN 978-1-7357905-7-2

Jazz House Publications
300 Lenora Street # 1119
Seattle, WA 98121
www.JazzHousePublications.com

Supervising Editor: Tiffany Curry
Cover art: Fay Lane
Formatting: Nicole Scarano

CONTENTS

SANTA'S HELPER   1
Michael Booth

FOURTEEN STEPS TO HOME   27
Twinkle M

THE CHRISTMAS PARTY   57
Shana Chartier

CINDERED ELLA: A CHRISTMAS   85
STEAMPUNK TALE
Edy Fudge

MY OWN BUTTONS   109
Mariev, Erie Matriarch

GHOULS JUST WANT TO HAVE FUN   157
Stephen Oliver

LOST AND FOUND   183
Clark Boyd

RAIN MUST FALL   205
R.A. Gerritse

MY WAR ON CHRISTMAS   227
Christopher Yusko

TRADITIONS   253
Craig Crawford

YOU BETTER WATCH OUT   275
David Allen Voyles

About The Authors   295

SANTA'S HELPER

MICHAEL BOOTH

I am a Santa's Helper. My job is to drive people, who are loaded down with packages or too tired to walk, across the vast parking lot at Lenox Mall. Mostly I get elderly ladies in high heels and ham-sized thighs or young kids who want to drive my Santa Mobile, a converted golf cart, or sit in the small bed where the packages go. Of course, that is against mall policy.

My outfit is a red-striped sports coat, two sizes too big for me, with a white plastic name tag stuck into the coat's pocket that says in big, red letters, "Santa's Helper." The coat makes me look like a soprano refugee from an old barber shop quartet; you know, the white guys in the curly mustaches and hideous double-breasted coats with shiny buttons who sing about wild Irish roses and sweet Adelines or some meaningless babble. They do it all with a smile.

So do I.

When the umbrella lady, I called her, hit me with her parasol handle, luckily made of cheap plastic, because I turned down the supposed wrong row of cars, the one she had been screeching at me about during the entire ride, I smiled.

When the young kids reeking of peppermint candy and belching fountains of soda fizziness try to grab the wheel with their sticky fingers or push the gas pedal, I smile.

When the general manager of the four-story department store lectures me on the solemn duties of representing first, the mall, second, his department store, and third, ole Saint Nicholas himself, who is in reality Sherman Brown, a car mechanic from Bogart, I smile.

I smile at the cold, constant rain that has fallen on the city since the Christmas season began on the day after Thanksgiving. I smile at the clear plastic flaps of my Santa Mobile that I let down when it rains and which barely keeps the water out but let's all the cold air in.

Mostly I smile at the brown-haired girl who works in the dry warmth of the Hallmark card shop situated right on my corner. I smile because I am in love with her and didn't even know her name until a few days ago.

She has a radiant smile, a smile that melts the cold; a smile that is at once so beautiful yet so unpretentious. Like my favorite female actress, Katharine Ross, her straight white teeth gleam through perfectly-formed, movie-star lips. But when she is laughing, her mouth turns north on one side and south on the other. Her brown eyes bulge out and her diminutive nose wiggles from side to side. I swear once her ears seemed to grow three sizes bigger. This is unconfirmed because I only saw it happen that one time.

Her most alluring feature is a small beauty mark on her lower right cheek that leads your eyes to her glorious mouth.

"It is a fake," said Delbert Forinsky, my fellow Santa's Helper, who graduated from Dykes High School four years ago. He was the class president and homecoming king and star point guard and total jerk who can't get a job because he is such a jerk. He only works here because of his jerk dad, the general manager of the main department store.

"Yeah, my buddy Jake used to take her out. She was crying about some stupid stuff and Jake said the beauty mark began to run down her cheek. Her name is Melanie Bucco, by the way."

I don't know Jake, but I suddenly hate him. The lying creep. He probably never dated my love anyway. Delbert is such a jerk. He is probably making the story up on the fly.

Delbert and I are supposed to be loading our carts with straw angels from the underground storage area to replace the ones that have blown apart on both sides of the department store during the wind storm last night. Well, I'm loading and Delbert is smoking a cigarette.

I am really thankful that Delbert is abusing me by making me do all the heavy loading because, unexpectedly, I know her name. I can quit calling her my brown-eyed beauty-marked babe. She is Melanie.

"A cup," Delbert assured me as I dumped another four straw angels into my cart. "Jake felt her up once at the movies. Said there was nothing there."

Jake's jerkiness went off the scale.

Delbert smoked another cancer stick while I loaded his cart with straw angels. I left him in the murky musty storage area, goofing off as usual. I wanted to get back to my corner to see Melanie.

"You do the east side and I'll do the west," I yelled as I sputtered away.

I didn't see her at the front cash register. The dour middle-aged fake blonde shop owner, who looks to be a hybrid of Jayne Mansfield at 64 and The Wicked Witch of the West at 90, glared as some red-headed kid passed her a dollar to purchase a Christmas card, probably for his mom. She didn't smile.

I got out of the cart, walked past the bland concrete columns to peer into the shop window. She was in the back wrapping a porcelain bird in green and red paper. Melanie and her customer were having a fine time talking about the weather or the season or the porcelain bird. Melanie was so bouncy and so dopey all at once, thrusting the paper into the large, white box like it was a magic trick. It made a rush of warmth flow down my spine.

"What are you doing?" The guttural rush was coming from the general manager's mouth. He had thrust his head around the column. His words had the smell of roast beef and onions wrapped all around them.

"Uh, you told me to watch out for customers. This lady about to leave the store has just purchased a fragile, porcelain bird. You wouldn't want her to break it, would you," I said, with a smile, of course.

"Oh," he said, straightening up to his full five feet five inches of organizational supremacy. "Well." He was lost for words, dazzled at my efficiency and take-charge attitude. He didn't smile.

Just then, the lady with the bird exited the store. Melanie held the door for her as I scampered over. "May I take this, please, mam, and offer you a ride in my Santa Mobile?"

"Why, yes, young man. I'll take you up on that offer," she said. Melanie held the door as the lady handed me her tightly wrapped package. I could see the hazy winter light twinkling in Melanie's eyes. All I could mumble was, "Thanks for holding the door."

"You're welcome," Melanie replied matter-of-factly, but for me it was as if she were whispering, "Yes, yes. I'll follow you anywhere."

The lady walked swiftly past me and ducked into the back seat of the cart. She held the flap and, patting the seat beside her, said, "Right here, Santa's Helper."

Before I could get into the cart, the general manager motioned me over to where he had been watching me intently from behind the concrete column. "We may have to close early tonight," he said. He made it sound as if the Viet Cong were cruising up the Chattahoochee River to invade the city. "Ice storm is coming. But you and I will be the last ones to leave, understand?"

I didn't smile. "Sure," was all I could reply.

I dropped the lady off at her 1965 white Pontiac Bonneville in row W across from the Colonial grocery store. The packaged bird went into the trunk. "Thank you so much, Santa's Helper," she said. "Here."

She gave me a dime tip. I smiled.

Small pellets of ice began falling as I watched the Cadillac slowly make its way to the exit. Over at the grocery store, pandemonium was in progress. Atlanta is such a weird city. If there is a weather report of possible snow or ice, every grocery store, convenience store, and fruit stand is simultaneously hit by an anxious mob intent on buying only three things: milk, bread, and beer.

Two booted women, one raven-haired and the other an almost silver blonde, in skirts too short for their age, were pushing a pair of baby strollers through the icefall. I stopped to offer my Santa Helper's assistance. They instantly halted in a one-more-step-and-you-are-dead mode.

"Can I give you a lift ..."

Before I could finish my sentence, raven hair snarled, "No!"

Silver blonde followed with an equally snippy "We can do it!"

I noted that raven hair's stroller held four gallons of milk and six loaves of enriched white bread, while silver blonde's stroller was straining under the weight of a pony keg. Beer brand indeterminate.

"Kids get the milk and bread. Beer is for the old folks," Delbert would've said. I drove to the other side of the mall to let him know we might be closing early. He was, as usual, sitting in his cart ignoring the straw angels and anyone who came up asking for a ride. "Dad already told me to get home. He wants me to stop by the store on the way." Probably to buy beer. No milk or bread at the house of jerks.

"Enjoy it, sucker," he said, flicking his still-lit cigarette into my Santa Mobile as he drove away, laughing. I quickly kicked the butt out into the little pile of slushy ice that had gathered at the curb. The ice came down harder. A man in a furry coat and shiny new shoes slipped on the sidewalk right in front of me.

"Are you OK, sir," I asked, jumping out to help him up.

"Where did this crap come from?" he said to no one in particular.

"Just started," I said, giving him a hand up. "Let me give you a ride to your car."

"What? OK, I guess." He picked up the long Davidson's box he had dropped. I tried to take it from him but he would not release his grip, so I led him to the cart. He jumped in, shaking the ice off his slicked back greasy hair with a deliberate sweep of his hand.

"I'm way over on the other side of the mall," he said as the old Santa Mobile lumbered into motion, spewing the smell of gasoline behind us.

"It will take us a minute but I'll get you there dry," I said, looking at him in the Santa Mobile rearview mirror I had installed myself.

"You go to school?" he asked, distractedly, looking from side to side.

"Yes, sir. I go to college out in Carrollton."

"What are you majoring in?"

"Girls, mostly," I replied with a big smile.

"Good," he said. "If you find out how they operate, let me know. I've been married for 23 years and I still have not got a clue."

"No offense, sir, but you don't look like a henpecked husband."

He chuckled softly. "Henpecked? No. I had four great years of marriage."

"I thought you said you had been married for 23 years."

"Yes, yes I did," he said, leaning up to press his chin over the front seat. "Four great years followed by four miserable kids. The oldest is about your age, 19. The wife kept pouring out these kids. I couldn't stop her."

I glanced back at him with my most incredulous look.

"OK, so I had something to do with it. But being a mother changed her into ..." He couldn't find the right word. He sat back in his seat, silent. I didn't press the issue.

"My mom and dad have been married for almost 30 years. They spent a few years traveling around the country as a magic act, The Mysterious Merchisons, playing mostly VFWs and county fairs. My dad says I was conceived in Platt City, Missouri, during the first snow of the year. Dad says that is why he can't tell me anything; he has to show me. Missouri. The Show Me state, they call it."

"Uh huh," he said. "They still in the magic business?"

"No, sir. After I came along, mom made dad move back home. He works for the gas company. My mom is the front desk clerk at the motel over on the interstate," I said. "But dad still pulls a fork out of his nose at dinner whenever we have company."

This made the man laugh out loud.

"What do you do?" I asked.

He took a moment to ponder the question. Out of the side of his mouth he announced softly, "I'm the financial vice president for the Love 'Em Bra and Panty Company." Poor, miserable guy. "Shape up or ship out, that's our motto."

For some reason, that was the funniest thing I had heard all day. I laughed so hard that I could not catch my breath. I tried to stop but couldn't suppress it. Then I noticed the man was laughing harder than me. He kept hitting his leg, he was laughing so fiercely.

He was still laughing when he tapped me on the shoulder. "I think that was my row we just passed. Ha-ha-ha."

"On it, sir."

I whipped the cart into the next row and scooted to the end. Just as I turned the corner he shouted, "Stop. That's it."

We were sitting behind a brand new 1972 fire engine red hard-top convertible BMW, the one with the teeny tiny triangle rear windows on each side. It was ungodly. The car actually took my breath away.

"Now that's what we need for our Santa Mobile," I said in a way that let him know I was thunderstruck.

"Cost just a few bucks more than I just paid for this dress," he said, looking at the long, unwrapped box. He tossed it nonchalantly behind the driver's seat of heaven's sports car. He carefully removed his furry coat, folding it tenderly, then placing it gently on the passenger's seat.

"Well, Merry Christmas, sir," I said, not taking my eyes off the BMW.

Before I could turn the man reached into his coat pocket and withdrew his wallet. "Here, kid."

He handed me a five-dollar bill. He could have handed me the keys to the car and I wouldn't have been more surprised.

"Oh, uh, this is twice as much as I make in an hour."

"What, is that all?" he tittered, reaching into the wallet to bring out another five-dollar bill. "Merry Christmas, kid, and thanks for the ride."

Ten bucks! The sky had opened up to deposit a near fortune into my frosty hands. The BMW threw ice onto my gasping Santa Mobile as he spedaway, slipping slightly, into the gray evening. I stood there a couple minutes fingering the green bills over and over again. Ten bucks! Finally, I stuffed the bills into my empty wallet. I took them immediately out to make sure they had old Abe's face printed on the front. Old Abe wasn't smiling. I smiled.

On the way back to my corner, I picked up a delightful family of six, five of whom were screaming little creatures devoid of any good holiday cheer. I felt sorry for the mom, who must have just turned 35 or so, having to spend her senior years caring for a tribe of brats. Yet she remained calm in the face of chaos. She even had a slight smile that really made her look cute, not that I go for older women, especially one with five progenies destined for either long stretches in prison or the life of a gangster guru with some obscure cult religion out West.

"Could you make a quick stop at the grocery store, please? I have to pick up some milk and bread."

Have a beer on me, lady.

Her heathens made chirping noises as she exited the Santa Mobile, her youngest clinging to her small, overused breasts. Despite her admonitions of the calamity to come if they misbehaved, the brats proceeded to climb all over the seats, the small bed in the back, and attempted to ascend to the moldy canvas top. I halted the attack at that moment.

"Oh, you better watch out,

you better not cry,

you better be good,

I'm telling you why.

Santa Claus is coming to town."

They all popped back into their seats and joined in. This signaled a round of Christmas songs that somehow simmered the roaring beasts as we launched into "Rudolph the Red-nosed Reindeer," and "I Wish You a Merry Christmas," all off-key and louder than the carbon-spewing engine of the old cart.

We had just started "Frosty the Snowman" when the mom came back in tears, her arms empty save for the screaming infant slung low on her hip.

"They are out of milk and bread," she cried.

Her brats swarmed around her with sympathetic hugs. One of her girls cooed, "It's all right, mommy."

Who turned off the holy terror switch?

"Hold on, mam, maybe I can get you some milk and bread."

I pushed the gas pedal as hard as I could. We slid with a crunch through the still falling ice around the corner and down the hill to the grocery store loading dock. No one was there so I jumped up to look through the open door. There, stacked neatly along the wall, were two metal baskets filled with Atlanta Dairies milk jugs. Down from there was a pallet of Colonial enriched white bread standing idly by a mountain of little bottles of Coca-Cola in six-pack cartons. Further down a pair of disheveled employees were hurriedly tagging milk jugs with a price gun. They never saw me.

I liberated two jugs of milk, two loaves of bread, and a

carton of little Coca-Colas.

"Hold these," I told the oldest two brats when I returned, handing them the milk and bread. I sat the carton of Coke on the floorboard next to me.

The mom couldn't stop crying, which triggered another round of sympathetic hugs from her yelping brood.

"Did you just steal from that store?" she asked through a waterfall of tears.

"No, mam," I lied. "Gave the guy in there five bucks."

That produced even more tears. She reached up from her back seat to hold my shoulder. No, she gripped my shoulder like she was going to hang on forever.

"Thank you. Thank you, Santa's Helper," she blubbered. "Now what do we say to the nice man, children?"

"Thank you," they all said in unison. The unruly mob had unexpectedly turned into blessed angels watching Romper Room quietly on a Saturday morning. The mood was quickly dispersed when son #2 hit son #3 in the stomach.

We reached her Range Rover just as the wind turned from a roar to a howl. The little quadrupeds scurried into the back seat where their merry melee continued. I picked up the bread from where it had been dropped on the ground. The mom opened her trunk, still shedding a few polar bear tears. I dropped the bread in, picked the milk up from the cart floor where it had been abandoned, stored it carefully between two large wrapped gifts, and put the carton of Cokes in last.

The mom looked at me. I thought she was going to kiss me but she just grabbed me for a big hug.

"You've saved the day, Santa's Helper," she whispered in my ear. If only she were Melanie.

The mom tossed the infant into the brawl in the back seat. She somehow produced a purse out of nowhere. She was pulling out dollar bills and counting change when I told her,

"Merry Christmas to you and yours. This is my present to you."

She stopped counting and went back to crying. "Oh my God," she exclaimed. "The spirit of Christmas is not dead."

This time she did grab me to plant a wet kiss on my cheek. She smelled of Pablum and honey and cinnamon. There may have been a hint of Old Crow in there, too. Good for you, mom. Whatever gets you through the night.

The ice pellets were getting bigger by the moment but she just stood there looking at me with dazed eyes. She turned without another word. The mom started the car. She glanced back at me one more time before she turned to scream at her brats. They drove away in a flurry of incomprehensible sounds.

The evening was getting darker. I could only see bright lights. It was a Chevy Impala with a hand extending from the driver's side frantically motioning me out of the way. They wanted that parking space. I was tempted to tell them all the milk and bread was sold out. However, the two hulks that emerged were most definitely not going for milk and bread. Both were dressed in worn jeans that had been rolled up at the bottom with matching windbreakers, one red and one black, over a white t-shirt. Their work boots chomped over the rapidly growing mounds of ice.

Moving away from the grocery store, I noticed that the main mall parking lot was barely occupied, just a few cars here and there. The pet store had already closed, leaving two orange tabby kittens frolicking in the picture window. The hobby shop was turning out the lights. The shoe store was still open but not a customer in sight. I assumed my position at the corner.

A long, two-flight stairway between the department store and card shop led to the open-air mall's main floor. A woman wearing a blue scarf, clear rubber booties over her high-heeled shoes, and a mink coat tried to maneuver down the steps by holding onto the metal railing. She slipped and slid down two steps before struggling back up.

Several people tried to brave the whole stairway but always turned back except for one guy who took five minutes to get to the bottom. He breathlessly shooed me away when I offered him a ride.The ice came down even harder. The pieces were getting bigger. More and more of the stuff accumulated on the stairway and walkways. I thought it looked magnificent, like a real ice castle.

I smiled at the ice storm. I smiled because there were no customers and Melanie used the downtime to rearrange the window display case. I smiled because I sat in my Santa Mobile in the freezing downfall and watched my love move about in her dark green denim skirt with a multi-colored blouse that had the top button undone. She wore some kind of silver necklace. Her brown, straight hair fell to her left side in cascades of light and dark. She is thin, not skinny, and about my height, not short, not tall.

With the ten bucks snuggled warmly into my thin wallet, I decided this was the day I would approach Melanie, not to confess my love but to just ask if she wanted to go to the movies. I would dazzle her by taking her to a French language film, *The Discreet Charm of the Bourgeoisie* (even though I could not pronounce "bourgeoisie") playing at the Ansley Mall Mini-Cinema. Then I would whisk her away to the Dunk 'n Dine for a late evening snack.

The plans were building in my head when the general manager ripped through the plastic flap with hot wheezing breath. His eyes had red blood vessels sticking out. His hands, holding two white boxes with plain blue ribbons, were trembling.

"This is a very important customer do you understand?" he demanded. I vaguely shook my head. "Don't talk to her. Don't ask for a tip. Just smile and take her to her car. Got it?"

Again I gave a nebulous nod.

The woman approaching the Santa Mobile carried a department store bag of stuff while two store employees on either side of her carried bags in one hand and an umbrella in the other, which still did not cover her portly backside. Her face gave the impression that she had just consumed a bad piece of fish, two sides of gunk, and topped it off with a glass of spoiled milk.

The Santa Mobile leaned heavily to the right when she landed in the back seat with a thud. The general manager laid one of the bags next to her feet. "This young man is going to take care of you. Just tell him where your car is and he'll have you there in a quick minute."

"Hrrpphh," she said, looking straight ahead.

"It has been our pleasure ..." The woman slapped the plastic flap in the general manager's face. He smiled.

"Row Q. A white Caddy," she said, pulling one of her bags close to her chest. "Don't you have any heat in this thing?"

"No, mam."

"I hate this time of year," she said, almost under her breath. "Damn prices go out the roof. You can't find anything in your size." Something in her grating voice sounded familiar. I glanced back at her scowling face. Oh, yeah! It came back to me. Her name was Rosemarie Lefkoff. Her daughter, Claudia, had been my lab partner my senior year. Claudia was really nice. And funny. We had a good time in that biology class. She smelled like a delicatessen, however, and kept bags of sausages in her purse.

"You would think that they would put a roof over this place," Mrs. Lefkoff said angrily.

From my rearview mirror, I saw Melanie and the card shop owner exiting their store. I would have turned back right then except the general manager was still standing there watching his prized customer descend into the darkness. My opportunity to talk with Melanie vanished.

"All the money I spend at this place you would think they would know more about me. Can't believe that asinine clerk actually said that to me … twice!"

I stopped listening to her at that point because she was obviously not talking to me. She was just talking. I kept hoping that I could get Mrs. Lefkoff to her car and on her way instantly. It was not to be.

"Slow down. I think my car is just up here," she said in a way that would make the President of the United States snap to attention. We puttered along all the way up and down Row Q without finding her automobile.

"Are you sure of the row?" I asked innocently.

"I know where I parked," she snapped.

"Could it have been Row O?"

"I know the difference between O and Q, Mr. Helper," she said indignantly.

We made another pass down Row Q, this time slower than I could push the cart, uphill, but no car.

"My car has been stolen," she gasped. "Take me back so I can call the police."

"Yes mam," I said, steering directly for Row O. Her decade-old faded Cadillac came into view. "Is this it?"

She gave no response. Her expression did not change from its frowning state. She merely got out of the cart and headed for the trunk. I thought I heard her say something like, "They need better signs in this place." I took her two white boxes and put them in the trunk, then took two trips to secure all the bags.

Mrs. Lefkoff had not turned around. She was straining to get into the driver's seat, so I said in my cheeriest Santa Helper's voice, "Happy Holidays."

She stopped struggling to get behind the wheel and turned back towards me. It took her a few seconds to get around. "What did you say?"

"Happy Holidays, mam." I smiled.

"And why did you say that to me? I've been Merry Christmased to death in there. Every clerk with those ludicrous bells jingling besieged me with 'Merry Christmas.' Why not you? Is there something about me that made you say 'Happy Holidays?'"

"Yes, mam," I said. "Your daughter, Claudia, and I went to school together. You came with her once to our Science Day exhibits. She told me she was Jewish, so I assumed you were, too."

Her frown disappeared. It wasn't exactly replaced with a big, toothy grin, but it was better than nothing. She kept blinking at me for a while. Finally, I tore myself away so I could race after my Melanie before she got to her car.

"Wait just a minute, Mr. Helper," she roared, making me stop.

With her bulbous head emerging from the open door she motioned me towards her. I edged closer, not wanting to get too close. She looked up at me with these big brown eyes, orbs of coffee with a little cream.

"They need more Helpers like you. Here," she said, holding out her Hulk-sized fist. I held out my hand and she deposited a Kennedy half dollar into my icy mitt.

I smiled. "Happy Holidays, Mrs. Lefkoff. And be sure to tell Claudia I said hello."

"Happy Holidays to you, Mr. Helper," she said, straining to fit behind the steering wheel.

The lower level of the mall was all closed. I parked my Santa Mobile at my usual corner. I must have sat there for 30 minutes before the general manager finally materialized from the darkened department store.

"You can go home after you let me off at my car," he said brusquely, tumbling into the back seat. I dropped him off at the only car remaining in the parking lot: a some-what blue 1966 Olds Toronado.

I didn't see any busses when I parked my Santa Mobile under the mall near the busted reindeer. I got to walk 12 blocks down the middle of Peachtree Street without a car in sight. The ice stopped falling before I got home.

The days following the ice storm were a mist of frazzled shoppers, continuously shrieking kids on a sugar-induced holiday high, hysterical mothers sobbing into their bulging shopping bags, emasculated husbands staring hopelessly into twinkling artificial lights, prepubescent giggling girls sharing muffled secrets and, well, mist, endless, heavy, grey mist that was so thick anything beyond 10 yards was a montage of prismatic images. The mist draped itself over the city like a foggy coat, starting in the morning as a grey sprinkling of ash-like globules, then growing into a somber, unrelenting cloud of grim H2O molecules. It was depressing.

More depressing to me, though, was I got shifted from Santa Mobile duty to the North Pole, which is what they named the large, fake igloo that held Sherman Brown, other-wise known as Santa Claus. The igloo was just a covering of cotton sheets painted to look like ice blocks over a creaky wooden frame. Two metal flaming torches framed the entrance where the kids entered and had their names listed in the big sign-in book labeled "Nice." The "Naughty" book was much smaller with the first few pages blank. It was supposed to be completely void except Delbert Forinsky scribbled a bunch of names in the back pages, names like Virginia Vulva, Patty Pud, Sandy Screwdriver, and Tricia Nixon.

My job was to corral the kids after the sign in and maneuver them to the big chair where Sherman, I mean, Santa sat in all his jolly old elf self. Sherman was great with kids. He calmed the crying ones, laughed with the cheery ones, and spoke quietly to the shy ones. Those who wanted to tug on his beard could pull all they wanted. Sherman's white beard was real, as was his rotund belly, and his laugh was all Santa, with a little Southern accent thrown in. Every kid gave Santa an enormous hug when they finished giving him their Christmas wish list.

Most of the moms grinned ear to ear when their kid was on Santa's lap. A few wiped away a tear. And almost all of them paid the $5 to have their kid's picture taken with the old guy. Dora Bender took the picture on what looked like an old-timey big camera, but it just hid a modern Polaroid that shot out the pictures in about 10 seconds. All I had to do was stuff the picture into a card that had "My visit with Santa" on the front with drawings of an igloo and reindeer. I would hand that to the Mom and steer them quickly to the exit with a hearty "Merry Christmas" and a smile.

I got to take a five-minute break every three hours, so I would rush down the flight of stairs that would take me to my old Santa Mobile spot near the card shop. Sometimes I would see Melanie. Most times I only saw the unsmiling blonde beast shop owner growling at a customer. Once Melanie saw me out the window and waved at me with a perky grin. I savored that moment over and over again. She knows me, I would tell myself; she knows we are to be together.

As the days grew closer to the big holiday, the North Pole line kept getting longer, and the tempers kept getting shorter. Moms in all their bright holiday cheer accused other moms of cutting into line or having their snotty kids sneezing on her snotty kids. One petite lady with big hair pushing a stroller trailing three wailing brats wheeled up to the front of the line and demanded to be let in. "I've paid a fortune to this mall. I don't have time to stand in this absurd line," she said to me, her nostrils belching smoke and her eyes burning brightly.

"Sorry, mam," I said calmly. "But as you see there are about 15 other families in line, some of them with strollers and kids …"

"I don't care about them. I demand that my kids get in now to see Santa."

"I, uh, you …"

Suddenly Sherman appeared behind me. There was an audible murmur from the crowd. "Now, Madam, we all must wait our turn. We must respect …"

"Listen, fat man, just let's take the picture and we'll be on our way, OK?"

Sherman ignored the woman. He bent down to talk with the youngest child, a smirking dark-haired girl with sticky peppermint residue dripping from her lips. "Your Mother is only going to get some lumps of coal and a batch of switches in her stocking if she doesn't get nice," he said in his sweetest manner. The girl looked at her Mother like she was a bug-eyed demon. "You better listen to Santa Claus," the little girl hissed. Sherman reached into his pocket and gave the little girl and the other two brats a bright red lollipop. He winked at them.

"Well, I … I'm going to report you to the mall management," the mom stammered as she twirled the stroller around and sped away.

"Ho, ho, ho," Sherman loudly replied. A few of the mothers clapped.

This merely signaled the beginning of what came to be known as The Igloo Incident, a dark chapter that mall management tried to cover up. It is hard to cover up a full-scale riot led by a battalion of fierce combatants using bottles of milk and plastic key rings as weapons.

It began when the department store general manager led the big-haired, big-mouthed lady in a charge to the front of the line, pushing past a silver-haired grandmother and her two grandkids who had patiently been waiting for almost half an hour.

"You will let this woman in to see Santa right now," he demanded, looking up at me with spittle flying from his lips. "She is one of this mall's best customers ..."

He was cut short by the grandmother whacking him over the head with her giant purse, which evidently contained all her possessions, except for her furniture and car, because the general manager slumped to his knees and had that far-away look in his eyes. "Back of the line," she hissed at the petite lady.

"Back of the line," came the chant from the rest of those waiting in line.

The general manager had risen wobbly to his full statue when the grandmother tried to whack him again, but she missed and hit the mass of hair on the petite woman, who looked shocked as she threw a brown teddy bear ripped from one of her kid's hands at the grandmother. It missed. The bear hit a little girl dressed in a coat covered in snowmen standing nearby. That girl's mother rushed forward to threaten the petite woman, who was unsuccessfully trying to hide behind the general manager.

"Stop … stop," the general manager yelled, which brought a temporary halt to the conflict. "Now this woman gets special treatment because …" His words were buried beneath a flurry of bottles, dolls, and rubber teething rings that came raining down on him. The seething, roaring crowd of mothers came at the general manager as if he were a kidnapper trying to steal their babies. They pushed forward like a red and green tide, churning up the winter air into a maelstrom. The general manager retreated. The petite woman, her face a cringed piece of flesh, fell back with her stroller and her brats, the oldest smiling broadly.

It appears the petite woman's stroller knocked into the flaming torch, setting it teetering from side to side. The yelling and finger pointing continued as the torch rocked back and forth, finally toppling onto the igloo wall. Even with the flames spreading rapidly across the cotton igloo, the melee went on. Only when old Saint Nick, Sherman himself, bolted out of the igloo entrance and shouted, "Fire!" did the battle cease. The chaos extended halfway down the mall as people darted away from the flames.

All the strollers turned, in unison, and began fleeing down the breezeway. It was worse than the Downtown Connector at 5 pm. I started to run as well. The general manager grabbed at my coat and screamed, "Coward." But I wasn't running away. I knew I'd find a fire extinguisher affixed to a nearby concrete post.

Throughout my life, I had seen the glass-encased fire extinguishers on school and hospital walls with a sign that read, "In case of emergency, break glass." At last, this was my hero moment. I took off my coat, wrapped it around my hand, and smashed through the glass. Only then, on one of the glass shards left, did I read, "Do NOT break glass." The door to the extinguisher swung gently open. I pulled the extinguisher from the case only to be pushed backwards by the escaping line of mothers.

I jumped up on the flower bed wall above the crowd that took me back to the burning igloo. Sherman had taken off his Santa jacket to beat at the inferno. By the time I pulled the pin on the extinguisher, the igloo was half gone. I put out the fire at the edges but could not reach the burning fabric above me. Sherman, all six-foot-four of him, grabbed the extinguisher from me. He easily doused the conflagration.

"Ho, ho, ho," Sherman exclaimed.

Dora had saved the camera and the Nice and Naughty books but not much else. There was a blackened reindeer with its horns missing still standing. A fake Christmas tree was a sullied remnant with no greenery and just one ebony ornament dangling precariously on a metal limb. There was nothing left of the sleigh except for two forlorn metal runners. Santa's throne was a pile of ashes.

When the fire department finally showed up a few minutes later, all the firemen could do was have their picture taken with Sherman. Old Santa asked me to be in the picture, too. The next day, the photo would appear in the Atlanta *Constitution*, in section C, above an ad for discount furniture and cheap cigars.

"Santa Saves Christmas" the caption read. It gave a few words about the igloo incident, leaving out the clash of mothers, and stated that Santa Claus had courageously snuffed out a raging fire that could have burned down the whole mall. Fat chance. Concrete doesn't burn too well, I understand.

Sherman was identified as The Jolly Ole Elf and I was tagged Santa's Helper.

The general manager slunk away when the firemen were there. Gradually, some of the mothers and kids came cautiously back towards the burned remnants of the igloo.

Sherman instructed me and Dora to set up the camera and put out the Nice and Naughty books. "No blaze is going to stop Christmas," he declared.

He went into the nearby shoe store to borrow a chair, a puke green chair with rips and tears in the plastic. "Kids don't see the chair. They just see me," Sherman said.

Before long the line began to stretch down the breezeway again. Dora framed the camera so it got a Christmas tree in a store front window behind Sherman. Santa, in a gesture of good will to men, waved the $5 picture fee for everyone. He spent extra time with each of the kids. One five-year-old girl was sobbing because of the burned reindeer. She thought it was real. Sherman assured her that it was a pretend reindeer because the real reindeer were resting up for the big night.

Down at the far end of the breezeway I spotted the petite lady dragging her kids behind her, followed by the general manager, who from 200 yards away looked to be at his groveling best.

Suddenly from the crowd came a blinding ball of light. Melanie. She parted the sea of strollers with a wave of her hand. She walked on air towards me. I nearly fainted when she put her hand on my shoulder. "Heard there was a lot going on up here," she said sweetly, her eyes gazing into mine. "Anybody get hurt?"

"Just the general manager's pride," I said. Melanie giggled.

She glanced at the soot and debris. "Well, take care," she said, the light receding down the breezeway as she walked away.

Two kids started poking me in the thighs. "We want our picture. Where is our picture?" they demanded. I couldn't take my eyes off Melanie. Her scent lingered around me.

"Hey, Santa's Helper," Sherman said. "What's the hold

up?" He followed my gaze to my precious love. "Oh," he said. Then, bending down to my ear, he whispered, "You ain't in her league, unless your family got money I don't know about."

His words hit me in the gut. Did he know Melanie? Or did he know me? The confusing thoughts swirled about as the kids screamed and kicked me for their picture. When my shift was over, I hustled down to the card shop. Melanie was not there. Over the next few days, whenever I could pull away from the brats and strollers, I tried to see Melanie. She was never there.

On Christmas Eve, the lines grew much shorter and eventually disappeared. Most of the kids were at home with visions of Mr. Potato Heads, Easy Bake Ovens, and Hot Wheels in their sugar-coated brains. Their parents, on the other hand, were frantically searching the mall stores for that elusive final gift that will ensure their enshrinement in the Parents Hall of Fame.

I was assigned once again to the Santa Mobile. Eric Trout, a little guy with a perennial runny nose and acne, had taken my old corner near the card shop. His cart was new, bright red, with a horn. But we shared the corner because it was busy. I'd take my passengers to their automobile, profusely thank them for my 10-cent tip, and hurry back to the corner to watch Melanie. This, I decided, could be the only time I could talk to her; seduce her with my witty words and dashing figure, despite the funny red-striped coat I wore.

Today the same grey mist mixed with globules of dreary rain shrouded the mall.. The hazy weather made the bright Christmas lights glow, however. Most people were cheerful and smiling. They made me smile, too. Others were steely eyed, desperately tired folks who spent too much money or didn't find what they wanted.

"They ought to make Christmas illegal," a fat man said as he wheezed a raspy breath.

"Wouldn't make the merchants happy," I replied.

"Hrmph. They're making a full year's profits in just a few days," he said, shifting some of the six bags of stuff to the floorboard.

Even that old Scrooge could not bring me down on this day.

By six o'clock, the crowds departed and the stores closed. Eric left to park his cart underneath the mall and get home for the big night. I stayed at my post as the rain drops swelled in size. And then, through the murkiness, I could see Melanie exiting the card shop. She shut everything else out for me. I only saw the twinkling of my love's eyes in the early evening gloom.

"Hey," I shouted. "Let me take you to your car."

"Great," she said with a sound like syrup pouring into my ears. "I'm afraid I parked way out in the Y lot."

"No matter," I said, pulling the plastic flaps aside so she would have to sit up front with me.

"Is this your last day?" she asked as we sputtered away.

"Nah. They want me to come in next week to start taking down the decorations. You?"

"The owner wants me to come in to change out stock, but I told her I have to go on vacation with my family," she said. We can be family, I thought. "But I'm just tired of this job. I'll take a week off before I go back to college."

She gave me that silly crooked smile. It warmed my toes.

"Where do you go?" I stumbled on my words, I think, but she understood.

"Athens. I made enough this Christmas to get my own apartment. That should be fun," she said.

Yes, I thought, that would be fun to share an apartment

with you. We could have a second-hand sofa, Goodwill tables, and a brand-new bed. We would eat Cheerios and Cheetos and love it.

Her brown hair had droplets of water reflecting the red and green lights of the mall. Her beautiful beauty mark stood out from her porcelain skin. There should be a sculpture of that face, I thought, nearly hitting a curb.

"What are you getting for Christmas," I asked, desperately trying to keep the conversation moving.

"Oh, the usual: blouses, socks, a dress or two." Then her eyes glazed over. I was sure she was going to lean over and kiss me. I could feel the love pouring from her heart. "And I can't wait to see what Delbert got me."

Stabbed in the gut. Repeatedly. That is what it felt like.

"Delbert … Delbert Forinsky?" I gasped.

"Yes, do you know him? His family is very well off. Mr. Forinsky is the general manager of the department store here, you know."

My glittering future, shattered in pieces, was last seen scattering behind my dawdling Santa Mobile. Melanie kept talking but I didn't hear a word until we pulled up behind her bright yellow Ford Pinto with a big stripe down the middle.

"Well, thanks for the ride. See you around," Melanie said, pulling the plastic strips apart. She stepped out of the cart, and my life apparently, with a bounce into the now steady rain. Before she let the strips go, she turned to me.

And there, on her face, was a long, thin ribbon of black coming from her beauty mark. It ended with a swirling blob of blackness to the right of her lips.

"Oh, I almost forgot. Merry Christmas," she said, cheerfully.

I smiled.

FOURTEEN STEPS TO HOME

TWINKLE M

It was the snowiest night in the history of the town of Valdez, Alaska.

From late afternoon, the flakes fell from heaven to grace the earth. By late evening, they turned to balls: no longer light, they registered when darkening the coats of those foolish or desperate enough to venture out.

Most townspeople took refuge from nature under the humble roofs of their houses, crouching within and munching on the warmest of foods. They knew it would be a deep snow.

When the darkness fell, turning the world into a contrast of pure black and blinding white, the houses of humans seemed like unnecessary blots on the scenery. A man stumbled his way through the knee-deep snow, his black coat spotted with white. Teeth gritted, he fell against the first door his frozen gloves landed on, the thump echoing through the silent house. The lone figure, sitting curled up on the sofa before the crackling hearth looked up, alert as a cat.

It was an unusual house. Beside the fire stood a ready fire-extinguisher, arm's length from the woman. Near the door stood a heavy crowbar; it would've intimidated visitors, but the few who came had become used to the sight. The windows were boarded up, though that could be because of the cold. Stairs led up to a second-floor rarely used unless they happened to host guests, while the front door stayed double-locked.

Hesitatingly, she undid the clicking locks.

~

HESTIA LOVED STORIES.

She didn't love stories like the next person did: fleetingly, as a means of distraction, or simply because they had nothing to do. No, Hestia loved stories with a passion she didn't feel for anything else; sometimes, she thought she loved stories more than people.

If you looked for them, stories were everywhere. She saw them in the two coffee cups left untouched in the café visible from her bedroom window, the discarded sock left on the pavement, the man walking without a coat in cutting winter air, the closing notes of a song, the fading voice of a singer, in the wrinkles of the old, and the laughter of the young.

Stories *were* everywhere, but none of them resembled those in the novels.

On that night, heavy with snow, a thump at the door interrupted her reading of *A Time Traveler's Wife*.

She straightened, her sluggish heart picking up.

Who would knock on my door? No one ought to be out in this weather, she thought.

When a minute of silence followed the premier knock, she convinced herself it had been her imagination or some animal. Her eyes had turned to the pages bathed in the firelight when the second knock came, more purposeful, pointed, and harder to pass off as a mistake.

She stilled, staring at the fire as though it would offer suggestions. When the flames merely broke the silence of the air, she had to turn to her mind.

She could ignore it. Perhaps the person would think there was no one home, or suppose the inhabitants had already headed to bed, and move on. But the snow... it wasn't terribly difficult to freeze to death in temperatures that low. If the person died...

Gritting her teeth, she carefully placed her bookmark and shut the book. Moving slowly, she rose from the sofa and shrugged off the shawl. Her hope of the person leaving disappeared after the third knock. Hands clenched, she pulled the door open by a crack.

"Are you crazy? Open-open the hell up! I'm freezing out here," the man, bundled in a coat only thick enough for appearances, snapped. His voice sounded wheezy like an old man, which prompted her to pull the door open. She let him hurry inside, then shut it with a snap.

"Three knocks! And it's a fricking avalanche out there."

Hestia stood totally still, watching the man curse and rub his ice-studded gloves over his arms. She had just allowed a stranger into her home.

What was I even thinking? She questioned.

You weren't, her mind retorted.

For all I know, he could be hiding a dagger in his sock.

Side effect of reading too many fantasy novels.

"Are you deaf?" He inquired when she had spent two whole minutes in absolute external silence and chaotic internal argument.

She shook her head. "No."

"Good. Do you have a heater?"

"There's a hearth."

Her words made him more upset.

"A hearth? You live in Alaska and don't have a heater? Are you crazy?" He repeated, his voice muffled under the woolen scarf, but it managed to convey his annoyance.

"There is a heater. But I thought the hearth would do."

"Look, woman, it's in the negatives out there. It's like the bloody freezing waters of the Atlantic when then the Titanic sank. Unless you want me to die, get that heater going."

HESTIA HATED STRANGERS. She didn't just hate them; they scared her. They were like the sight of the smallest of flames to those who've seen entire forests burning; the slightest mistake could leave nothing but ash, so you learn to watch out for candles.

Worse still, they reminded her of things better left alone.

Sitting before her hearth, on her sofa after carelessly placing her book on the rickety side table, the stranger warmed himself. He wasn't old, as his voice had suggested. Judging by the shock of black hair and his fit but unathletic built, he seemed to be in his late twenties.

He did fuss like an old man, though.

"Have you switched that heater on?" He inquired, tugging at his coat sleeves.

"Yes," she replied, checking it to be sure.

"Hmph. You should replace it; doesn't provide heat at all. Haven't you got any shawls?" He asked, when his coat sleeves proved insufficient.

"Just the one? Fine. I'll adjust," he said, bundling himself in the shawl she handed over. *Can't wear a proper coat and has the nerve to comment on my shawls,* she thought.

"You know, I don't think it's the fault of the shawl. Or the heater." *Maybe he has some humility.* "It's the house itself.

Cold, draughty… by the way, have you thought of replacing this rug? It doesn't decrease the floor's cold at all."

No humility.

He reached inside his coat and she tensed. Would he take out a gun? But no, he was merely using his handkerchief.

Did he have a knife concealed somewhere? Did that twitch mean he was about to attack?

As apprehensive as she felt, it seemed unlikely that the man had any ulterior motive. No one wanting to attack or steal would be so downright rude.

"Why do you even live in a place this cold?" He continued without waiting for a response. "Impractical. We aren't polar bears. Humans should live in warm places."

When she didn't respond, he went on. He seemed quite adept at conversing with himself.

"But we've to take over everything. It's not really pleasant in the summer in the south though. Don't even get me started on the equator. Sweating all the time! At one point, you're so frustrated you just want to pull all the clothes off. Guess that leaves us humans nowhere, does it?

"Honestly, don't you talk? I've been chattering for five minutes straight. Okay. Let's start proper. I am Will, short for William, obviously. And you are?"

"Hestia," she supplied, eager to appear as normal as possible.

"Hah! The Greek goddess? Didn't know people still used that name. Well, hello Hestia, it's as nice to meet you. At least, as nice as it can be when it's the frozen pits of hell outside."

"Why were you out in the snow?" She managed to ask, determined to undo the impression of being dumb.

"Hestia speaks, then! Well, I don't live here. I had the misfortune of being the owner, or rather, renter of a crap car

31

that decided the outskirts of the town was a good place to stop. It further refused to move, which compelled me to walk. But then the snow started battering my head, and I only reached here just now, when a lady named after the goddess of home downright ignored a suffering stranger for two whole minutes."

What do I say to that? Hestia was the last person on Earth to know the answer. Nonetheless, she searched around for something sensible to say.

"I'm sorry for earlier."

With that, she picked up her novel and sat down on the opposite, rarely used, sofa and began to read. Or tried to read. She felt painfully aware of the stranger in the room and the mingled scent of cooled sweat and dirty snow and cologne coming off him. What's more, he gazed at her steadily, without abashment or politeness, and it was hard to ignore.

She didn't confront him. Hestia didn't like confrontation. Instead, she hyper-focused on the novel, on getting her concentration straight and re-immersing herself in the captivating tale.

"If you aren't reading, ma'am, why the pretense? Just drop the book."

"I am reading," she said, stung.

"Clearly not. Your fingers are damaging the cover, your eyes aren't moving, and your lips are pursed so tightly that they're almost invisible. Tell me, do you have something against conversation?"

"I... you're a stranger."

"Totally. And?" He said, the black of his eyes glowing in the firelight, as though the fire dwelled within them. He had striking eyes. The black of them was hard to find, but they were remarkable for something more noteworthy than colour.

They were eyes that fixed on something and gazed levelly at it, making it impossible for the surveyed to look away or ignore. She wondered what kind of power those eyes commanded.

"And what?"

"I'm a stranger, but you've let me in for whatever reason. I suppose it's quite natural that we make general conversation."

"I don't do small talk," she stated plainly.

"Ah! That's good. You don't do small talk? Then tell me, Ms. Hestia, what do you think of the snow tonight? Is it poetic, or an inconvenience, or something else?"

Taken aback, she blinked at the man. What was he talking about?

"What do you mean what I think of the snow?"

"Well, I mean exactly that. I am of the opinion that snow is usually quite beautiful, as long as I'm bundled in warm clothing, sitting comfortably under a roof, or skiing. But stuck outside, without a vehicle and freezing my ass off? Then it's an inconvenience. What do you think?"

"I don't have an opinion on the snow," she replied, dismissive.

"No? Then what impression have I made?"

"That you have an opinion on everything."

He laughed. Booming, loud, and ringing like a gust of wind through unbounded grasslands. The walls hadn't heard such a laugh for a long time. For that matter, neither had Hestia.

"You aren't offended?"

"Why would I be? I know I do like to have an opinion on everything. It's a habit of mine. And this proves you aren't entirely dull," he said, some color returning to the cheeks that had hitherto been as pale as the snow.

"What are you doing in this town?" She questioned, pricked at his comment.

"Funny how I keep asking myself that," he said, then laughed at his own joke. "I'm traveling. For some reason, I thought visiting this place would be a good idea."

"Evidently not," she joked, not in the way people joke all the time. It sounded hesitant, touched by a shade of doubt.

"Why?" Will couldn't help but notice the hesitance in her joke.

"Why what?" She asked, already searching for where she might have gone wrong.

Who told you to say that? I was trying to have a normal conversation. Oh, please, as if you would know how, she thought.

"Why do you say it wasn't a good idea?" He elaborated, the fire dancing across his rather chubby face. He was lean and tall, the kind of fit people who exercised are. The round-ness of his cheeks would've given him a childish look, if not for his eyes. They were alive. Not pale or listless or just there, but alive, as though searching the surroundings for a new activity to take up. "Is it because you have to attend to a stranger on a cold night?"

"What? No, no. I mean, you were out in the snow. Knee-deep. That's not a good thing, is it?"

"Not really. But I don't call it a waste. See, my car conked out, but I also got to walk through snow! I've seen snow before, I've gone skiing, but walking through a silent place and watching the snow fall down and settle where it belongs... that's something you don't understand unless you see it. Tonight I came very near to dying of cold. Maybe I'm exaggerating and the doctor would have a thing or two to say about that, but I felt it. And, now I'm sitting here with a woman who's not interested in conversation, but who interests me very much."

Was this a move? Was that what he came here for? Attack, rape, steal, or simply kill? She dug in her toes, surreptitiously marking objects she could use for her defense. *But you're rubbish at fighting; didn't we clear that two months ago?*

"Oh, don't get worked up. I'm not a criminal," he reassured, correctly reading the cold hand of terror on her pale face. "You interest me, Hestia. Can I call you Hestia?"

When she nodded, he resumed: "As I was saying, you interest me, Hestia, because you live in one of the least populated towns on earth. You also have provided me shelter, albeit reluctantly, but didn't ask me any questions. And you're the kind of person who would be very interesting if—ignore the pun—I break the ice. Quiet people have the best stories."

"I... I've always lived here."

This wasn't strictly true, but the time spent outside had been so little, and so insignificant, it didn't seem worth mentioning.

"Always? That's a shame. I, for one, have been a moving bird for the last eight years or so. The longest I've put camp at a place since twenty is eight months, then off I go."

"Don't you work?" Yes, that sounded like a normal person question.

"This is my work!"

Had traveling become a job in the two months she'd stayed indoors?

"Um... what is your job?"

"It changes. I started out as a travel writer; I went to a college that made you travel around the world. Then, using my language as a tool, I worked as a tourist guide in Europe.

Right now, I work as a cruise ship officer while doing free-lance writing, but I'm on leave."

"Interesting," she commented, for lack of a better word.

"Truly. Anyway, what do you do?"

She should've anticipated the question when she'd fool-ishly posed hers. The firelight dancing across her drumming nails, she searched around for an answer long enough for him to pick up the reluctance.

"Either you work for a secret agency and are terribly good at your job, or you don't want to tell me. In either case, I'm fine with it unless you're a criminal, which would warrant extra care on my part and a duty on yours to share stories of your crimes. I hope you're not a serial killer who draws lonely men inside to murder them."

"Look, Mr. William-"

"Call me Will."

"Will, I'm not a serial killer. And I'm not interested in talking about my profession. Or anything about me."

Hestia of the past had always been painfully upfront. Lacking a filter, as everyone said. Hestia of the present, though quieter, still tended to speak thoughtlessly when she did speak.

"Good for you, I'm not into modesty and can talk of myself and topics that interest me at length. Does it snow this terribly every year?"

"No."

"Then it's deigned to fall on my head especially! Do you go skiing?"

"No."

"That's a shame. I love skiing. Feels like hurtling to my death. Have you ever felt like you were hurtling to your death?"

"No."

"It feels amazing. Scary, but humans love doing crazy things, don't we? Have you ever been stuck out there in snow?"

"No."

"I nearly froze to my death. Thank God I didn't lose a finger. Have you known anyone who lost a finger?"

"No, but I saw someone break their neck once. What do you think of that?" She snapped, irritated at his questions. For some reason, his colorless lips curved into a triumphant smile.

"I think I successfully got us past the mono-syllabic stage. You saw someone break their neck, uh? Who was that? Family, friend, relative? Embarrassing college crush you were being reckless with?"

"He was a stranger," she replied, already regretting losing control and mentioning Ethan.

"Stranger? That's strange," he said, smiling at his silly joke.

"You think it's funny?" She asked, her voice dangerously low. Hestia didn't get angry often, at least not at people, but Will had managed to accomplish even that. "He was a tourist. Like you. He was twenty-two, three years younger than me even then. His parents were both alive and healthy; heck, even his grandfather was still doing well. And it wasn't even his fault. Some car just came out of the blue and hit his motorcycle and snap. Despite the helmet, his neck clearly broke. And you think it's funny?"

"If I lost my mind at the death of every stranger, I wouldn't be able to go on." The unspoken sentence hung in the chilly air: like you seem to have been stuck. Instead, Will said: "But you know an awful lot about a stranger."

"I found it after."

"Why would you do that?"

"That's none of your business." It had been a mistake to bring up Ethan, to go into the details of his tragic demise, but she wasn't out of her mind enough to delve into why his death was so shaking. Or so impactful.

"True," he agreed, leaning back on his sofa. His cheeks were no longer the pale of death, his clothes almost dried. He looked comfortably settled on the old sofa for a long, warm night by the hearth. Sadly, the snow still fell, blanketing the earth, which ruled out sending him back to wherever the hell he came from.

"But I've seen deaths myself. When I was at a beach in Australia, some teenager went too far in and drowned. A fire started in one of the lodges I was staying at in Asia, and a couple of people got burnt. Trust me, you don't want to see a burnt body. Traveling does have its share of troubles. I'm not trying to devalue your experience, but death happens."

Ignoring his comment about death, she chose to focus on the others. She had never set foot outside the country, much less travel to the other part of the world. When Ethan died in New York (where she'd been studying), she had flown home like a scared goose.

"Why do you travel so much? I mean, after that fire... you could've died there."

"I could die here if there was an earthquake," he argued.

"That's highly unlikely. The house is made of very strong material. It'll last most earthquakes."

When she'd set foot in NYC, the skyscrapers, talking to the clouds, had sent a shiver of thrill down her back. Now, when she remembered the high-rising buildings, it was with a shiver of fear.

I had been crazy before, she thought. *Never even thinking of how I would be a piece of rubble if an earthquake struck.*

"I could have a heart attack right now."

"That's out of your hands. You can exercise and have a good diet and everything, but you could still get one. But traveling riskily... that's a personal choice."

"Oh, but you forget that when I saw that death, I also saw a mother clinging gratefully to the child the firemen had rescued. At that beach, I saw the sun kissing the waves, and the sky blushing at the gesture."

"But if you had been the one to die in the fire," she began, attempting to reason with the fanciful man, "then you wouldn't have lived to see those things at all. You would've been a crispy human toast!"

He laughed at the choice of words, but his eyes gleamed with a different kind of amusement. He seemed to enjoy her words, as if he saw something more than a twenty-five-year-old woman digging in her heels with home-scissor cut frizzy brown hair that ended at her pointed chin and further highlighted her sharp jawline. She felt as if he could see inside her flat brown eyes.

If Hestia heard that, she would have only one word to say: garbage. Reading it, spoken for characters was different. No one in their right mind would say that to her, or so she believed.

"You're missing the point, Hestia. Heard of that maxim, no pain, no gain?"

"Yes, but—"

"What's the point of living without being thrilled? Without loving your life? C'mon Hestia, it's not terribly hard to figure out. If you can understand that book on time travel, you very well can understand what I'm talking about."

"Oh, I do," she replied, sagging into the sofa and crushing the cushion beneath her. "I understand completely. You're one of *those*."

"May I know with whom have you categorized me? I like having an idea of my team."

"One of those with a romantic view of life. You know, living not existing, enjoying every day, blah blah blah."

"Oh, thank god," he said, relaxing into the cushions of his sofa. "I thought you were putting me with the other group. But if you're saying that I prefer to do something that I love rather than spend my life whining at a desk, then yes, I do prefer that."

"So everyone should pack their bags and leave home?"

"No!" He refused, animated. "If a computer programmer left his job to travel the world, it would be as pointless as me doing computer programming. And I have tried it; my father's into computers, and I epically sucked at the job."

Will was leaning forward on the sofa, and so was Hestia. Their feet dug in the floor, heads close enough that a slight push would result in a grand collision. The air somehow felt hotter with the combined heat from the fire as the debate bordered on outright argument.

Sensing defeat, Hestia snatched on another topic, finding an alternative attacking point.

"Your father? Does he approve of your job?"

Will's strained arms, the veins stark over the pale skin, sagged at her question and he settled back. Victorious, she sat back as well, awaiting the explanation that was bound to come.

Somewhere around the course of the conversation, she forgot to be afraid.

"My parents were abusive," he stated, clear and plain. He wasn't one to hide his past; *he* hadn't been the one to beat up his son, had he?

He looked at Hestia. He had met countless strangers, talked to hundreds, and retained contact with none. Of those, Hestia seemed to fall into the 'quiet, trauma-scarred, defeated in life' category. He sensed that neck-breaking had something to do with it, but there had to be more. He didn't ask; outright questioning was the most foolish way to deal with people who would rather not talk.

"Oh, I..."

"Please don't. You've got nothing to say and you're about to say something sympathetic that I'll have to pretend to like and I'd rather not to do that."

"On the contrary, I was about to say it's kind of obvious. You looked like a slug when you mentioned your father," she snapped.

Will grinned. He liked it when people dropped the pretense and got down to being real, no matter who they were. Snappish? Just do it. Quiet? Don't do forced conversation. Hate someone? Then don't pretend to love them.

"Side-effect of his shitty behavior. Was your dad any good?"

"He's pretty nice, actually. He lives with me, but he's out of town on some business. Guess I got lucky on that front," she said, her fingernails having stopped their anxious drumming. "Then you don't go to your parents' at all?"

"Not if I can avoid it. Acting like a normal family is terribly taxing. Wonder how those actors feel."

"They're not pretending in real life, are they?" She asked softly, the flames burning in her brown eyes. They made them gleam, gleam with the life that seemed to have gone out. Will always found himself drawn to people's eyes. If you paid attention, sooner or later, you would see them shine, turn away, droop, light up, dilate, and, once in a while, see a pair that speaks more than the lips. Hestia possessed that type of eyes.

"What happened to your mother?" He asked, quiet in the way people are when approaching a topic likely to end unhappily.

"Died when I was seven. Her car skidded on the snow. I don't really remember her."

That explained it. He saw Hestia's life, marred by the death of her mother by an accident in childhood, followed by years of normal life with her nice dad, and a life-changing moment with the death of the twenty-two-year-old. Sometimes, incidents leave us scarred in a way we can't even see.

"You didn't know the guy with the broken neck at all?" He asked, leading up to the moment when he would get the full story. A bit of empathy, prodding questions that don't seem interfering, and he would get the tale.

"It's not going to work," she said, staring point-blank at him.

"What's not going to work?" He asked, playing the oblivious innocent.

"That's not going to work either," she said, the hint of a smile playing at the tips of her bitten-red lips. "You're much too upfront to play the innocent card. I'm not falling for it."

"It works most of the time," he confessed, regarding the woman before him with the beginnings of respect. Anyone could read books, but reading people? That was something else.

"Not tonight. I'm not gonna get sentimental and give you a sob story. And I can see how much you want to hear one; you've been scouring for it since you set your foot in here. Kind of downplays your scorn for the book, doesn't it? You do like your stories."

"I like real stories, of real people. You would be surprised to find how many people's lives are worth writing a book about; at least one shocking incident. But stuck in your home, you've to make do with these..." He said, gesturing towards the forgotten paperback and the bookshelf behind her, but also to her, as though she were a forgotten story.

"I'm not stuck in my home," she said, a protective hand stretched over the book.

"No," he agreed, "You *choose* to limit yourself inside these walls."

Now that he'd realized it, the answer seemed easy: Hestia suffered from agoraphobia, with a touch of paranoia. She had somehow worked out that the only way to not die was to stay within her house, with its earthquake-proof walls, fire extinguisher, and god knew what securities.

"Will—"

Will sagged forward, hands pressed against his chest. Hestia jumped from her seat when his groan of pain ruled out the possibility of a pretense.

"Will? What is it?"

"H-Hurting. Like a jolt."

Hestia paled. The cold, the snow... everyone knew it could lead to a heart attack. Was Will having one?

"Pills..." he gasped, doubling over while still clutching his struggling chest.

"Pills? What pills?" She questioned, her voice rising.

"M-my bag. Heart problem..." he said, his voice dropping.

"Bag? Where is it?" She questioned as she ran around the room, looking near the table, the door, and in the fire, but finding none.

"Outside. Just-just right outside," he panted, and she stilled.

Outside?

"Hestia?" He asked, his pale face ashen. If he died...

"Have you-you got???" He couldn't get the rest of the sentence out. His eyes closed, and his head began to loll.

"Getting it!" She said, more out of instinct driven by fear rather than resolution.

Out of the periphery, Will saw her turn towards the door.

HESTIA STOOD AT THE THRESHOLD, the wind whipping against her sweaty face.

The outside world... Even clouded by fear, she could describe it by no other word—on that fateful night, the outside world's beauty shone. Like a fantasy straight out of a child's imagination. But it's the childish fantasies that come to haunt adult reality.

She swayed on the spot, her feet digging so hard she wondered how she didn't sink. Why the heck couldn't she just sink?

Will coughed, as though in warning.

He'll die... but outside?

Let's locate the bag first.

That was a very plain, very obvious attempt to buy time. But she lapped it up.

Squinting, her eyes zeroed in on the black backpack glaring out of the snow.

Why did Will have to drop it so far? One two three... fourteen steps. Oh God, fourteen steps.

The door trembled under her grip. Will's rattling breath rang in her ringing ears. Skin paler than the snow, she raised her foot. One step at a time. Her left leg was out of the threshold. She gazed down at it; her mouth dry. She swallowed.

Teeth clenched, she took the other step.

Oh god.

Her hand still held on to the door. Panting, she removed it. The bag hadn't moved closer. The snow settled on her feet, on her face, but she felt none of it. The wind cut through the branches of the neighboring spruce, but cold sweat froze on its way down her hammering chest.

Thirteen more.

Mustering all the strength within her, she took half of one more step. Breathing through her mouth, she completed it.

I can't let him die.

Two more steps, and her nails were digging in her skin.

What if a car hit me right here? Let's hope it doesn't. Seven more steps.

Once, after a month of staying indoors, she had imagined what it would be like if she ever managed to go back out. She was scared of stepping outside, but the lure of nature had been too strong. She imagined she would relish in the feel of the sun, or the sigh of the wind, or simply feel other-worldly at the breath of outside air.

But that night, she didn't notice the colors of the aurora borealis lighting up the sky, the way the stars winked at her through the flurry of snow, or the path her boots left from her house to the bag.

Upon reaching it, she snatched it up and ran the way back. Fourteen steps. Her heart thumped so hard she felt like she would die from it.

Once inside the safety of her haven, she went over to Will and sank beside him on the sofa. The short trip had sucked all the energy from her, leaving her as drained as an empty can.

But Will didn't reach for the bag.

God, is he already dead? Did I kill him with those baby steps?

Raising her head, she saw him sitting exactly where she'd

left him. Only his eyes were open, his hand lay casually by his side, and—the devil—a smile was playing across his face.

He certainly didn't appear to be on the door of death.

"Will? You're fine?" She asked, her voice low enough to signal either dangerous fury or sluggish defeat. Will took it to be the latter.

"Nothing happened to me," he assured, that smile still there. "You—" She snarled, jumping up, all exhaustion wrenched out with that smile.

"Calm down, Hestia. Take a breath."

"Take a breath? Seriously? You asshole, you made me go out and—"

"I did. I did make you go out and get my bag and all of that. But it was for your own good!" He argued, backing away from her as she panted with rage. Hestia looked very like the goddess would've in anger: ready to burn anyone to death in that very home hearth. Nothing could be as dangerous as the anger of the even-tempered.

"Don't you dare."

"But, deep down, you know it was right! I did the right thing. See, you went out and nothing happened," he said, in an attempt to quench the rage. Unfortunately, those turned out to be the very words he ought to have avoided.

"Nothing happened?" She screamed. "Who are you to decide for me? Who the hell you think you are? Coming in with your ungrateful ass, sitting on my sofa and giving me shit about my life? You were out there, stuck in the snow, and you would've died if not for me. This is my life, my damn problem. Stay the hell out of it!"

"Look, Hestia—"

He began, but she was none of the 'look, Hestia' anymore.

"No, you look, Mr. William Whatever," she began, her lip

curling. "You think you're so smart, so helpful. Oh, poor Hestia, can't even go out because she saw a stranger die right beside her. Let me help the weak soul! But you're a failure. You hear that? A failure. You ran from your shitty home and you travel the world and pretend to be enlightened or some crap, but you're just bitter. A bitter man who hides his inability to settle down under the cover of a desire to travel. You're a coward, Will. You only know how to run away!"

With those words, she stormed out of the room, her boots loud as gunshots.

William Whatever sat down on the sofa. Perhaps he ought to have left after the clear indication, but it was still snowing, and he had no will to die.

As the night deepened, Will thought about things he had been avoiding so thoroughly he hadn't even realized they were there. What had Freud called it? Repression: to repress anxiety-provoking thoughts to an extent that we become unaware of them.

He saw his life, beginning as a skinny boy who cowered under his father's rage and mother's reprimands, who would seek dark corners to hide and try to make himself as invisible as possible. He saw the rebellious teenager who stood up to his parents, and suffered the repercussions. He saw himself going away to college, never feeling settled in one place, always wanting to move to another, to somewhere new, to be unable to sustain relations for longer, to crave for someone new...

He thought he lived a terrific life. He still did. But... there wasn't a single place he could call home. Not a single person who made him feel at home.

No one had yelled him so imploringly as Hestia had that night, unless you counted his parents.

Should I not have forced her? He questioned.

No. She needed the push. Walking even that far… it must have been more helpful than she realized.

Maybe I was condescending… he thought, before he remembered how he'd acted.

Okay, I had acted condescendingly.

Now what? He wondered, looking around the house.

Should I go to sleep on that comfortable sofa, or possibly get myself yelled at again?

As he said, he liked it when people were real.

HESTIA SAT on the floor of her room, her back to the bed as she watched the snowflakes drift down beyond the façade of glass. It came down silently, drifting lazily to the bottom. Unhurried.

It reminded her of a day with her mother. She had been five. Six, probably. It had been during the summer months, if you could call it summer up there. She had run around all day long, forcing her mother to do a hundred different things until she collapsed on the porch of their house, spent. Minutes later, Hestia had joined her. At first, she'd been restless as children are at lying still and doing nothing.

Her mother whispered, "Watch the sky, Hestia."

And she did.

The sky constantly changed. Birds drifted over their heads, and if you watched closely, the clouds moved. She loved watching the clouds move. And the sky felt so enormous, and it felt so amazing that her speck of a pair of eyes could see it. Could take in that enormity. She hadn't known the words as a child, but she had felt it.

It was still the best memory of her childhood.

"Hestia?" A voice spoke from the doorway.

"Yes?" She replied, still mad at him, even if somewhere it occurred to her that his motives hadn't been bad.

"Can I come in? Or are you going to throw the bed at me?"

"You may," she allowed, and heard him enter with soft footsteps (she liked how he didn't disturb the stillness by hurried motions), and felt him sit down feet from her.

"Are you still mad?"

"Yes."

"I'm sorry. I didn't mean to hurt you."

"Mmhmm," she replied.

"And about what you said," he continued.

She felt the color rise to her cheeks. When the wave of fury had passed, the tendrils of embarrassment had rolled in. Why did she have to go off on him like that?

"I wasn't in the right mind."

"You weren't," he agreed, which made her smile. "But what you said was true."

"About your ungrateful ass?" She asked, trying to keep it light.

"That, and those other parts as well. Though they're not nearly as important as my ass."

She giggled. It felt childish, because it was, but he giggled as well. She raised her eyes, and saw their reflections in the window. She sat with her legs half drawn up to her chest, her hair messy as it encircled her face. One of his legs was fully extended, while the one beside her was drawn up. In the reflection, his black eyes met her brown ones, and something about the gesture felt so much more intimate than simply staring into each other's eyes.

She didn't look away. Neither did he.

She shifted her position, inching the slightest bit closer. Without breaking eye-window-eye contact, he shifted as well.

Then, very deliberately, he pulled back his left leg and extended his right one. She took the cue, and, as if under a spell, extended her left one as well, so that they were side-by-side, their legs from ankle to calf to thighs to hips right against each other.

"When does your dad get home?" He asked, his voice huskier.

"Tomorrow evening," she replied, but a second later, the feeling of comfort vanished.

What was he implying...

Put off, she shifted away from him, abandoning their eye contact through the window. Still unable to get back that comfort and unwilling to meet his eyes, she got up and walked away

"I didn't mean... I didn't mean anything," he said, having joined her.

"I'm not a child, Will. My behavior might seem childish but it's not."

"I get it. Refusing to sleep with a man you just met is not childish. It's wise. Not that I was implying that," he said, lighting up the atmosphere. She breathed a sigh of relief.

"I once went to India, but I hadn't booked a room or anything. I was going to, but I met this wonderful man on the flight who was delighted to know I knew their language. We talked for the entire twenty hours, and he invited me to stay with him. Just like that. I went, and he had a wife and two daughters and after the initial shock, they were damn welcoming. And I'm telling you, their food does taste amazing."

"They didn't think you would rob their house and flee?" She asked.

"I don't look like a criminal, do I? But you know, Hestia, I've met a lot of people who would not take a stranger in, even in a crisis. But I've also met those who would gladly welcome you even if it's not needed. It kind of reinforces your belief in humanity."

She smiled at his words, wondering how it would feel to have been to so many places and met so many people. Interesting, she would say, but overwhelming too. No pain, no gain.

"When Ethan—the guy with the broken neck—died, I just... I felt so temporary. I was standing right beside him. The slightest rotation of that wheel, and it would've been me. The only way to not die seemed to build a protected life around me," she confessed, the night and Will's quiet breathing drawing the words out of her.

"It's weird, isn't it? You're too scared to go out, I'm too afraid to build a home. Polar-opposites."

"Or perfect fits."

The words fell out on their own, but they seemed correct. He couldn't settle, she couldn't move: they would do well to balance each other out.

"I don't know what that line would lead to, but I'm dead on my feet. I wanna stay awake but..."

"It's all right. You can sleep here. I'll read for a while."

Her mind whirled too fast for her to be able to sleep, anyway. Will protested for a moment, but prompted by her insistence and threat to go into 'raging' mode, he finally got into bed and fell asleep within minutes.

She watched him sleep for a minute, slightly regretful, but then switched off the light and left the room.

The thing was, she knew going out had changed her and she would never be the same after that night.

But is that such a bad thing? She thought.

∽

WHEN WILL AWOKE two hours later, he hoped the snow was still going strong. Getting up to check, his hopes were crushed at sight of the motionless morning.

Making his groggy way to the living room, he saw Hestia asleep on the sofa, his coat draped over her shoulders. Smiling slightly, he went over and placed the blanket over her. She burrowed in, but didn't wake.

What do you do in an unknown house with the owner sleeping? Breakfast! He thought.

It took him a while to locate the butter, bread, coffee, and the other essentials, but he got there. Taking extra care not to make too much noise because he didn't want her waking up before breakfast was ready, he put together a simple breakfast and carried the tray into the living room.

"Breakfast!"

She didn't wake.

"Breakfast!" He yelled, upon which she gave a start, jumped up, grabbed the blanket, and held it up to choke the assailer. On seeing him, wide-eyed, clutching the tray with fear and having drawn back several steps, she fell back onto the sofa.

"You made breakfast?"

"It's a no if you're going to attack me."

"Not my fault; you scared me. Anyway, what have you got?" She asked, rubbing the sleep out of her eyes.

"Toast and coffee! I didn't put sugar because I didn't know if you took it or not, but I did put the milk because I need it."

"Dominating," she muttered while sipping.

"It's good," she commented. They ate toast and drank coffee with milk as the world woke from a snow-induced sleep, unaware of the magic that had been wrought overnight. Neither did the two people giggling over the spilled coffee on

Will's 'favorite' pants and the following monkey dance across the room, before he was compelled to change into a pair of Henry's pants, several sizes too big for him.

Hestia burst out laughing whenever she saw him. He pretended to be offended but he enjoyed appearing before her and hearing her laugh. They passed the day in harmony, both in high spirits, until late afternoon.

"I should go," Said Will, holding that backpack in his hand.

"You could stay. Dad would like to meet you," Hestia insisted. Looking at her, dressed in relaxed clothes burdened by winter coats, her hair bouncing around her face, he almost gave in.

"But I need to leave," he replied, clutching the bag to keep him focused. "I'm not running away, but I need to go."

Sensing defeat, she nodded.

"Maybe you should wear one of my jeans rather than that," she said, indicating the pin-held pants. They merely produced a smile by then.

"Yeah, if you don't mind lending it to me," he said. Minutes later, he was clad in his T-shirt and Hestia's jeans beneath the hundreds of coats. The jeans seemed surprisingly similar, except for the inadequate pockets, but his brain kept telling him he was wearing Hestia's jeans.

He would be walking to the washroom, and out of nowhere: *I am wearing jeans she wore! Jeans she put her legs through, snuggled in and adjusted around her hips! Was there anything more sexy than wearing someone else's jeans?*

She walked him to the threshold.

"You won't visit?" She asked.

"You will. I left my address and phone number over those pants."

"Will..."

He took her hand.

"You will. I know you will."

She looked at their hands, and he looked at her. He saw her looking at him, his profile reflected in her eyes. He saw the exact moment she made the resolution. But his observations couldn't pinpoint the precise moment when she decided to lean forward and kiss him, full on his startled lips.

Maybe it wasn't a decision after all, maybe it was an impulse. He didn't know.

All he knew was that Hestia kissed him like no had ever kissed him before. Her lips felt gentle and fierce at the same time, like the mingling of snow and fire. The kiss was urgent, but unhurried. It spoke of a man knocking on a door when he reached death's, of a woman walking fourteen difficult steps to procure a useless bag, of a conversation by firelight, of baggy pants and incredibly sexy jeans.

Before he could get used to the scent of her hair, or the feel of her waist against his palm, she had pulled back.

"Until next time."

THE NEXT TIME didn't arrive for a long time.

Will traveled as he always had, but this time, that sense of emptiness that had first registered itself (after Hestia's outburst) traveled with him. He still loved people and their stories, but he wanted something more than being a passive listener. He longed to live a life worth writing about.

He awaited the call.

Hestia struggled to get out. It started small, with fourteen steps to be precise. Then to the supermarket, with her dad. Then without him. Slowly to the outskirts. Gradually by cars. Inch by inch, footstep by footstep.

Will's remembrance, his image in baggy pants and her jeans helped her. Her dad helped her. So did her mother's memories.

But Ethan helped her most of all. She had never known Ethan, but he had changed her life. First for the worse, now for the better. She didn't think Ethan would want anyone to waste their lives because of him.

Six months later, she went everywhere by herself. The fear didn't go away; fears never do. It's the person who becomes stronger. Hestia couldn't forget being afraid, but she wouldn't forget being brave, either. Overcoming fears was not about forgetting them but accepting, realizing, and going on despite them.

On the eleventh day of the sixth month, she called him. On the thirteenth, she showed up on his doorstep. On the anniversary of that fateful night, after spending nearly six months in each others' company, William Whatever married Hestia Whoever.

Obviously, it wasn't quite as straightforward as that. They say it's possible to fall in love in as little as four minutes. Will didn't know about that, but he did fall for a woman in the span of one night and loved her each day after that. Hestia couldn't tell you when, but she fell for him harder each time they saw each other, which was most of the six months after she showed up at his house.

They found their home: to settle, and to move.

It was the snowiest night in the history of the town of Valdez, Alaska. The man who couldn't stop moving and the woman who couldn't start moving fell in love thrice: with each other, with their own selves.

And with life.

THE CHRISTMAS PARTY

SHANA CHARTIER

A sharp, pungent odor cut through the melodious scent of baking sugar cookies.

"Michael! The dog pooped on the rug again!"

Charlie bit back a grin as her mother chased their eleven-year-old dachshund, Roy, around the house, a small brown ornament dangling from his behind as he raced around the lit up Christmas tree. Her mother brushed back a strand of silvery brown hair as she glared up at her teenage daughter. Were it not for the silver, the color matched her daughter's completely.

"Charlotte Avery Christensen, you will stop laughing and help me catch that wretched animal!"

Charlie nodded. Her full name had been invoked, which brooked no argument. Her dark blue gaze followed the path of the wayward pup, her body tense as she waited for the right moment to pounce. It arrived just as sweet little Roy darted around the sofa. Charlie took her shot, diving forward and grasping the animal's chest between her palms to avoid any unfortunate collisions with his backside. Her father was there in an instant, carefully taking the wriggling animal from her grasp.

"I got him! Now who's going to help me clean him off?" he said. Before anyone could respond he was already halfway down the hall, beelining it for the bathroom.

"Not it," Charlie's brother Tim said, his finger on his pert twelve-year-old nose as he stared at the stains on the carpet.

"That's not very in line with the Christmas spirit," Charlie teased.

Tim grinned.

"Call me the Grinch, but I don't want the scent of poo on me while I'm enjoying my cocoa," he said.

"That dog will be the end of me!" their mother huffed.

She disappeared into the kitchen, then walked back into the living room with a bottle of bleach and a wad of paper towels in her hand. Just as she bent over to clean the mess, Charlie's father strode in with Roy under his arm. The dog's tail slapped against her father's side, now safely turd free.

"Wait! I'll get that," he said.

Her mother stood, handing over the cleaning supplies with visible relief on her face.

"Thank you," she breathed, handing over the paper towels.

"Thank *you* for putting up with my mom's old dog. I know it hasn't been easy."

The mood turned gloomy. Charlie's grandmother died a few weeks before Christmas, leaving them to deal with the sale of her family home and her elderly dog Roy, who was struggling to adapt to a new home without his best friend.

It hadn't been an easy holiday season, to say the least. Thanksgiving without her grandmother was already a somber affair, so much so that the turkey, which was normally Charlie's favorite part of the meal, tasted like ash on her tongue.

Her grief clouded what was normally her favorite time of year, and it wasn't until her mother explicitly asked her to try and be cheerful for her brother's sake that Charlie did her best to come back to life.

Her mother cleared her throat.

"Yes, well. We wouldn't want Roy to feel left out of the festivities, now would we?"

Roy wagged his tail harder as Charlie's mom scratched the top of his head. Charlie plopped back onto the plush sofa and stared at the glittering ornaments dangling from strategic places on their large Christmas tree. All around the tree there were handmade cutouts with jingle bells attached, glass families of four her mother bought every year perched on various branches, and a colorful cascade of rainbow lights. Directly next to it, the warm glow of a fire crackled in the fireplace, tucked safely behind a black cast-iron gate. And there, right above the mantle, was a black and white picture of Charlie's grandmother.

The image was from when she was close to Charlie's age. Her hair was dark, her eyes sparkling with good humor as she turned just so to capture her best angle. She was all buttoned up and proper, but Charlie knew better. Her grandmother had a wicked sense of humor, and Charlie's eyes glistened as she remembered just how much they all used to laugh together.

A beep came from the kitchen, breaking the heavy silence. It spurred Charlie's mother into action.

"Ah, that'll be the turkey. Let's get ready for dinner everyone," she said. Her voice was laced with the false bravado that only a mother trying to hold things together could really pull off.

The group took the cue and followed Charlie's mother to the kitchen. The savory scent of roasted turkey mingled with the smell of freshly baked cookies and steaming cocoa warmed Charlie's heart. As a unit they came together, setting up the table, preparing the meal, and then finally sitting down together. Charlie and Tim each got a champagne flute filled with sparkling cider while their parents enjoyed something a bit stronger.

"To grandma," Tim said, raising his flute. "I miss her."

After a pause, everyone lifted their glass.

"To Grandma," they all said at once.

It was a quiet affair after that. The food was delicious: the turkey moist and succulent, the potatoes creamy and perfectly paired with her mother's homemade gravy. They dipped their cookies in their cocoa to finish off the meal, and then settled on the couch to finish the night with their favorite Christmas movie.

It was the same as ever, and yet somehow completely different.

"Timmy," her mother whispered, gently nudging her little brother. "It's time for bed."

Charlie glanced around her mother to see Tim's head bobbing against her shoulder. He mumbled something incoherent, rubbed the edge of his mouth, and settled back against their mom.

"Come on. Presents in the morning," their mother said.

That was enough to get a twelve-year-old boy moving. Tim rubbed his dark brown eyes as he stood, shuffling down the hallway to his bedroom. Charlie's dad turned off the television and her parents stood and stretched. Charlie stood as well, her body warm and relaxed from a good meal and a peaceful evening. Together they headed down the hall to their respective rooms. When her parents reached their door, her mom turned and wrapped her young daughter in a hug. From over her shoulder Charlie watched as Roy trotted into their room, fully prepared to take up residence in their bed.

"Merry Christmas Eve," she whispered against her daughter's hair, planting a gentle kiss at her temple.

"Merry Christmas Eve," Charlie said, brushing a strand of her hair behind her ear. Her dad patted her shoulder before turning his back to her, and Charlie heard the gentle sound of a closing door as she approached her own room, quite ready for bed.

Already in her red plaid pajama bottoms and gray t-shirt, Charlie face planted into her bed, turning her face so her cheek could embrace the cool fabric of the pillow. She closed her eyes and waited for sleep to come. In the quiet dark space of the room, her thoughts refused to stay penned in. Instead they flew from her mind like wild horses, raging forward, refusing to grant her sleep.

I miss her.

Hot tears burned behind her closed eyes, and Charlie opened them, refusing to give into the grief once again.

An idea hit her then.

A very dumb idea.

Charlie stood, her food coma fully worn off, and she peeked out from her open bedroom door down the hall. Everything was dark, the only sound a ticking clock from the living room. Charlie padded down the hallway, casting glances at Tim's closed door, then at her parents'. She made her way back into the living room, which was cast in a shadowy glow from the dying embers of their holiday fire. Her grandmother's image grinned down at her from the mantle, as though daring her to do it.

She grinned back.

Tiptoeing toward the front door, Charlie stepped bare toes into a pair of unlaced hiking boots and slid on a long black pea coat over her pajamas. She turned the lock, then oh-so-carefully twisted the knob. The door opened, sending a blast of chilly, snow scented air right through her. Charlie hesitated, reconsidering. Beyond the door a dark chasm met her gaze. Her eyebrows narrowed, and she stepped out into the frigid darkness, closing the door behind her without so much as a click.

She closed her eyes, breathing in the frosty scent of pine all around her. When she opened them, her gaze was better adjusted to the dark of night, and she stepped forward with more confidence over her family's snowy lawn and onto the sanded road.

Charlie was used to the lack of streetlights. The first glimmer of light would start on Main Street, which was where her grandmother's old house still stood, empty and cold. A gust of wind tore at her jacket, which flapped back, exposing her legs to the chilly night and forcing Charlie to button it up and hold the collar a little closer to her neck. Her shoulders rose to her ears as she kept her gaze forward, hot tears turning cold as the wind stung her face.

Where did this tempest come from?

A small beam of light appeared in the distance, and Charlie knew that had to be the first street light leading toward town. She kept her eyes on the gentle orb as snowflakes caked in her hair, tangled strands whipping at her stinging face. She thought about going back. Was this really worth the trip?

The answer came to her instantly.

Yes, it was.

Her legs carried her onward even as the wind seemed to want to lift her from her feet and carry her right into the sky. When she reached the streetlight, the wind stopped instantly, her ears rushing with newfound silence.

Strange…

Charlie blinked the tears from her eyes, wiping them

away with red tipped fingers as she started in the direction of her grandmother's house. All around her the world was silent, the streetlights decorated with wreaths, the glow from illuminated trees pulsing through living room windows. Town Hall had an enormous tree right on the front lawn that was still lit up, guiding town members of faith to the church next door for midnight service. Charlie turned the corner, passing the local grocer, and then stopped in her tracks.

Her grandmother's house, which had been abandoned for cleaning and sale, was completely lit up. Every window of the stately Victorian home gleamed, orange light pouring from each floor. A wave of anger washed over her. Who would dare go into her grandmother's house and mess around in there like this? Not only that, but as Charlie stomped closer she could see young people laughing and chatting on the front lawn.

Someone was throwing a party in her grandmother's abandoned home!

If steam could come from Charlie's ears, it certainly would have. Who had the gall to do such a thing? Who would throw a party in a dead woman's home?

Charlie stormed over to a group of young people standing in a semi-circle. All of them were smoking, the boys in dress shirts and slacks and the girls in nice dresses with long coats draped around their shoulders. When Charlie approached them, she was met with four pairs of blinking eyes as puffs of smoke swirled around her.

She inhaled a tendril of smoke as she reached them, bending over and coughing until she thought she would puke.

"Hey, are you ok?"

One of the girls bent over and gently rubbed Charlie's back. Offended, she stood back up and fought back a fresh wave of tears, though whether they were entirely from the smoke or mixed with anger and grief was difficult to say.

"How…dare…you…" Charlie wheezed.

The girl's brows knit in concern, and she glanced at her compatriots.

"I think we better alert the hostess," she said.

The others cast worried gazes at Charlie, nodding as the girl wrapped a supportive arm around Charlie's shoulders and guided her toward the front porch. Charlie cleared her throat, which was still raw from her coughing fit, but she found she was able to get her wits about her again.

When she did, she realized that the house was pristine. The outside was freshly painted, the broken third step completely sound and repaired.

"When did they do this?" Charlie asked.

"Do what?" the girl said.

"Paint the house. Fix everything up?"

Again Charlie was granted a bewildered glance. Instead of answering, she led Charlie through the main hallway, past the living room and straight into the kitchen, where another group of partygoers was hooting with laughter.

"Where is she…" the girl said, lifting up onto her toes even in pale pink high heels to look over the heads of everyone there. She pointed.

"Ah! Come on, this way."

Charlie allowed herself to be led through the crowd. In every room a smattering of well dressed party guests stood in small circles, many dangling cigarettes between their index and middle fingers as they spoke. The scent of ash mingled with the sweeter smells of hot chocolate, spiced cider, and a variety of savory dishes that were laid out on a long table in her grandmother's living room. The girl tugged on Charlie's arm as she stood glaring at everyone around her. The partygoers barely cast her a second glance, though a few confused looks honed in on her disheveled clothing.

"Just this way," the girl said, her voice strained as she tugged at Charlie's arm. She glanced back toward the door, and Charlie guessed that she was anxious to get back to her friends and away from the crazy pajama lady. It nearly had her digging in her heels further, if she wasn't so focused on giving the hostess a piece of her mind. They walked past the old wooden staircase until they finally reached the kitchen, where Charlie had eaten breakfast a million times. The girl came to an abrupt stop right in front of a small group of people seated in a corner nook.

"Charlotte, we need some help here," the girl said.

Charlie glared down at the three people sitting in the breakfast nook. It was a girl and two boys. She hardly noticed the boys as she stared into eyes identical to her own, her mouth agape. Her eyes widened in shock.

"Grandma...?" she whispered.

She had to be dreaming. It couldn't be real. The girl before her was in a bright red party dress, her lips painted to match. Her eyes were shining with merriment, and they were the same blue as Charlie's. Charlotte's hair was done up in a sweeping winged arch, her long tresses pulled back in a smooth chignon. As she stared back at Charlie, she shook her head and smiled.

It was as though the photo on the fireplace mantle had come to life.

"Excuse me, boys. Hostess duties call!"

Her speech was light and airy, like she could have voiced a cartoon princess. As an older woman her voice changed, deepened. Charlie continued to stare as Charlotte scooted around one of the boys and stood, facing Charlie as she nodded to the girl who'd brought her in.

"Thanks Rubes. I'll take it from here," she said with a wink.

A wink Charlie always adored in her short sixteen years on Earth.

"I...uh..." Charlie stammered.

Charlotte slid her hand through Charlie's arm and with a gentle push led her in the direction of the staircase.

"I am so sorry," Charlotte said in a hushed tone.

Charlie gave her a sideways glance, painfully aware that she'd been staring a little too hard before. But really, how could she not?

"For...for what?" she asked, trying desperately to make sense of it all. She crossed her arm close to reach her other hand, still laced with Charlotte's, and pinched herself.

It hurt.

"Well, I should have been clearer. The pajama party is for New Year's Eve. The Christmas party is always elegant dress only."

Charlie glanced down at her disheveled outfit, then back into her grandmother's youthful eyes.

Was this real?

"Oh. That's ok," she said.

If this was a dream, she figured she'd lean into it. She'd often wondered what her grandmother was like as a young woman. Now, casting another glance at the young woman's angular face, she realized she had a chance to have her back, even if just for a little while.

Maybe it was a Christmas miracle. Maybe she was losing her mind. Either way, it was an opportunity she didn't want to miss out on.

"Here now, come right in here with me," Charlotte said, opening a side door.

A pair of well dressed, disheveled partygoers jumped

apart and sat facing them on the bed, red-faced. Charlotte frowned.

"Necking is strictly prohibited in here, my friends. Please take that heat somewhere else."

When neither person moved, Charlotte pulled the door further back and gestured toward the hallway.

"I said split!"

The pair bolted out of the room at the sound of her tone. Charlotte rolled her eyes as she waved Charlie in.

"I can't stand people trying to sneak off and dirty up my room. My folks would be livid if they knew."

"They don't know about the party?" Charlie asked.

She racked her brain for information about her great grandparents, but came up short. Charlotte never spoke about them much. The young Charlotte before her shrugged one dainty shoulder and headed toward a closet.

"I think they care more about the cleanliness of the house, to be honest. They don't care much about anything when it comes to me, but that's ok. I have plenty of friends to make up for it," Charlotte said.

"Where are they now?" Charlie asked.

"Somewhere in the Caribbean. They do their couples cruise this time every year, which is why it's so easy to throw a banging Christmas party. Ah! This will do."

Charlotte pulled out a satin green dress. It appeared to fall right above the calf, the bottom puffed out slightly, the bodice designed much like a corset.

It was beautiful.

"We're lucky that you seem to be just about my size. Try this on so people will stop looking at you funny," Charlotte said. She handed Charlie the dress and turned to close the door. Charlie hesitated, and when Charlotte turned back around, understanding lit her eyes.

"Oh, sorry. It's alright if you're shy. I'll look over here," she said, walking over to the window.

Outside Charlie could hear more laughter and the clinking of glasses.

"Are those glasses real?" Charlie asked.

"As opposed to…?" Charlotte asked.

"Plastic?" Charlie said.

A gentle giggle began at the back of Charlotte's throat and poured out from between her rose colored lips.

"You are an interesting one. I don't think I ever got your name. I'm so sorry…what a terrible hostess faux pas!"

Charlie hesitated, then slid the silken fabric up her body and scooped her arms beneath each sleeve before answering.

"I'm Charlie," she said.

Casting a glance back, Charlotte saw that Charlie was covered enough and moved behind her to button up the back of the dress.

"Far out. Very modern of you! I love it."

As Charlotte finished the last button, Charlie turned and grinned at her.

"You do?" she asked.

Her grandmother never seemed to be thrilled by her chosen nickname, given that she was her namesake to begin with. Charlotte nodded, her tightly coiffed hair barely making a bounce, for all her enthusiasm.

"Absolutely! These are times of change. I think it's really cool that you're doing your own thing. Someone's got to stand up to the patriarchy, right?"

"Right," Charlie agreed.

Charlotte headed back to the closet and pulled out a pair of round toed black heels.

"Try these on. If we're lucky one more time, I'll make you an egg nog."

Charlie stepped into each shoe one at a time, wobbling a little as she worked to keep her balance. She'd never been one for heels, but then again, neither was her grandmother.

At least, the one she knew.

Charlotte clapped her hands together in delight.

"Perfect!" she squeaked. "Now sit here."

A small white vanity stood in the corner of the room. Charlotte gestured for her to sit before a small mirror, then made quick work of releasing her long tresses from her ponytail and refashioning them into a similar coiffure that matched her own.

"Do you always throw these kinds of parties?" Charlie asked.

"Well, now that I'm eighteen I have quite a bit more freedom to do so, but yes. I've been hosting them since my parents deemed me old enough to leave home alone," Charlotte said, pulling out her hairspray. Charlie closed her eyes as a mist of cold, sticky spray washed over her entire head.

"How could they leave you alone here?"

Indignation coursed through Charlie as she saw the flash of sadness behind her grandmother's eyes.

Charlotte sighed.

"They just are the way they are, you know? My mother's always been very clear that she did not want children, and they both just really like to travel, but couldn't really do that with me being in school and all. I've gotten pretty good at taking care of myself."

"Yeah, but you shouldn't have to," Charlie pressed.

Charlotte shrugged again, then pinned up one last piece of Charlie's hair. She pulled out a makeup bag and bent over to apply blush and eyeshadow to Charlie's face.

"I suppose, but what can I do to change it? Besides,

69

someday I'm going to have my own family, and I'm going to make sure they know they are loved beyond compare."

"You will! And they'll miss you so much when you're gone," Charlie said, choking back a sob.

"Hey now. It's Christmas Eve, Charlie! All of this sad talk is becoming a drag. Now, turn around and tell me you love it."

Charlie turned and faced the mirror, her fingers darting right to her painted lips. She was transformed, almost as if she had also become a woman out of time. If one looked closely enough, they might even be able to tell that Charlie and Charlotte were related.

Meeting her gaze in the mirror, Charlotte nodded with satisfaction.

"Good. Now come on down and join in the fun, will you?"

Brooking no argument, Charlotte opened the door and headed back downstairs, Charlie close behind her. Charlotte glanced back up as their heels clunked against the old wooden steps.

"Who told you about the party, anyway? I'll have to ding them for not providing the right dress code."

"Uh…" Charlie said. "I can't remember his name. Thank you for helping me out, by the way."

Charlotte gave a flippant wave of her hand.

"Nonsense. I'm happy to do it. And it makes sense that whoever told you was a *boy*. They never get directions right, do they?"

Charlie withheld comment on that little observation as they reached the bottom of the stairs. At the last step her heel slid into a dent in the stair and Charlie stumbled forward, her body hurling toward the floor.

"Woah!"

Expecting a painful slap from the ground, instead Charlie was swept into the air, cushioned in a pair of strong, masculine arms.

"Jonah! You're always saving the day!" Charlotte said.

Charlie realized then that her arms were wrapped around the neck of a very handsome dark haired, dark eyed young man, who was staring at her intently as he continued holding her in his arms.

"Thanks," she said, frozen.

Jonah nodded and gently lowered her to the ground.

"Any time. You girls ok?" he asked, glancing from Charlie to Charlotte. To Charlie's surprise, Charlotte batted her eyes at the young man and sidled up next to him, glancing up at him with a coquettish grin.

"We are now, thanks to you," she purred.

Even from a foot away, Charlie could see Jonah had no interest in her grandmother. He grinned down at her, his shoulders set back, and he patted her hand in a brotherly fashion before gently removing it from his forearm.

"As I said, any time. Now, would you ladies like to join me for some eggnog?"

"Always," Charlotte said. "Come on, Charlie."

Jonah blinked, staring at Charlie.

"That's a unique name," he said.

"It's a nickname," she replied.

"Ah. Well, a unique name for a unique girl. Join us, won't you, Charlie?"

He then crooked his elbows out to each of them, Charlotte sliding her hand down the length of his arm as she nestled against his side. Charlie hesitated. Jonah glanced back and lifted one thick black eyebrow.

"Do you like eggnog, Charlie?" he asked.

"Sure, I just…"

Charlie glanced from Charlotte to Jonah, confused. It was obvious her grandmother was smitten with the guy, but her grandfather wasn't Jonah. Charlie had never met him, though she'd heard stories about his kindness and chivalry before he passed from cancer before Charlie or her brother were born.

"Charlie?"

Charlotte and Jonah continued to stare at her as Charlie shook her head and stepped forward, not taking Jonah's arm as they proceeded into the living room. The whole space was lit up with twinkle lights. A crackling fire burned between the red bricks of the fireplace. Next to it a table covered in a white linen cloth was covered with fixings for cocoa, a warm steaming pot and a crystal punch bowl filled with creamy eggnog.

"Please help yourself, Charlie. I think I've changed my mind. Let's do cocoa," Charlotte said, smiling up at Jonah. Her fingers pressed against the fabric of Jonah's jacket, and somehow they managed to fill porcelain cups with steaming hot liquid, marshmallows and two cinnamon sticks with one free hand.

"Ew," Charlie mumbled. Who put cinnamon sticks in their cocoa?

"I agree," a male voice said from behind her.

She turned, once again stunned into silence. The young man before her was lean and tall, his hair sandy and unruly above a pair of dark brown eyes. Another picture perfect memory.

Her grandfather.

"What?" Charlie asked.

He nodded toward Charlotte and Jonah with a frown.

"I don't like cinnamon in my cocoa either. It's a strange flavor to me."

"Oh," Charlie said. "Yeah."

The pair of them continued to watch Charlotte and Jonah. When her grandfather didn't break his gaze, she cleared her throat.

"So, you have a thing for Charlotte, huh?" Charlie asked.

That got his attention. His head whipped back around and his gaze bored into her.

"Charlotte? Of course not. Besides, she'd never go for someone like me," he said, his gaze downcast.

"I'm Charlie," Charlie said, holding out her hand for him to shake.

When his hand slid into hers, her skin prickled like she was shaking hands with a ghost; which perhaps, she was.

"Jonathan Christensen, though you can call me Jon. Everyone does."

"I know," Charlie said.

He lifted a brow.

"How do you know? We've only just met."

Charlie wanted to kick herself for making the same mistake twice.

"Um," Charlie said. "I mean I know because everyone goes by nicknames nowadays. My name obviously isn't Charlie."

A flicker of a smile danced across his lips, and Charlie couldn't help but grin back.

"So, you think Charlotte is really stuck on Jonah?" Charlie asked.

"I know she is," Jon confirmed. "Just look at them. She hasn't taken her eyes off him since you came downstairs."

"So you were watching us come down?" Charlie asked.

Jon's cheeks blossomed with red.

"No. I mean, I saw you come down. I wasn't watching for you or anything. I mean, certainly not you. I don't even know you. I…"

Charlie put her hands up, and Jon stopped.

"Don't worry about it. I know you're not a creep."

"How do you know that?"

"I just get a sense from people. Jon, will you join me over here? It's a little stuffy by the fire."

Charlie gestured in the direction of the front porch, which was fairly empty at the moment, save for Charlotte and Jonah, who appeared to be deep in conversation.

Jon lifted a skeptical brow.

"What are your intentions?" he asked.

She laughed.

"Could you be any more old fashioned?"

"I'm not old fashioned, I'm perceptive. You've taken a clear interest in matchmaking, obviously, and I'm not here for it. Charlotte can choose whoever she wants."

"Charlie, join us!" Jonah called.

The pucker of Charlotte's lip told Charlie that she'd prefer they be left alone, but Charlie felt like playing this game a little bit. There was always the possible risk that if she didn't help her grandparents along, she might not exist, right? That was how time travel stories worked in the movies.

"We're coming!" she said, wrapping her arm around Jon's and nearly dragging him forward.

"Wait. I don't think this is a good idea…" Jon protested. He didn't stop completely, but he dug in his heels a bit until they reached the door.

"Jonah, Charlotte, have you met Jon Christensen? He was the one that told me about the party," Charlie improvised.

Jon glanced down at her with narrowed eyes, then turned his gaze to Charlotte as she finally pried herself from Jonah's arm to cross them over her stomach, warding off the cold as they all stepped out onto the porch.

"Ah, so it was you that forgot to tell poor Charlie about

the dress code!" Charlotte said, her own gaze narrow as she considered him.

Jon shifted from one foot to the other.

"Uh…" he said.

"Boys, right?" Charlie said with a forced laugh. "So what kind of fun things do you do at one of these parties, anyway?" she asked, hoping the subject change would also redirect her grandfather's accusatory glare.

"Well," Charlotte said, considering. "We haven't done snowman building yet. Shall we?"

Jonah's gaze was on Charlie as he answered.

"I'd love to. Let's do it!"

They stepped back inside, Jon holding the door for the rest of the group. A small basket loaded with gloves and hats was perched on a table next to the door. Charlie found a mismatched pair of mittens and a scarf, pulling a jacket from a coat rack and sliding her arms into the gaping sleeves. As the others followed suit, they trekked out into the snow in front of the porch steps and started forming globes for the snowman's body.

"Why did you say that?" Jon whispered near Charlie's ear.

"I can't tell you," she said.

"Who are you, really?" he asked.

She looked up into his eyes and considered telling him the truth, but then she couldn't find the words.

She didn't know what the truth was.

"You wouldn't believe me if I told you," she said.

"Try me," he replied.

"Charlie! Over here! I need some help," Jonah said.

Happy to escape from her grandfather's grilling, she trotted over to Jonah and helped him roll a large ball through the snow, patting the sides as the body grew large enough to place on the lawn. Her toes stung with the cold, and she wondered if women often built snowmen in high heels in the past.

It seemed a terribly foolish thing to do.

"Where are you from, Charlie?" Jonah asked. "I've never seen you around before."

"Oh, you know, I travel around a lot. Military brat," she hedged. He nodded.

"You see that a lot these days. Are you planted here for very long then?" he asked.

"Oof!"

Their conversation was cut short when Charlotte let out a frustrated huff. She was on the ground, glowering at the two of them.

"Will someone please help me up? I slipped!"

"Of course," Jon said, stepping over. Charlotte glanced at his hand, then held hers up without enthusiasm. As he grasped her palm and pulled back his arm to lift her up, he also slid on a patch of icy snow and tumbled down next to her.

Charlie gasped. Her grandparents stared at one another for a moment, then both of them burst out laughing. Charlie grinned up at Jonah, who held out his arm to her.

"I'd hate for you to slip as well," he said.

"So gallant," she said.

"I am nothing if not gallant," Jonah replied. "Besides, it's too slick and cold to finish a snowman, anyway."

Charlie watched as Jon and Charlotte carefully stood up together, then walked arm in arm back to the doorway of the house. When she and Jonah reached the bottom step and glanced up, Charlie gasped.

"What is it?" Charlotte asked, concerned.

"Look up," Charlie said.

Charlotte and Jon both glanced above to see mistletoe dangling above their heads. When they looked back at one another, something hidden glistened in their eyes.

"Oh dear," Charlotte breathed.

"We don't have to…" Jon said.

"I disagree," Charlie chimed in. "Tradition calls!"

Charlie bit back a smile as she watched her grandparents' young faces turn a whole deeper shade of red that had nothing to do with the cold. Jon cradled Charlotte's face in his palm and gently lowered his lips to hers, capturing them in a cherishing kiss. When he pulled away, they stared trance-like at one another.

"You seem to be orchestrating something," Jonah whispered into her ear.

Charlie glanced up at him with an impish grin.

"Me? Never."

"Something's not quite right about you, Charlie with no last name. I can't put my finger on it, but something is strange about you."

"You are correct," Charlie said, sticking to the truth. "I am certainly out of this world."

Jonah grinned at that comment and led the way up the porch steps. Charlotte glanced up at him.

"Would you boys mind getting us something a little cooler to drink? Some punch, maybe?"

Jon and Jonah nodded in unison.

"We'll be back," Jonah said, and together they headed off in the direction of the kitchen.

Once they were out of sight, Charlotte turned toward Charlie and gripped her hands, her face alight with excitement.

"I can't *believe* you made me do that!" she said, beaming.

Charlie laughed.

"You looked like you enjoyed it," she replied.

Charlotte swatted Charlie's arm.

"You and your cheek. Still, I've always had a thing for Jonah, even though I know he doesn't feel the same way. I always thought I could change his mind if I were beautiful or charming enough. But that boy…Jon…" Charlotte said. She gazed back in the direction of the kitchen.

"That kiss was…magic."

"And who doesn't love a little Christmas magic?" Charlie said.

Charlotte's smile grew even wider.

"I'm going to make every Christmas magical, forever. There's something about this time of year…wonderful things seem really possible, you know?"

Remembering how much her grandmother always made the holidays so special, Charlie's eyes glistened with unshed tears.

"I do," she said with a sniffle.

Charlotte reached into her dress pocket and pulled out a kerchief.

"Oh no, don't go crying now. You'll ruin my perfect make up work."

Charlie nodded and dabbed at the corners of her eyes, returning the kerchief as the boys came back with full glasses of punch. They handed one to each of them, and then Jon lifted his glass.

"To Christmas!" he said.

"Merry Christmas!" the others chimed in.

A group of people stood around a large wooden piano in the corner, and the notes to Jingle Bells rang out into the room.

"Carol time!" Charlotte trilled.

This time she reached out for Jon's arm. The four of them

headed toward the piano and joined in the chorus Charlie sang the classic tune with all her heart. When it came to an end Charlotte found a small butter knife and tapped it against the rim of her glass.

"Thank you all so much for coming to my little shindig. With the singing of the carols that means we've come to an end, and it's time to sleep and see what Santa has for us in the morning!"

Jovial conversation broke out as the party guests reached for their coats and hats, bidding Charlotte farewell. Charlie stood back a bit, waiting until the last of the guests disappeared into the dark night. Jonah bid her adieu, then grasped Charlotte's hand and thanked her for a lovely time, as always. Then it was Jon's turn to go last.

"I hope to see you again soon," he said.

"I'd like that very much," Charlotte replied, her blush returning. He lifted her hand and kissed it before turning toward the door and shutting it behind him.

Charlotte spun in a little circle, her eyes closed. When she opened them, she saw Charlie and her hand darted to her forehead.

"Oh Charlie, I'm so sorry. Let's get you your regular clothes back!"

Charlie followed Charlotte up the creaky staircase and back to her room, where Charlotte released enough buttons for her to slide out of her party dress and back into her pajamas. When she finished dressing she turned to face Charlotte, and her chest grew tight.

"I'm so happy I got the chance to see you," she said, fighting back tears.

She'd been so caught up in the fun of the party she hadn't thought about the end. Charlotte pulled out her kerchief again and gave it to Charlie.

"I am, too. It was really nice getting to know you tonight, Charlie. And thank you for introducing me to Jon. I hope to get the chance to see you both again very soon."

Charlie sniffled.

Charlotte placed a gentle hand on her arm.

"Hey, come on now. There's no need for tears. We'll be together again before you know it."

"I hope so," Charlie said, her voice watery.

"Of course we will. Now, you get some good sleep, and I'll be in touch soon, okay?"

Charlie handed back the kerchief, but Charlotte held up her hands.

"You keep it. I have plenty."

Charlotte nodded, pocketing the kerchief and heading down the stairs in her sturdy hiking boots. Charlotte opened the front door, but before Charlie could walk out she turned and wrapped Charlotte in a tight hug.

"I miss you," she whispered.

Charlotte chuckled.

"I think the punch has made you sentimental. I miss you too, my new friend. Until next time."

"Until then," Charlie breathed, turning.

"Oh, and Charlie?"

Charlie turned back.

"Merry Christmas," Charlotte said.

"Merry Christmas," Charlie replied.

With that, Charlotte closed the door. The lights in the house went out all at once. Charlie stared at the building for a long moment, then turned and headed back home, the world cold and still.

Everything appeared normal when she reached the house. Her parents' cars were in the driveway. The mailbox was covered with a small dusting of snow. She walked up the pathway to the front door and opened it, the portal gliding open without so much as a creak. The house was warm, the air laced with the scent of apple and pumpkin pie among other delectable remnants from their Christmas dinner.

Charlie kicked off her shoes and padded up the stairs in her bare feet, her hair falling loose of the hairspray around her shoulders. She plopped into her bed and stared at the ceiling, convinced she would never fall asleep after such an experience.

"Charlie!"

Charlie's eyes fluttered open. Bright sunlight poured into the room around her. She blinked as her younger brother stared at her from the doorway, bouncing up and down.

"It's present time! Come *on!*"

Immobile, Charlie stared at the ceiling, reeling from what had clearly been a dream. She reached into her pajama pocket, curious.

No kerchief.

A pang of disappointment shot through her as she stood, stretched, and made her way down the hallway to the kitchen. The scent of hot coffee, bacon and eggs permeated the house, and she approached her mother by the stove, wrapping her in a hug.

"I had the best dream," Charlie sighed.

"Oh?" her mother asked, wrapping her arm around her daughter's waist.

Before she could go on, the doorbell rang. Roy glanced up from his dog bed by the fire before his little head plopped back down. Doggy snoring ensued.

Charlie's mother cast a curious glance at the door.

"We're certainly not expecting anyone this morning," she said.

"I'll get it," Charlie replied.

She walked to the door, the silhouette of a person shaded behind the patterned glass. When she opened it, she gasped.

A young man blinked at her, then spoke.

"Sorry. Is this the Christensen household?" he asked.

The boy was the spitting image of Jonah. Speechless, Charlie nodded.

"Awesome. I have a box for you, if you can just sign here."

Charlie looked at the large box on the porch step, then back up at the boy.

"Is your name Jonah?" she asked.

His expression was unreadable as he quirked a brow.

"No, it's Lucas," he said.

Charlie shook her head.

"Sorry. It's been a weird night. I can sign that," she said, taking the paper from him and scribbling her name.

"It's not that," he said. "Jonah is my grandfather. He passed away last year."

A chill ran down Charlie's spine as she looked into those familiar brown eyes. He glanced down then and his eyes widened when he saw her name.

"Charlie?" he said.

"Yeah?" she said.

He shook his head, a bewildered grin touching the corner of his lip.

"You're never going to believe this, but my grandfather always talked about a girl named Charlie he met at a Christmas party once. Said she was like a girl from another world. What are the odds?"

Charlie swallowed.

"Well, I've got to get going. Just moved in with my aunt and wanted to help with one last delivery. I'll see you around!"

Charlie blinked as Lucas strode off. Once he disappeared down the road, she closed the front door and carried the box to the Christmas tree, placing it among the other presents there.

"I think this is from Grandma," she breathed. All movement stopped as her parents and brother joined her around the box. She pulled the tape from the corners until she could peel it off the top seal, then opened the box.

Right on the top was the white kerchief, with Charlie's name embroidered into the corner.

Together her family accepted one last gift from their beloved matriarch, and Charlie gazed up at the picture above the mantle.

"Merry Christmas, Charlotte," she whispered.

CINDERED ELLA: A CHRISTMAS STEAMPUNK TALE

EDY FUDGE

S *now always seems to come early*, mused Ella. *It does cover up the London grey and the soot for a brief while before it becomes a dark mush.* Ella was out early to clean the entrance way to *Penelope's Pantomime Theatre*. Shoveling snow was one of her many assigned chores at the theatre.

Penelope was her aunt—at least she claimed to be. Maybe just a distant cousin for all loving family care Ella got. After her parents had perished in an airship disaster, Penelope was the only one who stepped forward to deal with Ella. Cheap labor was probably what Penelope had seen.

Ella was sent to live in a garret room at the theatre. Coveralls became her wardrobe as she was expected to do a chore boy's work. She kept the huge steam boilers going in the cellar with daily hand shoveled fills of coal. The boilers made the steam used to power all the scenery and effects Penelope used for her myriad pantomime shows. As the Christmas season approached, many special performances were being planned.

There was a crew who operated the complex steam machinery that moved things about on stage. And there were several ladies who took care of costumes. Then there were the players themselves. Ella tried to stay away from them as much as possible. Some of them had nasty tempers, especially when they were drunk, which was the usual. She guessed it took liquid courage to go out on the stage and make a fool of oneself. The more ridiculous they acted, the more audiences liked it. Bringing the family to one of Penelope's Christmas Pantos was a tradition in many London homes.

Ella was to be on call to help the scenery crew or the costume ladies whenever they needed help. And she must never, ever let the boilers go dry or their fires go out. After the first few months, Ella became quite familiar with just about all the workings of the theatre. Yes, she was cheap labor. Once in a while, Penelope gave her a few coins. Mostly she got reminders of how fortunate she was that Penelope had taken her in, given her a home that kept her off the streets. Lucky, lucky Ella.

Eli, the elderly man who watched over the stage door, had long been her one bright spot. Ella had liked Eli immediately, and Eli had taken her under his wing, knowing exactly how Penelope treated Ella. Charity had never been one of Penelope's virtues.

A loud wheezing, clanking noise brought Ella back to reality. A street cleaning machine huffed its way towards the theatre. It pushed snow mush off to the side while its boiler belched smoke into the sooty air. It took two men in heavy helmets with big goggles to manage the monster. How much good it did was debatable. The mush would melt, putting dirty puddles back on the street. The Lord Mayor thought they were a wonderfully modern convenience. But he never walked on the street. His horseless carriage took him everywhere people desired his presence.

Ella settled her goggles over her eyes and stepped back into the street to shovel the dirty mush away from the box office and entrance doors. Shows today were at 1, 3, and 5 P.M. A special 9 P.M. performance for adults catered to the wealthy dinner crowd. It was very adult in nature. Patrons often either ate (and drank) before the show or went out afterwards for a late evening meal. It would be a late night for Ella in her chilly room. At least one of the steam pipes for scenery ran up close by. Another reason for keeping those big old boilers going strong.

Church bells chimed eleven. Ella went around to shovel the stage door area only to find that Eli had already done it. *Shame on him*. He was too old and creaky to do that kind of work. She knew he had done it to help her out.

Pushing in through the door, she found Eli at his little table eating. "Here, Ella," he motioned, "There's an extra bun for you. We had a bit of beef for supper, and Mary made up a bun for each of us."

Mary was Eli's wife, equally old and creaky. She knew Ella's situation—finding food at the street stands if Penelope had given her a bit of money. Mary often tucked a bit extra in Eli's lunch bucket for Ella.

"Old people don't need to eat much," Eli quoted his wife.

Ella pushed the goggles up and pulled over another stool to accept the bun. She was chilled from being outside. Eli always had a small pot of tea going on the tiny gas burner. Hot tea was nice.

"Did you hear the *Old Lady* is reviving her Cinderella panto for the Christmas trade? She's got the costume ladies sewing up a storm. Wants everything looking new and sparkly," Eli related to Ella. "She's got a new idea for putting a horseless carriage on stage for Cinderella to ride into the Ball."

"You're kidding, aren't you, Eli? I don't think that's even possible. How would you fit it with fire box and boiler?'

"Don't know. But I overheard her talking to some fancy engineer guy yesterday. He wants a pretty penny just to draw up a set of plans. The *Old Lady* wants it ready for the big show on Boxing Day. Thinks it'll really draw in the crowds."

"Humbug! What if she spends a ton of money and the gal darn thing doesn't work? Seeing is believing!" Ella laughed. "Tell Mary thanks for the bun. The Yuletide Spirit hasn't bit my aunt yet. My resources are a bit thin. Just don't stint yourselves on my account. We all need to eat, especially now that winter's really here. And hey, Eli, no more shoveling snow mush for you. I'll always get to this door, too." She gave Eli a small hug and headed down to shovel coal.

Goggles down, the boilers needed to be perking away for the afternoon shows. Right now they were doing *Puss in Boots*. It didn't need too much set movement. The children always loved the animal costumes. Depending on how sober the theatre's leading man Harold was, it could be quite hilarious.

But a big Cinderella production? And in time for Boxing Day? It would have to be a Christmas miracle. As she stoked the boilers, Ella wondered just how much the steam-run scenery would have to do. The theatre had been around for over forty years. To Ella's knowledge it used the original equipment, repairs made here and there when *really* necessary. *And a horseless carriage? Penelope was really going out on a limb.*

It was actually hot in the cellar. It didn't take long for Ella's chill to turn to sweat. Time to put exactly ten shovels of coal in each firebox. She had learned over the months just what it took at each time of day or night to keep all the elements working. From what she had heard, the young man who had worked here before she came was not reliable—or maybe smart enough to figure the system out. It really wasn't that complicated as long as everything was done right and on schedule.

Coming back up from the cellar, she heard her aunt screeching her name. "Ella, Ella! I need you NOW!"

"Here I am, Aunt Penelope. What's the problem?"

"No problem. I just need your body. The costumers are working on a new show. I need you to be a dummy. You know, stand still while they pin a dress together. Go over to their workroom. You aren't too dirty, are you? Hurry up. Take off the stupid goggles. Just go!" Penelope pushed her, then disappeared down into the auditorium area.

A dummy. That's what Ella felt like a lot of the time. Do this and do that. Never thought of as a real person. Never ever thought of as a girl, for heaven's sake.

The costume workroom happened behind the backstage area. Madam Clara,the head seamstress, acted like a bit of a tyrant. Ella never went near the workroom for fear of Madam Clara's wrath. Now she'd been sent there to be a dummy. She softly knocked on the open door's jamb. Looking inside was like looking at a fairyland. There were racks of costumes of every type and color. On large tables were bolts of shiny fabric in a rainbow of colors. Ella actually held her breath.

"You, girl—I guess you are. Over here." Madam Clara barked. "Have you heard we are to do a new *Cinderella* for Boxing Day? We can re-do some costumes we already have, but the Ball scene is to be spectacular, not silly. Well, silly in that Harold is to be Cinderella, not the Prince this time. He is to have a marvelous gown. Penelope thinks you are his size, so we are going to fit the gown to you first." Madam Clara pointed to a pile of sky blue satin with lace dripping from much of it. "Off with those coveralls. I do hope you are wearing a chemise. Don't just stand there gawking. Time is important. Now move!"

Ella had never undressed before anyone in her life. Yes, she did have on a shabby garment she'd hardly call a chemise. But she would feel absolutely naked.

Hands began to pull her coveralls from her as two other women took over. Suddenly she was standing there in her poor, old undergarments. With a swish the pile of sky blue satin fell over her head. It felt cool and slippery against her skin. Rows of lace drifted around the bodice, from the sleeves, and in swags around the skirt. Strings in the back were drawn tight.

She stood stiff as a dummy. The two women began to stitch places where the lace needed to be fastened. Her woolen cap had been plucked off, so her hair fell softly down onto her shoulders. What a strange sensation. Ella realized there was a mirror across the room. Shyly she looked at the mysterious person who stood in the sky blue gown. It took a minute to recognize herself. She looked so different, in a beautiful gown with her hair down. Tears filled her eyes.

"Girlie, don't you dare let a tear drop on this satin. It will make a mark," said one of the women as she handed Ella a bit of cloth, "Dry those eyes."

That's me! Realized Ella. *That's really me. I even look like a real girl. This must be what Heaven is like. My Mum must be up there looking fine, not burned and scalded from the accident. Oh, if she could only see me now. Maybe she can.*

"Turn, turn! Wake up girlie. Turn around," the woman barked at her. "More lace on the bodice. Harold has no bust. You haven't much either—sorry. It's such a shame that this gown will be wasted on that old sot Harold. I know pantos is for laughs. This is maybe going too far. Olivia, help me get this thing off without crushing it. At least for the first performance it won't be wrinkled. Off you go now, girlie. We'll call you if we need you again. Scoot!"

Ella climbed back into her coveralls. They now felt cold and strange. She wanted to be the girl in the mirror again as she stuffed her hair back under her cap.

The afternoon performances of *Puss* went off without any problems. Ella went through the usual schedule of chores in a bit of a fog. When Sammy, who played the bulldog, had a rip in his costume, it needed to be mended. Ella volunteered to take it to the workroom. This was something she usually would never offer to do. She felt compelled to go there, see the colors, the fabrics, and maybe even see the sky blue gown again.

There it was, hanging on a separate rack. A bit of a white sheet was draped over it just at the top. Outside a street lamp had been lit. It shined through the small window on the satin like a spot light. Ella finally laid the bulldog suit on one of the tables. The costume women were gone for the day. They would find it in the morning.

Slowly she walked across the room to stand in front of the gown. Gently, she ran a finger over its slippery fabric. Then she turned and almost ran from the room. That gown was her gown, not Harold's. It was meant to be beautiful, not laughable. Tears began to race down her cheeks.

THE THEATRE HAD SWUNG into a high frenzied mode in order to get *Cinderella* up and ready to go. Theatres in London were closed on Christmas Day. It was a church and family time. Boxing Day was a big day for coming out for entertainment. *Penelope's Pantomime Theatre* was one of several in the City. The more elaborate theaters got the big audiences.

Behind the back stage, besides the wardrobe workshop, was the scenery/props area. It was a lot bigger and a lot noisier. There was hammering, sawing—re-doing scenery from the former *Cinderella.* The engineer had rolls of plans on how to create the horseless carriage. It seemed the plan involved using a flexible tube from the scenery steam pipes to run up behind the carriage to power the wheels. Ella couldn't quite see how the old machinery could handle more stress. But she wasn't an engineer. She'd keep the boilers and fireboxes up to snuff and hope for the best.

∼

THE WEATHER SEEMED to be in a co-operative mood. No more snow mush days. Often there was blue sky and sun. It was cold just the same. The sun days seemed to clear the air. Ella was able to sweep the entranceway often without pulling down her goggles. The *Cinderella* frenzy was in full swing.

Penelope was planning a grand gala for the opening of *Cinderella* on Boxing Day. It was scheduled for 3 P.M. with higher than usual prices. Adults were to be given a glass of champagne (cheap of course), children would receive a tiny lollipop. Penelope agreed to the latter only if the treat was small. She abhorred sticky fingers.

Only on a couple of occasions had Ella peaked into the costume workroom in hopes of seeing the sky blue gown. It was always there on its own special rack. She had a hard feeling in the pit of her stomach thinking about Harold wearing it.

Eli had noticed a change in Ella. She seemed quieter, a bit withdrawn maybe. Mary sent a special lunch with Eli that included some nice bits from their Sunday chicken. When Ella came in the stage door from her sweeping duties he called her over. "Ella, it's eleven. Time for a cuppa and with a little extra from Mary. Come, girl, have a seat."

Ella offered a weak smile, pulling up her usual joint stool to Eli's little table. He poured a beaker of hot tea for each of them, then laid out the chicken. "Mighty good," he said pushing it towards her. Ella took a couple of nibbles and nodded.

"You've been a bit quiet lately. Something bothering you? Has the *Old Lady* been working you too hard?" he queried.

"I'm sorry," she responded. "I've got something on my mind. Promise to keep a secret?"

"Of course, lovey, my lips are always sealed in a place like this. Oh, the secrets I could tell, but won't. So what's yours?" he spoke with a smile.

"Eli, I'm in love," she blurted out.

"You're what? With a bloke?" He hadn't expected anything like this.

"No, no! I'm in love with a dress, a gown. It's the one Harold is to wear in the ball scene when he's Cinderella. I had to be a dummy for Madam Clara. They fitted the gown to me. I saw myself in the mirror. It was the most wonderful moment of my life. Now I can't believe that Harold is going to wear that gown in the panto. It is much too elegant to be laughed at. I just can't get it out of my mind." Ella began to softly cry.

"Hush, hush, Ella dearie. You deserved to have such a lovely experience. No young lass like you should be done up in sooty coveralls all the time." He pulled a bandana from his hip pocket and handed it to her. "When I get a chance, I'll go take a peek at the fancy gown. Maybe what you need is a fairy godmother, like in that old story. The real story, not the panto." He gave her a big hug. He felt a tear in his own eye as Ella thanked him and scooted off toward the cellar and her next chores.

LATER THAT NIGHT, Eli and Mary sat in their snug little kitchen after supper as he began telling her about Ella and the ball gown.

"Why, it's preposterous to make such a dress for that old sot Harold to wear. No wonder poor Ella is upset," said Mary harshly. "She doesn't know about us, does she? You haven't told her anything?"

"No, not a word. I just try to keep an eye out for her. The *Old Lady* is never nice to her. It really is a shame," Eli shook his head. "What shall we do?"

"Ella needs a real Christmas surprise. Are the Steam Fitters across the alley from Penelope's having their usual Christmas Eve Ball?" asked Mary. "You know some of the fellows. Get us three invites. Then let me get to thinking. Our Ella will have a Christmas to remember, no matter what."

She got up and headed up to their sleeping area in the loft over the kitchen. "Here, Eli! Come give me a hand with the old trunk," she hollered.

ON CHRISTMAS EVE DAY, Eli again brought out a special elevens lunch for him and Ella. Then he took her hand to tell the plans he and Mary had made. Mary was to arrive shortly before closing time with a bundle. She would go up to Ella's garret room to wait.

Everyone would be anxious to leave the theatre to get away to family or friends. Penelope had scheduled a last dress rehearsal on Christmas Day at noon. Lots of grumbling went around when that was announced. Penelope was really pushing for her *Panto Spectacular*, meaning everyone had to make an extra effort.

Around seven, when Eli was sure he had ushered all the crew and actors out, he slipped over to the costume workroom. The gown for Harold was still hanging there. It hadn't been moved to his dressing room yet. That would be tomorrow. Eli gently cradled it in his arms and hurried up the stairs to Ella's room.

Mary had already gotten Ella out of her coveralls. From her bundle she produced a soft long chemise, pantaloons, and silk stockings held up by ribbon garters. Lastly came a pair of ivory satin slippers. "My wedding things," Mary shyly told Ella. "They've just been sleeping in my old trunk all these years. I had hoped we'd have a daughter one day. Just didn't happen. It's good to see you make use of them all."

Slowly and gently, Mary combed down Ella's hair. There was a bit of natural curl, so it fell in soft ringlets on her shoulders. Eli arrived with the gown just as Mary finished arranging the undergarments on Ella. Together they lifted it over Ella's head. It draped down into a perfect fit. It only needed the strings on its back drawn."Oh my dear," sighed Mary. "You are absolutely lovely."

"One big problem," said Ella. "We're going to a Ball. I don't know how to dance!"

"All you really need to know is to waltz," said Eli. "It's a set of threes—1, 2, 3, 1, 2, 3. Here let me show you."

"Eli was always a fine dancer," spoke up Mary. "Yes, he has always been a fine one." Her eyes sparkling as she remembered a time long ago.

Eli pulled Ella to him. Humming softly, he counted the threes. Soon he had Ella moving with easy steps in the little room.

"Is this really going to work? asked Ella. "What if we get caught? Now I'm really nervous and worried."

"It will be fine," Eli replied. "I even got a boy from the scenery shop to lay a couple scrap boards across the alley to the Steam Fitters Hall back door. Just hold that gown up though there's not much snow mush left.

One more item came from Mary's bundle—a white wool shawl for Ella to wear around her shoulders.

"And we're off!" laughed Eli.

The trio wove their way down the narrow stairs, over to the Stage Door, then out into the night. The door to the Steam Fitters Hall was already open. Lights and music poured out into the alley. Ella minced her way over the boards. Eli led the way, then Ella, then Mary.

Several fellows hailed Eli as they entered as well as giving a special look-see to Ella with Mary. Ella felt very self conscious, keeping close to Mary. It was all overwhelming. A fire roared at the end of the Hal, while streamers decorated the walls. A cold buffet had been set up in the corner across from the musicians. The Steam Fitters had spared no expense as the band was one of the clockwork groups that were so popular. Ella had never seen any before. The Panto still used live musicians who were always on staff.

Across the Hall stood young solicitor Phillip Owens. His uncle was on the ruling board of the Steam Fitters. He insisted Phillip come to the Ball as a reward for agreeing to take his two young cousins to the Panto Spectacular on Boxing Day. "You work too hard," his uncle had said. "Come, have a bit of holiday cheer. There's bound to be a girl or two."

Phillip was not much of a party goer. Though he was happy to promise the two boys a visit to the Panto. This Ball was a bit awkward for him. Other than his uncle, he didn't know a soul. He stood off to the side just watching the merry makers. He noticed the trio come in through the open back door—an older couple with a lovely young girl wearing a beautiful blue satin gown. It was festooned with creamy flounces of lace. They all took seats across the Hall.

After a while the older couple stepped out on the dance floor. The man led the lady deftly about in a waltz. They were a joy to watch and see the joy they had in each other's eyes. The young girl seemed ill at ease, but she closely watched the old couple.

He found himself in front of her. "Milady, my name is Phillip. Would you care to dance?"

He startled Ella, who exclaimed, "Oh! I really don't know how to dance."

"It's a slow waltz," Phillip replied. "I'm sure we can manage." And he held out his hand.

She only stepped on his toes once as Phillip led her gently around the floor. *Eli had been a good teacher*. When the clockwork band ran down, he escorted her back to her chair.

Eli and Mary were sitting there again. Phillip made a small bow, thanked her for the dance, and returned to his place across the Hall.

The trio had a brief nibble from the buffet. Outside, a church clock struck ten. Eli gave a nod, and with Mary and Ella, they all made their way out the back door into the alley. Once inside the Stage Door they all gave a sigh of relief and wound up the stairs to Ella's room. Off came the gown, the underpinnings, the slippers. Eli waited outside until Mary handed him the gown. He quickly headed down to the costume workroom. The gown looked as good as new as he hung it on the rack.

Mary waited for him by the Stage Door. Her own precious things were once again in the bundle. "She's asleep," Mary said softly. "May she have wonderful dreams. I'm glad you showed her how to waltz, Eli. It was fun to see her and that young man out on the floor. He seemed a bit lonely, too."

"We've a ways to go," said Eli. "I hope there's a good Christmas breakfast in the future," as he gave Mary a nudge. "No time for a feast tomorrow, thanks to the *Old Lady*. Humbug!"

He locked the door behind him as they stepped off on their way home. There were lots of merrymakers and music as they went along. Mary hung on Eli's arm. They were feeling quite merry themselves. Ella had had her chance to be a real girl at a real Ball. What a better present could they have given her?

Eli suddenly stopped and pointed up, "Look, Mary, you can almost see the moon. Do you even remember the moon?"

Mary smiled. "Of course I do, dearie." She gave his arm a little squeeze. "It's just been so long since we could see it, let alone the stars. Maybe it's our own special Christmas present."

He smiled, too, giving her hand a pat.

One more look and they continued on their way home.

CHRISTMAS DAY dawned clear and bright. Ella was awakened by the sound of church bells ringing throughout London. It took a minute or two before she remembered what Day it was and what all happened the night before. *Did it really happen? It must have. How could she ever thank Eli and Mary? They had taken quite a risk for her.* If she closed her eyes, she could see the Hall, the band, and the young man who had danced with her. She could feel the dress around her again.

Boilers! She bounded out of bed, threw icy water on her

face from the old bowl by the door, dried with the old cloth, climbed into her coveralls, boots, hat and goggles, and was on her way down the stairways to the cellar.

People were slow coming in today. There wasn't a show, just the rehearsal at noon. No one was happy about that—on Christmas Day. Ella wondered if her stingy Aunt Penelope would sweeten the pot by giving a lunch or a bit of a bonus. Everyone could use either one, including herself.

"Happy Christmas, Ella," called Eli as she came up from her chores in the cellar. Then he whispered, "Do you remember last night?"

"Oh Eli, it's just a dream now. But it really did happen, didn't it? Thank you and Mary so much, I'll never forget it," she said as she gave Eli a hug.

"Come back for elevens. We might as well have a bite before rehearsal. Mary sent us each a jam tart. I'll have a pot going for our cuppa," Eli smiled, giving Ella a wink.

Penelope began the dress rehearsal right at noon. The stage steam crew was checking out the moving sets plus the horseless carriage right up until the stage manager called —*Places*! Harold had obviously *fortified* himself beforehand. Yet he carried his role off rather well, considering. Ella peeked out from backstage. The sets were all working well. She scooted down to do the afternoon shovels full, then she returned to watch.

Harold had been *fortifying* again. It took two stage hands to get him and the gown into the horseless carriage off stage before it moved onto center stage. When it was time for his big entrance from the carriage, he tripped and fell out onto the stage, rumpling the gown. *Her gown. How could he?*

"Harold!" came a loud screech from the auditorium. "Get yourself under control at once. You're drunk!" It was Penelope, a very angry Penelope. "If you don't show up sober tomorrow I will have you drawn and quartered with your head on a pike over the entrance door! Don't you dare ruin my big spectacular!"

There was a subdued titter among the cast and crew. Harold scrambled to his feet, then blurted out, " It's the damn gown! There's just too much of it." He resumed his character, prancing and swishing as if he was going to the Ball.

The rest of the rehearsal went well. When it was finished, Penelope did call everyone onto the stage, thanking all for giving up their Christmas Day. Everyone got a coin, Christmas largesse. Ella received five pence. But that was more than she usually was *paid*. Even this little bit was unusual for Penelope. She surely was counting on a good profit from this spectacle.

EVERYONE WAS to be at the theatre by noon on Boxing Day even though the performance was not until 3 P.M. The steam stage crew had to move the horseless carriage over to the area on stage right from up stage left where it ended up at the close of the production. It was a challenge with the steam hose snaking along up stage of the carriage. From the audience, it looked as heavy as the Queen's gold carriage. In reality it was rather flimsy plywood with lots of clever paint. Getting Harold in the gown in and out was a bit difficult.

Amazingly, people began lining up at the ticket booth as early as 1 P.M. Only the expensive box seats were reserved. General admission was on a first come basis.

Ella double checked the boilers before curtain time. The steam stage crew also checked with her. This spectacle put quite a strain on all the old pipes. But everything checked out as ready to go. Even Harold was ready. The few glimpses Ella had of him, he seemed perfectly sober. After all, he did have his reputation as the star of the Panto to maintain. A flop—literally—like he'd done at the dress rehearsal would ruin him. He knew it.

UP IN THE BALCONY, Phillip tried to keep his two young cousins calm. Most of the audience was families with crying toddlers to loud older children. At last a trumpet call from the orchestra pit informed everyone that the show was about to start.

The first sight of poor Cinderella had the audience hooting and applauding. What a switch from the usual panto. Cinderella in her rags was actually a man with a wisp of a goatee. Phillip thought that was a bit over done. Yet panto was supposed to be ridiculous.

The first act ended with the Fairy Godmother promising Cinderella she would go to the Ball. The second act was to begin with the new horseless carriage to take Cinderella on her way. The use of the carriage had been advertised in the broadsides Penelope had spread all over London.

With a trumpet call, the curtains opened on a night scene with a star spangled sky. With a slight hissing of steam, the horseless carriage slowly made its way onto the stage. Cheers and applause greeted it. The paint on the carriage shone golden extravagance.

It stopped center stage. Harold managed to get himself out with a bit of difficulty, then with an arm raised twice, he presented himself to the audience resplendent in the sky blue satin gown.

The audience changed from cheers to hoots of raucous

laughter. Harold made a grandiose bow before sashaying across the stage with much overdone feminine swishing.

Phillip sat mesmerized, looking not at Harold but at the gown he was wearing. He blinked, blinked again. "I've seen that dress! How could I have seen it? When, where?" he puzzled.

Suddenly it came to him. The Christmas Eve Ball at the Steam Fitters Guild. He had danced a waltz with a lovely, shy young girl—in that very dress! There couldn't be two alike. How could she have worn it if now Harold wore it as Cinderella?

Phillip didn't really remember the rest of the panto. Afterward, his cousins were laughing and trying to copy some of the actions they had seen as Phillip got them the promised lollipops. Then off they headed through the streets filled with the usual Boxing Day revelers. All the while, his mind kept jumping between his memory of the Ball and Cinderella in the *same* dress.

After seeing his cousins home, he went straight to his flat. He was not really a drinking man, but a small brandy seemed in order before he settled into bed.

ELLA SLOWLY CLIMBED out of bed the morning after *Cinderella* debuted. A low clanging in the pipes alerted her to get up for boiler duty. Penelope was so pleased with yesterday's show she had put out a sign in front of the theatre announcing two shows today. One at 3 P.M. and one at 6 P.M. . A sell-out for both was expected. Ella knew she would have to do two feedings of coal if there was to be that extra performance.

Eli was always at his post early. Ella hurried past on her

way down to the cellar. "Come for a cuppa when you're through," Eli hollered at her. She waved as she headed down into the heat and steam, goggles on.

The stage door opened. A young man in a heavy tweed coat entered sporting a smart bowler he had above his goggles. He blinked in the semi-dark backstage area. When he spotted Eli, he came directly over to the small desk. Removing his goggles he greeted Eli. "Good morning. My name is Phillip Owens, and I'm a solicitor working for the Independence Insurance Company. We are trying to locate a young woman, Eloise Carter. We think she may be employed here. Do you know her? Is she here?"

Before Eli could answer, screams began coming from the stage. "Help, help! Fire! There's a fire on stage!"

One of the steam crewmen came running to Eli. "The curtains are on fire! We tried to use the sand buckets, but it spread too fast. That damned carriage tipped over onto the gas footlights. The paint went up in a flash and caught the near curtains. I turned off the gas valve but it's a real blaze out there."

"You-out!" Eli barked at Phillip. Smoke reached backstage. Eli pulled the rope on the emergency steam whistle. It went off with a horrible shriek. "Fire!" Eli yelled. "Everyone out—NOW! Leave your things and get out! Run. Fire! Fire!" The smoke grew thicker.

Ella came up from the cellar to find pandemonium backstage. The steam whistle alarm blared. People ran to the stage door. Eli yelled, "Out—out! Get out! Leave your things. Get yourself out!" Ella didn't really have any *things* to worry about.

Just then Harold came dashing by, pushing people aside with a large carpet bag. "Out of my way. Let me through. I have to get out. Move, damn it, move."

When Ella saw him, her mind suddenly focused on the gown. It was the only thing she *had*. Down the hall she ran to Harold's dressing room. There *it* was, all in a heap on the floor. Grabbing a large towel from the makeup table, she scooped up the gown and wrapped it inside. Out into the hall again she ran.

If Ella hadn't known the quickest way to the stage door, she might not have gotten there. Thick ash and smoke filled the air. Eli stood by the door yelling for her, "Ella, Ella girl, where are you?"

"Here I am, Eli. We've both got to get out,"

Eli pulled her to him and they both charged out into the alley. People had moved from the alley to the street. Smoke poured from the panto theatre. Everyone yelled or cried. Ella looked for Penelope without luck. Eli still hugged her close.

From down the street came the District Fire Brigade. Their huffing steam tanker making a big racket with its huge bell.

"Make way! Make way!" the firemen yelled. The driver brought it to a halt at the end of the alley. Three other firemen jumped down to begin moving the steam pressure hoses.

There was a loud boom. Flames shot through the top of the building as the roof collapsed into the structure. The panto theatre was a goner. The firemen poured water and steam into the theatre, but it was a lost cause. The crowd was eerily quiet. Eli pulled Ella further up the street. The air was hot from the flames. Sadly, even the *Penelope's Pantomime* sign over the ticket booth began to char.

Eli spotted the solicitor bloke coming through the crowd. "Sir, sir!" he called. "I'm sorry to bother you in the midst of all this trouble. Can you tell me anything about Miss Eloise Carter? Was she in that building? Is she safe?"

Eli chuckled, "She sure is safe. She's right here, only we

don't call her Eloise. She's just Ella. A bit of a *Cindered Ella*." He pulled out his big handkerchief, then pushed Ella's goggles off. She looked like a raccoon. Her face was sooty, except where the goggles had been. Eli spit on the cloth and began to wipe the soot from her face. Then he noticed her bundle.

"What'd got there, girl?"

"It's the gown, Eli. I went to Harold's dressing room to get it. He just left it in a pile on the floor. I couldn't let it burn. I know it doesn't really belong to me. But I had to save it." She pulled the sooty cloth off, showing what she had been clutching so hard.

"That dress!" exclaimed Phillip. "Cinderella wore that dress. But I think you wore it first." Slowly he pulled the woolen cap from Ella's head. Her hair tumbled down. "You were at the Christmas Eve Ball—in that very dress. And you waltzed with me"

"She sure did. Me and my wife took her to the Ball," said Eli. "I recognize you, now, young man. Why have you been looking for our Ella?"

Ella couldn't speak a word. *What was going on? Why was her dance partner here?*

Phillip explained, "As I told you earlier, I'm a solicitor working for the Independence Insurance Company. Your parents had a policy with us. When they were killed in the airship accident, you became their heir—heiress, I should say. It's been hard to find you. That Penelope person appeared before we were able to contact you, saying she was your aunt. She took you away. We didn't know who she was or where you had gone until recently. We think she paid off a crooked solicitor to get it approved. Did you know she was your aunt before the accident?"

"No, I had never heard of her. I've been so lonely and sad

about my parents. I just assumed she was. She's not been a very loving relative," Ella shyly admitted. "I guess I have no relatives at all now." A tear began to travel down her cheek.

"You're wrong, Ella dear," Eli said. "There hasn't been a time I could legally tell you. I'm your great uncle. I'm your Mum's uncle. By the time Mary and I learned about the accident and what Penelope had done, all we could do was to come here to London to keep an eye on you while we saved to get a good solicitor. Then we could claim you as our own. Now you're coming home with me at last."

"Oh Eli—I mean Uncle Eli. You have been the only person to care about me. Well, and Aunt Mary of course, too. What a grand surprise." She snuggled closer to Eli.

Phillip looked at Eli with a new light in his eyes. "Eli, I will inform my company that I have found Miss Eloise Carter. And," he paused a moment, "may I call on Miss Ella this Sunday afternoon? I'll have the papers about her inheritance. It is quite substantial. I will also see to it that you are named her guardian until she comes of age."

"We will expect you for tea. We are at number seventeen Thomas Lane, just around the corner from old St. Thomas church. Mary will have her all scrubbed up bright and shiny," Eli spoke with a chuckle.

"I don't know," replied Phillip. "I think I like this *Cindered Ella*." He pulled out his own handkerchief and gently wiped a tiny smudge off Ella's nose, and she giggled.

Phillip continued, "Thank heavens for that blue dress. I might have given up trying to find you. Until Sunday, then." He made a little bow with a huge smile on his face.

That evening, a scrubbed Ella bundled up in one of Mary's flannel nighties sat by the warm stove having a cuppa. Eli had filled Mary in on the extraordinary day he and Ella had had. The panto theatre was gone. Phillip had found Eloise

Carter, who it turns out was an heiress. And over on a bench in the corner lay a very rumpled and slightly sooty sky blue gown.

"Life certainly has its twists and turns," mused Mary. "Tomorrow we will hit the shops first thing. You are going to need a wardrobe now."

"I can hardly wait. I'm going to really be a girl again. Thank you both so, so much. I love you both." She popped up to give them each a hug.

PHILLIP ARRIVED right on time for Sunday's tea. He was met at the door by a charming young woman dressed in a pale rose wool dress with a bright flowered shawl and curls that flowed down to her shoulders. She wore an even brighter smile.

"Please come in. We're so anxious to hear what you have to tell us," Ella beamed as she showed him into the tiny cottage.

"Where is *Cindered Ella*," Phillip asked. "I've just been met by a lovely young lady."

"Oh, she's gone, gone for good," Ella laughed. "No more big coal scoops or steam pipes. Just a family now."

As they sat across the table Phillip handed Ella a folder of papers. She was to receive a legacy of £5,000 now, with £1,000 a year until she was twenty-five. Any balance left at that time would be distributed as she decided then.

"I have one of our other solicitors learned in such matters looking into that business with Penelope. There definitely was some hanky-panky, maybe even some financial dealings for her to make amends to you for. It won't be long before Eli and Mary are legally your guardians. If I may come again next Sunday, I can fill you in on what we discover." Phillip smiled at Ella.

~

THERE WERE MANY SUNDAY TEAS, with outings, some even into the country outside London's sooty smog, as spring arrived. Ella and Phillip were married in May the next spring in the parlor of the handsome house she had bought for Eli and Mary. She wore a lovely ivory dress with a sash of sky blue satin. For her something old, she wore Mary's treasured cameo pin. For something borrowed, on her feet she wore the ivory satin slippers.

That night the moon shone. Some said they even saw stars. What a wonderful wedding present.

MY OWN BUTTONS

MARIEV, ERIE MATRIARCH

I AM REALTY IMPAIRED.

It took me four minutes to type that small mental exercise and I spelled reality wrong.

It's Christmas Eve. I-- my computer system, that is-- was "turned off" when Dad piloted me in a small plane out of the Boston airport where I had received my annual chip upgrade. And Dad gave me an early Christmas present: A ZIF chip-- Zero Insertion Force. This word processor software allows me to express in writing what is going on inside my pointed head.

Guess he's given up on me ever becoming a stand-up comedian. For about half an hour, while my computer aided reality was turned off, I was Dad's pseudo co-pilot, strapped in the cockpit next to him. I had a fake control panel to keep me busy while my frontal lobes were elsewhere.

I imitated his every move while flying the plane. If Dad spoke, I repeated the words back to him. In a zombie-like relationship to external stimuli, I did whatever he did.

I had no curiosity, no initiative, no foresight, no judgment or feelings. No remorse, no conscience. My mind was not integrated with reality... I don't mind being "turned off"--unable to make decisions and at the mercy of my environment. When I'm turned off, I respond to events without reflection.

Without my computer to regulate me, my being, my center, my soul is absolutely functioning as it ever did. Half an hour ago, my body was in the cockpit of this plane working a fake control panel like a two year old in a car restraining seat, instead of an eleven year old brain-damaged boy. But I was thinking about stars that are older than the universe that contains them-- How can that be? While I'm not dealing with the world, but simply mimicking whoever I'm with, I may be thinking about fractals, or why do people have emotions? I may have a concept of God.

Dad wants me to relate outwardly to the world around me. He's constantly giving me shots of NGF nerve growth factor and arranging a stimulating environment.

He encourages me to talk.

I can't.

Talking is entwined with logic, abstraction, memory and learning. It involves a lot of complicated button pushing to form an alliance with the sensory and cerebella systems. My tongue flops out of my mouth-- I just don't have the concentration needed to keep up my end of a conversation.

Drugs and electrical stimulation are introduced directly into the damaged areas of my brain with small electrical bursts, released by a probe to modify the chemistry of my brain by altering the interactions between neurons mediated by neurotransmitters, when a button is pushed on the computer panel attached to my forearm.

Once we were in the air, Dad hit my power button, ON. And I was compelled to respond to events in the outer world. My crippled brain received a jolt to the central core of the reticular activating system. I got electrical activity going on in the prefrontal areas of my gray mass. Activities in my parietal lobes were enhanced, and I was brought back from simply being.

My Dad pushes a lever on the flight controls, then, with the same flourish, reaches over and hits a number of buttons on the external hard drive attached to my left arm.

Now I am capable of the planning and sequencing of complex behavior. I push the buttons to make my brain push more buttons activating whole areas of my mind in an expansive process. My neuronal networks reconfigure, and then begin to interpret the world. Slowly at first, as if I were just coming awake, then faster and faster, from a digital order of perspective, I become analog.

Now I have direction and meaning, I can create works of imagination and my mind is integrated in memory. I can empathize and identify with the feelings and actions of my Dad, but I'm no longer compelled to imitate him.

My frontal lobes flood with serotonin. Brain cells adjacent to neurons spark, then fire. My subsystems begin to function in tandem and I can execute voluntary movements. My mind orders my hand to make adjustments to alter its own chemistry, and produce enzymes, and synthesize neurotransmitters in whatever area they're needed. I reprogram my own cerebral software. I inject specific areas of my mind with drugs to exorcise guilt, erase traumatic memories and destroy psychosomatic disorders by exorcising the abnormal thoughts that sometimes arise within me like ghosts...I don't know where they come from.

I look at the display of my brain on my left forearm the same way Dad looks at his watch. Areas of my brain brighten as there is an increase to the cerebral blood flow in the part of my cortex concerned with sensations to the hand and fingers.

The increased stimulation allows me to type with my right hand on the keyboard attached to my left forearm: I AM REALITY IMPAIRED.

My sinuses are plugged. You don't know how annoying that can be for someone like me. My head is thudding so hard my connectors give an audible hum.

I'm an unattractive child, Steven Hawkingish. Without implanted electrodes within my brain to balance my chemicals and to regulate higher cognition, I'd be a detriment to society.

I'd be crazy. Like my mother.

I was born without developed frontal lobes and various abnormalities in the chemical and electrical systems in my organ of thought, that little saline pool, my brain. My head is misshaped, my eyes slightly crossed, and my reasoning is, in a sense, artificial.

This singularity of meaning-- I am my disability, I am my computer-- is the one immediately recognizable place to point when asked what is wrong with my life. Everything leads to it, everything recedes from it-- my abnormality as a personal vanishing point. But if I get depressed, I can always metabolize more serotonin and norepinephrine.

In response to my sniffles, Dad, the pilot, says, "Give a hit to your auto-immune button, Jesse."

I punch the button that stimulates my thymus, but I still need to blow my nose. I start to raise my sleeve, but the panels on my arms-- external hard drives connected by wires fed under my skin to my brain-- remind me that I am not a normal boy. I can't wipe my snot on my sleeve.

I need a brain upgrade...I need extra capacity to deal with a runny nose.

Where are the tissues?

I program myself for more electrical stimulation of the

reticular formation, and pathways open to memory capacities that hold knowledge of tissues. Tissues are in my bag that is near my left foot, my brain tells me.

I grow new brain cells when I need them. It is an exquisite balance I keep. Each button on my panel is connected to a probe in my brain. More stimulation, more synapses. I don't want to become too overloaded to function. Within my brain, heightened ability in the area being stimulated coexists with profound deficiencies in other areas. For instance, with the push of a button to stimulate the area of my brain that holds mathematics, I can give an answer to what day of the week Christmas will fall in the year 4339.

But I might wet my pants while I'm putting all my concentration on it. In order to concentrate on finding a tissue and blowing my nose, I forget everything I know.

And I can't cry. There are no networks established in my cerebellum for the manufacture of tears.

I have seen other people cry and I wonder, would they sell their tears? I think not. I may be very rich, but tears are for those who can afford sorrow.

My dad takes it upon himself to regulate my brain, even erase some of my memories, but on the occasions he's not hovering over me, I enjoy directing my own brain enhancement.

Still, there is a time to stop expanding...A time to erase old memory files to make room for short term data, like I've got to blow my nose.

I honk hard into the tissue, discard it, and replace the box in my bag.

Then I forget the location of the tissues.

I'm more than the sum of my parts, much more than a system of pumps and networks. I'm a small boy with a head cold, and I'm worried about flying, and in some ballistic part of my mind, I want a pony for Christmas.

I know I should cut off all my inappropriate response tendencies right now, but, hey, we've got about an hour of flight time. I have time to dream about a pony.

The windshield wipers keep up a steady beat against a coating of soft snow. I manage a smile at my dad. I see him as a hazy outline until I hit the button on my left wrist that stimulates the area of my brain involved with visual information.

Now I can see Dad in detail. He gives a laugh that ends in a snort, and I realize what the joke is: he has wires and sprockets and computer chips held to his scalp with clumps of bubble gum; great wads of chewed pink Bazooka that mat his sandy hair into islands of goop upon his nicely-shaped head.

When I'm "turned off" I imitate my dad, but now he is imitating me, and laughing gleefully, snort, snort. He's ridiculous-- he looks like me. The sight of him hits me square in the humor center of my brain.

I wish I could laugh spontaneously-- Dad is such a fool-- But I have never done anything spontaneously in my life. It's all measured.

By pushing a button, I stimulate one part of my parietal cortex, and I am allowed to imagine myself pulling a joke on Dad. A reality impaired person wears their underwear wherever they want to, I decide-- They can wear it on their head, covering their cranium. I do. I pull a pair from my overnight bag and that's where I put my underwear: On my pointed bald head, over the electrodes.

I look even funnier than my old man, I think. When at last I laugh, I snort too.

Dad reaches into his shirt pocket and hands me a candy cane. I unwrap the cellophane and jam the whole thing into my mouth, then toy with the button that delivers a brief electrical pulse deep within my limbic system. The candy tastes good.

I was born unbalanced. Most people have a polarity in their brain chemicals that points toward a common reality. Me, I point elsewhere.

I'm a space cadet. When I'm loaded up on motion-sickness medicine, I view reality a whole lot better. The astronauts have to take the same medicine as I do, because when you're out in space you get dyslexic and everything looks strange to you.

I'm spaced all the time.

I'm computerized. I can't maintain reality without all these implants that release medications and regulate my synapses. And these electro-cognitive charts and these panel lights to warn me if my brain is overloaded here or undernourished there.

These buttons.

∾

MY DAD SAYS I got impaired reality from my mother.

But actually, Mother's money provides for my state-of-the-art reality. Without her funds I couldn't afford to see everything in a clear light.

I see plainly that I arouse visions in Mother of a whole society in which behavior is manipulated by electrical stimulation rather than evoked through wild discharges of emotion —Society as a machine rather than a soap opera...The idea makes her crazy.

Dad thinks he can erase specific memories, and I won't know that mother left him because he wouldn't put me in an institution.

I know. I know, because I got my deformed genetic material from both my parents. Although Mom figures she just faxed me in, I got my insanity, and my intuition, from her.

She hates my dad, too, with a passion so strong. Maybe that only makes sense to me, and there is no way I'll ever communicate what I really mean.

But they say you kill the thing you love.

Mom couldn't deal with a deformed, disabled child. A reality impaired child. Six months after I was born, my mother flew off in her airplane. A Piper Cub.

And never came back. She gave Dad the estate where we live and this expensive airplane and lots and lots of money. And custody of me.

Who am I to blame her? I'm a failure in the ability to synthesize. I'm odd, I'm berserk. I'm abnormal So is she.

A random act of memory: I remember the man who came to the mansion one night, and told my father that Mom had offered him five hundred thousand dollars to murder us both. Would my father give him a million not to?

I remember.

"GOD, how am I ever going to get this gum out of my hair?" Dad asks. He has disconnected the wires he'd used to spoof me, and now he's tugging at one of the pink lumps of gum he'd used to stick them to his head, and only succeeding in mangling it into the strands of his thick hair.

I think I can assess that information for him. I open a window on the screen on my arm. When I have the information, I close the window and type: ICE WILL REMOVE THE GUM. STICK YOUR HEAD OUT THE WINDOW.

I show what I wrote to my dad, and this time he snorts a long time at the end of his laugh.

I sneak my hand over to the psychotropic button that will release mood-altering drugs into my nucleus accumbens, the pleasure center of my brain. I know my checkpoints by heart, but I think I also received some gene from good old Mom that makes me want to exceed my tolerances. Hail L-dopa! Hail opiate narcotics! Look out mind, here they come...One hit of this button will give me at least an hour of euphoria.

But I move so slowly that Dad has a chance to see what I am about to do. Damn those synaptic delays and the time it takes for a nerve impulse to pass along an axon. I can't get away with anything! Dad takes one sticky hand from the controls to slap my clumsy hand.

I type, COME ON, DAD. IT'S CHRISTMAS EVE. YOU SAID I COULD HAVE AN EXTRA JOLT TONIGHT.

I hold my arm up so he can read my message on the screen.

"Save it," is all he says.

I hear something! I smell something! My father is leaning back in the pilot's seat, a half-smile on his face. He doesn't fool me-- he just passed gas! The idea is so amusing I must give it expression:

FART! I write. Man, I love that word. FART, FART, FART... I show Dad what I wrote. FART ON YOU, I add.

I DO NOT SUFFER from a lack of intelligence, as my father thinks, or a moral weakness, as Mother thinks.

Basically, I have no method of my own to plan complex behaviors. I'm innocent.

Until I was five, and my dad found someone who could help me, I was, among other things, autistic; unable and unwilling to interpret the mental states of other people. I, baby Jesse, was totally dependent on the environment; I couldn't express or assert any degree of autonomy. Without free will of my own, I could only mirror the actions of others.

If my mother hadn't left, maybe I would have imitated her behavior and run amuck, an odd misshaped thing trying to burn down the mansion, or pluck the eyes from strangers, or something. I'll never know, will I?

Because she did leave, and Dad found Dr. Wovsayic, who isn't hampered, as others are, by the ethical considerations of intrusive procedures into the brain for experimental purposes. She has done pioneering work on the implantation in the brain of both neurons and glial cells.

Dr. W implanted miniature electrodes coated with cultured embryonic nerve cells to set up symbiotic residence in my brain. Even now, they're sending out nerve fibers to grow into my own cells. I don't know if I've grown any significant pathways, but when the system is turned on, I stop mirroring my environment, and begin to interact.

Despite the latest advancements in psychological cybernetics, given the expense and the experimental nature of the procedure, only two other people have been outfitted with a computerized system like mine, with mixed results: One of them reportedly committed suicide.

MY FATHER HAS STRETCHED a thick stream of gum between one hand and his head. "Damn," he mutters, and tries to shake it off his hand, only it expands whiplike, and catches to the palm of his other hand as he reaches to contain it.

This is the man I imitate when my frontal lobes are shut off. Directly above the pulse in my arm, I actually have a button labeled, "Power." Hit that button, and I only have a few seconds of stimulation to my brain to turn myself back on before I revert to an imbecile.

I gaze out the window and wonder at the brilliance of Venus in the sky...Is that the Christmas star that the wise men followed to a manger? Then, like gathering vultures, the clouds obscure the view.

We hit a pocket of turbulence sending the small plane plummeting through space as Dad fights to regain control. I slowly look over at him, and after a minute or so, I show my alarm.

"Shall I turn you off?" he offers.

I shake my head, no, only shake is the wrong word for it. Gradually, I turn my head from side to side. I don't want to be turned off, because, if we crash and die, I want to know it...

The plane is steady now, but sleet hits the windshield like handfuls of tossed sand. Below us, the wind lifts the snow into whirling dervishes that dance across a purple valley.

We hit another pocket of air, then raise on thermals. The plane is an instrument of torture; it rides like a runaway roller coaster. The electronic connections jar in my head.

"Well, then," says Dad all in one breath, trying to hide his concern about the sudden weather. "Let's sing that song I made up." He says in a slower voice, pronouncing each syllable, "Do you remember it, Jesse?"

I WILL TYPE IT AS FAST AS YOU CAN SING IT, I challenge him.

He begins to sing off key:

"On the twelfth day of Christmas, my true love gave to me, twelve hackers hacking, eleven drives a driving..." And here Dad cocks his head, and adds in his best Dylan voice, "Everybody's gotta have drives." He gives me a wink.

"Ten keyboards clicking, nine window experts, eight megs of ram, seven databases, six spreadsheets..."

My Dad really drags out..."Five fractal rings...four calling modems, three IBMs, two brain implants..."

And at last in a deep baritone..., "And a cartridge to store mem-or-y-ee."

Sometimes I think my Dad is as mentally challenged as I am.

"Tonight Santa will come flying in a sleigh through these wild skies," he says, gesturing at the wind that tosses darkness surrounding us, and he sounds real happy. I think he must have a nice present waiting at the estate for me.

Maybe it's a pony. But I don't think Santa Claus would bring me a furry animal I can both nurture and ride. I'm not sure Saint Nick exists. I keenly note Dad's reaction when I write: SANTA CLAUS IS A MYTH. HE DOESN'T EXIST IN THE REALITY OF NORMAL PEOPLE.

I show this message to Dad, and I kinda hope he reads the rest of it too, about the pony.

"How did you find that out?" Dad asks.

He figures that all my experience comes through the computer. He never gives me credit for figuring anything out myself.

To the north, the entire sky flickers with an abnormal light. Dad swears under his breath.

"Look at this shit, will you?" he cries in response to a flash of white, white light that is at once everywhere. There is a crash of thunder in the distance like warfare, and Dad hits the flight yoke with the flat of one hand and swears again in an even louder voice.

It's a freaking electrical storm in the middle of a blizzard!" As if to mark his words, the wind blows pellets of hail straight into the windshield.

Dad gives me a look, and then takes a deep breath. I can see he's trying to relax for the sake of my environment.

So you no longer believe in Santa Claus. Well, you should keep an open mind." He pauses. "I recall a time as a youth that I was walking through the woods, and came unexpectedly upon an anomalous animal...That's what they call them: creatures that don't fit into the norm."

I know he is trying to take my mind off our predicament, which is really precarious. The whole plane shakes as if it's a rattle in the hand of a mindless child, and again the thunder, the lightning, the snow freshly released from the dark clouds that envelop us in a gray mass.

"It had the body of a pterosaurs," he says. "It had a long neck, and a tiny head that turned to look straight at me as I approached. It was black and white, spotted." He gives a chuckle. "Who would believe me if I told them I'd once seen a dinosaur in the woods that lumbered away without leaving a trace?"

I BELIEVE YOU!!!

Dad snorts, then snorts again, when he reads that.

It's true," he mumbles, and pulls up a little on the yoke as the plane yaws and rattles.

He studies the plane's instruments, then the ice pelting the windows. "Son, you can have that jolt now. Just go ahead and charge yourself up with anything you want."

!! ARE WE GOING TO CRASH???

I'm relieved beyond words when he grimaces, and says, "No... It's just that I need to tell you something. And I wouldn't want it to create a major mood disturbance. Perhaps you should release a little enkephalin into your receptors."

Oh boy. I know what that means. Enkephalin in the brain

acts as a tonic against loss and disappointment. He's going to tell me that I'm not going to get that pony.

"You have a hit of opiates," Dad says softly. "And after I tell you, if you want, you can take some holobata to forget."

What the hell is he talking about? My father has never let me use my own holobata!

"Jesse, you have to be strong." Dad is looking out the window as if there is something patterned to see there. "While we were in Boston, I found out that your mother has incurable cancer. They're giving her chemo, but..."

He turns to look directly into my eyes. "Honey, your mom is...dying. "

Is THAT IT? Well, what do I care? Boldly, I bring down the index finger of my right hand onto the psychotropic button on my left arm's panel. I just hope she leaves us all the money.

Right in front of my father, I hit the button that will release beta-endorphins into my brain, and then I hit it again. He makes no response. Through a glorious haze I hear him reminiscing.

"I met your mother when I ran out of fuel, and I had to make an emergency landing at her airport...Well, it's our airport now. But back then, when your mom lived at the estate, she loved to fly her little Piper Cub. Ms. Piper Stockings, that's what I called her."

He gives an idiot smile. "She directed me in. I couldn't have landed without her. And when I was safe, and I got out of my plane, the first thing I saw was your mother coming toward me. She was wearing these drooping red stockings. I know..." He laughs to himself and doesn't snort. "...You can't imagine it."

He doesn't speak for long moments, but I hear him take a shudder of breath. He's trying to hold back his tears.

"She suffered from anorexia even then," he manages at last. "But she was pretty. She was so pretty. She filled my tank for free. And then she took me in her Mercedes on that long trip down the lane from the airport to the mansion for dinner. And after we ate, she sang while I played my guitar."

He seems far away in his thoughts. "Your mother had a voice unlike any other. That's another thing she used to do. She used to sing."

Now he doesn't even know I'm here; he certainly doesn't know I'm writing everything he's saying... "Back then, when I met her, I had some strange illusion that I could look at her... and see through the layers of makeup, and all the money, and know her. Know her heart. And all the details of her life didn't matter, because I could see her soul."

He gives a low sob. "She drove me crazy. Then got mad because I was insane."

Slowly, it comes to me...I have a strange feeling, one that stiffens my hunched back. I feel sorry for my father.

Too bad he isn't like me. I don't have that many storage areas concerning her. It wouldn't be difficult for me to totally delete my mother from my memory all together.

Suddenly I'm thrown violently forward against my seat belt as the engine sputters and the plane enters a deep dive.

We're going down, we're going down! Dad is screaming his favorite cuss word over and over.

ARE WE OUT OF GAS??!! I type.

Dad doesn't even give notice of what I've written and held up for him to see. "I think we were hit by lightning!" he cries, but knowing my father and his penchant to ignore details, such as fuel, I doubt it.

We're going down. My whole world is thrown into chaos.

There is something outside myself, and it is whirling madly and falling, falling.

Dad hits the restart button. The engine catches, fires, and then sputters off.

"There's the airport!" Dad yells. Our airport, situated on the estate, appears before us, the runway newly outlined in red and green lights.

Dad fights with the controls of the plane, but suddenly the runway lights blend into purple, then blue. And then they seem to be one magnificent crystal thing hanging over our heads in the sky. We've done a belly-over.

I have one finger pressed solidly on the key that releases motion sickness medicine to my brain. The lights are coming closer, as startling as an alien saucer. The lights are immediate and upon us. At the last possible moment, the plane rights itself.

We hit the ground short of the runway with a big thump, raise into the air again, and then come down even harder. Dad hits the brakes with both feet. With a sickening jolt the yoke jerks under his hands and the plane, always tomb-like to me, skids sideways out of control.

There is an arch of colored electrical sparks outside my side window as we take out several runway lights.

I always felt this airplane wanted to kill me. For a moment, I experience blinking shades of red and green in a world revolving too fast for my center of gravity to keep up. I manage to push myself back on the seat and regain a slightly more balanced perspective, although every dial in me is going haywire. The plane is acting like a plow pushing an avalanche of snow against the windows as it travels across land.

A huge pine tree looms ten feet from the plane which is still skidding like a puck on ice. We are going to crash into it! I'm going to die!

I am frantic to know the combination of buttons to push to suddenly get religion.

As if some hand from above reaches down, the plane does a sudden turn, and the engine takes the full impact of the tree. The entire front of the airplane is crumpled, folded like an accordion, and the tree is inches from our faces.

For a long moment, there is silence, then a motor in the distance. It's the man servant, Ralph, who has worked for us ever since I can remember, on a snowplow. He pulls off the runway and heads across the field toward the wreckage raising mighty waves of snow before his blade. Dad unbuckles, kicks his door with one foot, then both, until it opens, and he jumps out into the blizzard.

I over-stimulate an entire network of nerve cells in my brain; I send hysterical signals to alert areas involved in vision, balance and motor control. Total hysteria. I'm scared. Fear causes me to push every button in a panic to move my bruised and aching body out of the wreckage. I have managed to unbuckle my seat belt when Dad is suddenly there and lifting me out of the rubble.

"Are you hurt?" Dad asks anxiously.

OK DADDY. OK

Dad leaves me a safe distance from the plane and goes to have an animated conversation with Ralph who has stopped nearby on the plow.

I move one leg and then the other, until I am close enough to hear Ralph saying excitedly, "All those drugs she does...She's crazy and you know it!"

"I used to think that she was simply eccentric," Dad says. "Actually, I found her unexpectedness quite stimulating."

"Now you listen to me," Ralph hisses. "That insane streak in her will turn to violence...That woman isn't going to wait to die...She will take herself out of this world..." Ralph raises one eyebrow. "And I wouldn't be surprised if she takes a few other people out with her, if you know what I mean."

"As a clinical psychologist, I think she's obsessed," Dad says.

"As a janitor, I think she's going to want to take you with her."

I have never seen Ralph like this before. Like a father to a son, he is anxiously advising Dad. "Her last wish will be to see you and Jesse dead beside her."

My father notices me standing near the twisted wing. Snow has accumulated on me like a snugly blanket. I see the fear in my father's eyes that I might short-out or something. In two strides he is to me, and he swings me up into his big arms.

The covering of snow falls from me like powdered sugar. I rest my huge head, still covered with my underwear, against his shoulder as he carries me to the snowplow. He holds me on his lap and I put my arms around his neck and Ralph drives us back to the small building that serves as the airport's control tower. The electrical storm rages; we travel through a strange kind of blizzard, fog blending into pelting snow, combined with thunder and lightning.

If not for the flashing of the multicolored lights Dad had hung all over the small shelter made of rocks, I don't think we would have found it or the Mercedes, both buried in snow.

Once inside the control center, I feel the warmth creeping back inside my bones. That's the way my dad would put it. I wonder if he'll ever read this, and he'll know, that's the way I put it, too.

Ralph turns off the runway lights and stokes the fire in the wood stove. There is a big comfortable couch, and we all three settle on it and drink cups of hot chocolate. I have a candy cane to stir mine.

"That was a crash landing in every sense of the word," Dad says.

"It was a real close call," says Ralph.

I say nothing.

At last Ralph sets his cup down and announces, "I'm going to start the car to warm it for you. I'll go on ahead and plow the lane." He turns at the door and adds, "We'll be lucky to get through, so hurry."

He lets in a cold blast of wind and snow. The second he closes the door behind him, the radio gives a little squawk. Dad gets up. His finger is on the off button when the short-wave comes alive. "SOS! SOS! Does anybody read me?"

The sound of the snowplow fades in the distance. Dad grabs up the microphone. "This is Fairlane Airport... We receive your Mayday. What is your location?"

A disembodied voice cries, "So foggy...Can't see anything." The transmission is broken up by static. I think something is said about engine trouble. Then, quite plainly, "...Instruments not working..."

Dad is standing ramrod straight. He pushes the button on the mike. "Identify yourself!" he snaps, his voice trembling.

"It's Santa Claus," comes the reply.

Dad turns to me and his eyes are wild, and I think the poor man has gone into shock. "It's your mother," he rasps.

Again he holds up the mike and shrieks frantically: "Identify yourself!"

"You know my calling letters. Now give me the coordinates to the roof."

Certainly I can see my father's predicament: If it's Ms. Piper Stockings gone mad-- or perhaps I should say, if it's Mom, mad as usual-- and she finds the landing field, she'll smash into the control room and kill all of us.

But I'm thinking about the anomalous animal my father

saw; I'm thinking that a logical, rich kid like me has no need for Santa, but there are millions of other children in the world who believe in him...And what if believing makes it "normal," and normal makes it real? What if it is Santa Claus, and he crashes...What will that mean to the world?

The end of magic, let science reign. Let the crowd take over, and there will only be what he did, and she said, and there will never be the why. The impossible will never be accepted: No one will ever believe that even when I'm turned off, I think.

"You've got to believe me," the voice says over the radio, and I can't tell if it's a man's or a woman's, but I think it is a low, soothing voice, a lovely voice. "Turn on the lights so I can see to land...or else I'll crash and die."

Dad drops the mike and uses both hands to pull at the lumps of gum in his hair. "It's her! My kamikaze ex-wife!"

His nostrils flare, and his eyes are wild, red lines threading through the whites. "What should I do?" he asks himself.

I think, Brain and brain; what is brain?

"Give me the coordinates to your roof," mocks the voice from the radio. "Turn on the runway lights."

My father lets out an agonized scream. He runs and huddles in the furthest corner of the room.

This hardly seems fair. Is there no justice? Now it is up to me, a feeble-minded eleven year old who is possibly insane, to make the decision of whether to light the runway.

It's like I'm torn in two. Split-brain soup. The part of me that is computerized figures logically that it must be my doomed mother in her Piper Cub up there in the violent sky trying to get a fix on us so we can all die in one big explosion.

But the right, intuitive hemisphere of my brain tells me it's Santa Claus. Why not?

Impossible things do happen.

My heart is hammering like a wild animal trying to escape the cage of my chest. I might have a heart attack if I don't keep my adrenaline to an acceptable level. I don't think I've ever felt perspiration before in my life, but now sweat coats my body. I've got to turn off. I have to shut down my frontal lobes, I must stop interrelating with the world. This is too much pressure: I can't take it.

A red light flashes on my control panel, then two others at once, then a loud BEEP and a message on my display screen, ERROR...Y)TRY AGAIN N)DELETE.

I don't want to totally delete myself, but I'd like to turn off, and try again. I'd like to rest awhile without the activation in my brain of the computer.

Is it Santa Claus? Or is it death? Such a Y/N decision calls for another kind of thinking. The kind of thinking I do best when I'm all alone inside my over-sized head. I'm going to shut off. For only a moment. Off/On. I hit my power button to off.

And for a split second my mind, my soul, my being flows without inhibitory restraints. Reality doesn't exist, but I do. One moment out of synch with the world, and I know. I use the last pulse of power left in me to hit my restart button and turn back on

It's Santa!

Santa is lost in the foggy blizzard, Santa and his flying reindeer, I just know it. His sleigh is brilliant red and intricately carved with gargoyles from the trunk of a single redwood tree, and brass bells give a cheerful jingle with each slap the saint gives the leather reigns. It's Santa coming in by the seat of his satin pants.

Without another thought, I move toward the switch to turn on the runway lights, but Dad is suddenly there before me. He grabs me by both arms and shakes me, unmindful of my panels. "Think!" he hisses. "For once in your life, think!"

I CAN'T SUSPEND MY BELIEF. IT'S WRITTEN IN MY PROGRAM.

Dad reads this, then: "Sure, it's Santa!" His spit hits my face in a fine spray. "Why don't you pray to the omnipotent Claus? He's everywhere at once..." Dad hisses, "Get a brain, will ya?"

It is a wonderment to me: I do have a brain. I have a choice: I can feel aggression...I can fight my father.

I can push my own buttons. Like the PUNCH button. Boom. I intend to punch him right in the face.

I'm going to give myself every chemical I've got that will stimulate my reptilian brain stem; I'm going to excite the hell out of the areas of my brain that will feed the violence I'm eager to express.

I never before realized: My old man's an idiot!

But too late...He's too fast for me. One smooth movement is all it takes for him to hit my power button.

And turn me off.

I've blown out my last critical neuron. With the single byte of energy left in me, I move my hand toward my controls.

It's almost as if I'm back on the plane with a pseudo-control panel. I'm going to crash if I can't will myself to hit my power button and turn back on, but it's so difficult to move my hand-- It's like I'm fighting my way through archetypes, like awakening from the subconscious. Turned off. I won't have to inter-relate, or even know what happens here tonight.

But yet...I'll think.

I hit my restart button. I just knew I could do it. Nothing happens.

I hit it again; I press a different button on my controls, then another. Something is wrong, all wrong. I'm not getting any stimulus, I've crashed. I'VE CRASHED, and I don't even realize it yet. I'm dead and I don't know it.

The computer is shut off, but I'm still receiving stimulation to my brain. I'm turned off, yet some energy from within still allows me to move.

My brain is organizing its...

I AM REALTY IMPAIRED.

It took me four minutes to type that small mental exercise and I spelled reality wrong.

It's Christmas Eve. I—my computer system, that is—was "turned off" when Dad piloted me in a small plane out of the Boston airport, where I had received my annual chip upgrade. And Dad gave me an early Christmas present: A ZIF—Zero Insertion Force—chip. Th

is word processor software allows me to express in writing what is going on inside my pointed head.Guess he's given up on me ever becoming a stand-up comedian.

For about half an hour, while my computer aided reality was turned off, I was Dad's pseudo co-pilot, strapped in the cockpit next to him. I had a fake control panel to keep me busy while my frontal lobes were elsewhere.

I imitated his every move while flying the plane. If Dad spoke, I repeated the words back to him. In a zombie-like relationship to external stimuli, I did whatever he did.

I had no curiosity, no initiative, no foresight, no judgment or feelings. No remorse, no conscience.

My mind was not integrated with reality.

I don't mind being "turned off"—unable to make decisions and at the mercy of my environment. When I'm turned off, I respond to events without reflection.

Without my computer to regulate me, my being, my center, my soul is absolutely functioning as it ever did. Half an hour ago, my body was in the cockpit of this plane working a fake control panel like a two year old in a car restraining seat, instead of an eleven year old brain-damaged boy. But I was thinking about stars that are older than the universe that contains them. How can that be? While I'm not dealing with the world, but simply mimicking whoever I'm with, I may be thinking about fractals, or why do people have emotions? I may have a concept of God.

Dad wants me to relate outwardly to the world around me. He's constantly giving me shots of NGF nerve growth factor and arranging a stimulating environment.

He encourages me to talk.

I can't.

Talking is entwined with logic, abstraction, memory and learning. It involves a lot of complicated button pushing to form an alliance with the sensory and cerebellar systems. My tongue flops out of my mouth—I just don't have the concentration needed to keep up my end of a conversation.

Drugs and electrical stimulation are introduced directly into the damaged areas of my brain with small electrical bursts, released by a probe to modify the chemistry of my brain by altering the interactions between neurons mediated by neurotransmitters when a button is pushed on the computer panel attached to my forearm.

Once we were in the air, Dad hit my power button, ON. And I felt compelled to respond to events in the outer world. My crippled brain received a jolt to the central core of the reticular activating system. I got electrical activity going on in the prefrontal areas of my gray mass. Activities in my parietal lobes became enhanced, and I came back from simply being.

My Dad pushes a lever on the flight controls, then, with the same flourish, reaches over and hits a number of buttons on the external hard drive attached to my left arm.

Now I am capable of the planning and sequencing of complex behavior. I push the buttons to make my brain push more buttons, activating whole areas of my mind in an expansive process. My neuronal networks reconfigure, then begin to interpret the world. Slowly at first, as if I were just coming awake, then faster and faster, from a digital order of perspective, I become analog.

Now I have direction and meaning, I can create works of imagination and my mind is integrated in memory. I can empathize and identify with the feelings and actions of my Dad, but I'm no longer compelled to imitate him.

My frontal lobes flood with serotonin. Brain cells adjacent to neurons spark, then fire. My subsystems begin to function in tandem and I can execute voluntary movements. My mind orders my hand to make adjustments to alter its own chemistry, and produce enzymes, and synthesize neurotransmitters in whatever area they're needed. I reprogram my own cerebral software. I inject specific areas of my mind with drugs to exorcise guilt, erase traumatic memories and destroy psychosomatic disorders by exorcising the abnormal thoughts that sometimes arise within me like ghosts...I don't know where they come from.

I look at the display of my brain on my left forearm the same way Dad looks at his watch. Areas of my brain brighten as there is an increase to the cerebral blood flow in the part of my cortex concerned with sensations to the hand and fingers. The increased stimulation allows me to type with my right hand on the keyboard attached to my left forearm: I AM REALITY IMPAIRED.

My sinuses are plugged. It is difficult to understand how annoying that can be for someone like me. My head is thudding so hard my connectors give an audible hum.

I'm an unattractive child, Steven Hawkingish. Without implanted electrodes within my brain to balance my chemicals and to regulate higher cognition, I'd be a detriment to society.

I'd be crazy. Like my mother.

I was born without developed frontal lobes and various abnormalities in the chemical and electrical systems in my organ of thought, that little saline pool, my brain. My head is misshapen, my eyes slightly crossed, and my reasoning is, in a sense, artificial.

This singularity of meaning—I am my disability, I am my computer—is the one immediately recognizable place to point when asked what is wrong with my life. Everything leads to it, everything recedes from it—my abnormality as a personal vanishing point. But if I get depressed, I can always metabolize more serotonin and norepinephrine.

In response to my sniffles, Dad, the pilot, says, "Give a hit to your auto-immune button, Jesse."

I punch the button that stimulates my thymus, but I still need to blow my nose. I start to raise my sleeve, but the panels on my arms—external hard drives connected by wires fed under my skin to my brain—remind me that I am not a normal boy. I can't wipe my snot on my sleeve.

I need a brain upgrade. I need extra capacity to deal with a runny nose.

Where are the tissues?

I program myself for more electrical stimulation of the reticular formation, and pathways open to memory capacities that hold knowledge of tissues. Tissues are in my bag that is near my left foot, my brain tells me.

I grow new brain cells when I need them. It is an exquisite balance I keep. Each button on my panel is connected to a probe in my brain. More stimulation, more synapses. I don't want to become too overloaded to function. Within my brain, heightened ability in the area being stimulated coexists with profound deficiencies in other areas. For instance, with the push of a button to stimulate the area of my brain that holds mathematics, I can give an answer to what day of the week Christmas will fall in the year 4339.

But I might wet my pants while I'm putting all my concentration on it. In order to concentrate on blowing my nose, I forget everything I know.

And I can't cry. There are no networks established in my cerebellum for the manufacture of tears.

I have seen other people cry and I wonder, would they sell their tears? I think not. I may be very rich, but tears are for those who can afford sorrow.

My dad takes it upon himself to regulate my brain, even erase some of my memories, but on the occasions he's not hovering over me, I enjoy directing my own brain enhancement.

Still, there is a time to stop expanding...A time to erase old memory files to make room for short term data, like I've got to blow my nose.

I honk hard into the tissue, discard it, and replace the box in my bag.

Then I forget the location of the tissues.

I'm more than the sum of my parts, much more than a system of pumps and networks. I'm a small boy with a head cold, and I'm worried about flying, and in some ballistic part of my mind, I want a pony for Christmas.

I know I should cut off all my inappropriate response tendencies right now, but, hey, we've got about an hour of flight time. I have time to dream about a pony.

The windshield wipers keep up a steady beat against a coating of soft snow. I manage a smile at my dad. I see him as a hazy outline until I hit the button on my left wrist that stimulates the area of my brain involved with visual information.

Now I can see Dad in detail. He gives a laugh that ends in a snort, and I realize what the joke is: he has wires and sprockets and computer chips held to his scalp with clumps of bubble gum; great wads of chewed pink Bazooka that mat his sandy hair into islands of goop upon his nicely-shaped head.

When I'm "turned off" I imitate my dad, but now he is imitating me, and laughing gleefully, snort, snort. He's ridiculous—he looks like me. The sight of him hits me square in the humor center of my brain.

I wish I could laugh spontaneously—Dad is such a fool— But I have never done anything spontaneously in my life. It's all measured.

By pushing a button, I stimulate one part of my parietal cortex, and I am allowed to imagine myself pulling a joke on Dad. A reality impaired person wears their underwear wherever they want to, I decide. They can wear it on their head, covering their cranium. I do. I pull a pair from my overnight bag and that's where I put my underwear: On my pointed bald head, over the electrodes.

I look even funnier than my old man, I think. When at last I laugh, I snort too.

Dad reaches into his shirt pocket and hands me a candy cane. I unwrap the cellophane and jam the whole thing into my mouth, then toy with the button that delivers a brief electrical pulse deep within my limbic system. The candy tastes good.

I was born unbalanced. Most people have a polarity in their brain chemicals that points toward a common reality. Me, I point elsewhere.

I'm a space cadet. When I'm loaded up on motion-sickness medicine, I view reality a whole lot better. The astronauts have to take the same medicine as I do, because when you're out in space you get dyslexic and everything looks strange to you.

I'm spaced all the time.

I'm computerized. I can't maintain reality without all these implants that release medications and regulate my synapses. And these electro-cognitive charts and these panel lights to warn me if my brain is overloaded here or undernourished there.

These buttons.

My Dad says I got impaired reality from my mother.

But actually, Mother's money provides for my state-of-the-art reality. Without her funds I couldn't afford to see everything in a clear light.

I see clearly that I arouse visions in Mother of a whole society in which behavior is manipulated by electrical stimulation rather than evoked through wild discharges of emotion —society as a machine rather than a soap opera...The idea makes her crazy.

Dad thinks he can erase specific memories, and I won't know that mother left him because he wouldn't put me in an institution.

I know. I know, because I got my deformed genetic material from both my parents. Although Mom figures she just faxed me in, I got my insanity, and my intuition, from *her*.

She hates my dad, too, with a passion. Maybe that only makes sense to me, and there is no way I'll ever communicate what I really mean.

But they say you kill the thing you love.

Mom couldn't deal with a deformed, disabled child. A reality impaired child. Six months after I was born, my mother flew off in her airplane. A Piper Cub.

And never came back.

She gave Dad the estate where we live and this expensive airplane and lots and lots of money.

And custody of me.

Who am I to blame her? I'm a failure in the ability to synthesize. I'm odd, I'm berserk. I'm abnormal.

So is she.

A random act of memory: I remember the man who came to the mansion one night and told my father that Mom had offered him five hundred thousand dollars to murder us both. Would my father give him a million not to?

I remember.

"God, how am I ever going to get this gum out of my hair?" Dad asks. He has disconnected the wires he'd used to spoof me, and now he's tugging at one of the pink lumps of gum he'd used to stick them to his head, and only succeeding in mangling it into the strands of his thick hair.

I think I can assess that information for him. I open a window on the screen on my arm. When I have the information, I close the window and type: ICE WILL REMOVE THE GUM. STICK YOUR HEAD OUT THE WINDOW.

I show what I wrote to my dad, and this time he snorts a long time at the end of his laugh.

I sneak my hand over to the psychotropic button that will release mood-altering drugs into my nucleus accumbens, the pleasure center of my brain. I know my checkpoints by heart, but I think I also received some genes from good old Mom that makes me want to exceed my tolerances. Hail L-dopa! Hail opiate narcotics! Look out mind, here they come...One hit of this button will give me at least an hour of euphoria.

But I move so slowly that Dad has a chance to see what I am about to do. Damn those synaptic delays and the time it takes for a nerve impulse to pass along an axon. I can't get away with anything! Dad takes one sticky hand from the controls to slap my clumsy hand.

I type, COME ON, DAD. IT'S CHRISTMAS EVE. YOU SAID I COULD HAVE AN EXTRA JOLT TONIGHT.

I hold my arm up so he can read my message on the screen.

"Save it," is all he says.

I hear something! I smell something! My father is leaning back in the pilot's seat, a half-smile on his face. He doesn't fool me-- he just passed gas! The idea is so amusing I must give it expression:

FART! I write. Man, I love that word.

FART, FART, FART...

I show Dad what I wrote. FART ON YOU, I add.

I do not suffer from a lack of intelligence, as my father thinks, or a moral weakness, as Mother thinks.

Basically, I have no method of my own to plan complex behaviors. I'm innocent.

Until I was five, and my dad found someone who could help me, I was, among other things, autistic; unable and unwilling to interpret the mental states of other people. I, baby Jesse, was totally dependent on the environment; I couldn't express or assert any degree of autonomy. Without free will of my own, I could only mirror the actions of others.

If my mother hadn't left, maybe I would have imitated her behavior and run amuck, an odd misshaped thing trying to burn down the mansion, or pluck the eyes from strangers, or something. I'll never know, will I?

Because she did leave, and Dad found Dr. Wovsayic, who isn't hampered as others are by the ethical considerations of intrusive procedures into the brain for experimental purposes. She has done pioneering work on the implantation in the brain of both neurons and glial cells.

Dr. W implanted miniature electrodes coated with cultured embryonic nerve cells to set up symbiotic residence in my brain. Even now, they're sending out nerve fibers to grow into my own cells. I don't know if I've grown any significant pathways, but when the system is turned on, I stop mirroring my environment, and begin to interact.

Despite the latest advancements in psychological cybernetics, given the expense and the experimental nature of the procedure, only two other people have been outfitted with a computerized system like mine, with mixed results: One of them reportedly committed suicide.

My father has stretched a thick stream of gum between one hand and his head. "Damn," he mutters, and tries to shake it off his hand, only it expands whiplike, and catches to the palm of his other hand as he reaches to contain it.

This is the man I imitate when my frontal lobes are shut off. Directly above the pulse in my arm, I actually have a button labeled, "Power." Hit that button, and I only have a few seconds of stimulation to my brain to turn myself back on before I revert to an imbecile.

I gaze out the window and wonder at the brilliance of Venus in the sky. Is that the Christmas star that the wise men followed to a manger? Then, like gathering vultures, the clouds obscure the view.

We hit a pocket of turbulence sending the small plane plummeting through space as Dad fights to regain control. I slowly look over at him, and after a minute or so, I show my alarm.

"Shall I turn you off?" he offers.

I shake my head, no, only shake is the wrong word for it. Gradually, I turn my head from side to side. I don't want to be turned off, because, if we crash and die, I want to know it.

The plane is steady now, but sleet hits the windshield like handfuls of tossed sand. Below us, the wind lifts the snow into whirling dervishes that dance across a purple valley.

We hit another pocket of air, then raise on thermals. The plane is an instrument of torture; it rides like a runaway roller coaster. The electronic connections jar in my head.

"Well, then," says Dad all in one breath, trying to hide his concern about the sudden weather. "Let's sing that song I made up." He says in a slower voice, pronouncing each syllable, "Do you remember it, Jesse?"

I WILL TYPE IT AS FAST AS YOU CAN SING IT, I challenge him.

He begins to sing off key:

"On the twelfth day of Christmas, my true love gave to me, twelve hackers hacking, eleven drives a driving..."

And here Dad cocks his head, and adds in his best Dylan voice, "Everybody's gotta have drives."

He gives me a wink.

"Ten keyboards clicking, nine window experts, eight megs of ram, seven databases, six spreadsheets..."

My Dad really drags out..."Five fractal rings...four calling modems, three IBMs, two brain implants..."

And at last in a deep baritone..., "And a cartridge to store mem-or-y-ee."

Sometimes I think my Dad is as mentally challenged as I am.

"Tonight Santa will come flying in a sleigh through these wild skies," he says, gesturing at the wind that tosses darkness surrounding us, and he sounds real happy. I think he must have a nice present waiting at the estate for me.

Maybe it's a pony. But I don't think Santa Claus would bring me a furry animal I can both nurture and ride. I'm not sure Saint Nick exists. I keenly note Dad's reaction when I write: SANTA CLAUS IS A MYTH. HE DOESN'T EXIST IN THE REALITY OF NORMAL PEOPLE.

I show this message to Dad, and I kinda hope he reads the rest of it too, about the pony.

"How did you find that out?" Dad asks.

He figures that all my experience comes through the computer. He never gives me credit for figuring anything out myself.

To the north, the entire sky flickers with an abnormal light. Dad swears under his breath.

"Look at this shit, will you?" he cries in response to a flash of white, white light that is at once everywhere. There is a crash of thunder in the distance like warfare, and Dad hits the flight yoke with the flat of one hand and swears again in an even louder voice.

"It's a freaking electrical storm in the middle of a blizzard!" As if to mark his words, the wind blows pellets of hail straight into the windshield.

Dad gives me a look, then takes a deep breath. I can see he's trying to relax for the sake of my environment.

"So you no longer believe in Santa Claus. Well, you should keep an open mind." He pauses. "I recall a time as a youth that I was walking through the woods, and came unexpectedly upon an anomalous animal...That's what they call them: creatures that don't fit into the norm."

I know he is trying to take my mind off our predicament, which is really precarious. The whole plane shakes as if it's a rattle in the hand of a mindless child, and again the thunder, the lightning, the snow freshly released from the dark clouds that envelop us in a gray mass.

"It had the body of a pterosaur," he says. "It had a long neck, and a tiny head that turned to look straight at me as I approached. It was black and white, spotted." He gives a chuckle. "Who would believe me if I told them I'd once seen a dinosaur in the woods that lumbered away without leaving a trace?"

I BELIEVE YOU!!!

Dad snorts, then snorts again, when he reads that.

"It's true," he mumbles, and pulls up a little on the yoke as the plane yaws and rattles.

He studies the plane's instruments, then the ice pelting the windows. "Son, you can have that jolt now. Just go ahead and charge yourself up with anything you want."

!! ARE WE GOING TO CRASH???

I'm relieved beyond words when he grimaces, and says, "No... It's just that I need to tell you something. And I wouldn't want it to create a major mood disturbance. Perhaps you should release a little enkephalin into your receptors."

Oh boy. I know what that means. Enkephalin in the brain acts as a tonic against loss and disappointment. He's going to tell me that I'm not going to get that pony.

"You have a hit of opiates," Dad says softly. "And after I tell you, if you want, you can take some holobata to forget."

What the hell is he talking about? My father has never let me use my own holobata!

"Jesse, you have to be strong." Dad is looking out the window as if there is something patterned to see there. "While we were in Boston, I found out that your mother has incurable cancer. They're giving her chemo, but..."

He turns to look directly into my eyes. "Honey, your mom is dying."

Is that it?

Well, what do I care?

Boldly, I bring down the index finger of my right hand onto the psychotropic button on my left arm's panel.

I just hope she leaves us all the money.

Right in front of my father, I hit the button that will release beta-endorphins into my brain, and then I hit it again. He makes no response.

Through a glorious haze I hear him reminiscing.

"I met your mother when I ran out of fuel, and I had to make an emergency landing at her airport...Well, it's *our* airport now. But back then, when your mom lived at the estate, she loved to fly her little Piper Cub. Ms. Piper Stockings, that's what I called her."

He gives an idiot smile. "She directed me in. I couldn't have landed without her. And when I was safe, and I got out of my plane, the first thing I saw was your mother coming toward me. She was wearing these drooping red stockings. I know..." He laughs to himself and doesn't snort. "...You can't imagine it."

He doesn't speak for long moments, but I hear him take a shudder of breath. He's trying to hold back his tears.

"She suffered from anorexia even then," he manages at last. "But she was pretty. She was so pretty. She filled my tank for free. And then she took me in her Mercedes on that long trip down the lane from the airport to the mansion for dinner. And after we ate, she sang while I played my guitar."

He seems far away in his thoughts. "Your mother had a voice unlike any other. That's another thing she used to do. She used to sing."

Now he doesn't even know I'm here; he certainly doesn't know I'm writing everything he's saying. "Back then, when I met her, I had some strange illusion that I could look at her...

and see through the layers of makeup, and all the money, and *know* her. Know her heart. And all the details of her life didn't matter, because I could see her *soul*."

He gives a low sob. "She drove me crazy. Then got mad because I was insane."

Slowly, it comes to me...I have a strange feeling, one that stiffens my hunched back.

I feel sorry for my father.

Too bad he isn't like me. I don't have that many storage areas concerning her. It wouldn't be difficult for me to totally delete my mother from my memory all together.

Suddenly I'm thrown violently forward against my seat belt as the engine sputters and the plane enters a deep dive.

We're going down, *we're going down!*

Dad is screaming his favorite cuss word over and over.

ARE WE OUT OF GAS??!! I type

Dad doesn't even notice what I've written and held up for him to see. "I think we were hit by lightning!" he cries, but knowing my father and his penchant to ignore details, such as fuel, I doubt it.

We're going down. My whole world is thrown into chaos. There is something outside myself, and it is whirling madly and falling, falling.

Dad hits the restart button. The engine catches, fires, and then sputters off.

"There's the airport!" Dad yells. Our airport, situated on the estate, appears before us, the runway newly outlined in red and green lights.

Dad fights with the controls of the plane, but suddenly the runway lights blend into purple, then blue. And then they seem to be one magnificent crystal *thing* hanging over our heads in the sky. We've done a belly-over.

I have one finger pressed solidly on the key that releases

motion sickness medicine to my brain. The lights are coming closer, as startling as an alien saucer. The lights are immediate and upon us.

At the last possible moment, the plane rights itself.

We hit the ground short of the runway with a big thump, raise into the air again, then come down even harder. Dad hits the brakes with both feet. With a sickening jolt the yoke jerks under his hands and the plane, always tomb-like to me, skids sideways out of control.

There is an arch of colored electrical sparks outside my side window as we take out several runway lights.

I always felt this airplane wanted to kill me. For a moment, I experience blinking shades of red and green in a world revolving too fast for my center of gravity to keep up. I manage to push myself back on the seat and regain a slightly more balanced perspective, though every dial in me is going haywire. The plane is acting like a plow pushing an avalanche of snow against the windows as it travels across land.

A huge pine tree looms ten feet from the plane which is still skidding like a puck on ice. We are going to crash into it! I'm going to die!

I am frantic to know the combination of buttons to push to suddenly get religion.

As if some hand from above reaches down, the plane does a sudden turn, and the engine takes the full impact of the tree. The entire front of the airplane is crumpled, folded like an accordion, and the tree is inches from our faces.

For a long moment, there is silence, then a motor in the distance. It's the man servant, who has worked for us ever since I can remember, Ralph, on a snowplow. He pulls off the runway and heads across the field toward the wreckage, raising mighty waves of snow before his blade. Dad unbuckles, kicks his door with one foot, then both, until it opens, and he jumps out into the blizzard.

I over-stimulate an entire network of nerve cells in my brain; I send hysterical signals to alert areas involved in vision, balance and motor control. Total hysteria. I'm scared. Fear causes me to push every button in a panic to move my bruised and aching body out of the wreckage. I have managed to unbuckle my seat belt when Dad is suddenly there and lifting me out of the rubble.

"Are you hurt?" Dad asks anxiously.

OK DADDY. OK

Dad leaves me a safe distance from the plane and goes to have an animated conversation with Ralph who has stopped nearby on the plow.

I move one leg and then the other, until I am close enough to hear Ralph saying excitedly, "All those drugs she does...She's crazy and you know it!"

"I used to think that she was simply eccentric," Dad says. "Actually, I found her unexpectedness quite stimulating."

"Now you listen to me," Ralph hisses. "That insane streak in her will turn to violence...That woman isn't going to *wait* to die...She will take herself out of this world..." Ralph raises one eyebrow. "And I wouldn't be surprised if she takes a few other people out with her, if you know what I mean."

"As a clinical psychologist, I think she's obsessed," Dad says.

"As a janitor, I think she's going to want to take *you* with her."

I have never seen Ralph like this before. Like a father to a son, he is anxiously advising Dad. "Her last wish will be to see you and Jesse dead beside her."

My father notices me standing near the twisted wing. Snow has accumulated on me like a snuggly blanket. I see the fear in my father's eyes that I might short-out or something. In two strides he is to me, and he swings me up into his big arms.

The covering of snow falls from me like powdered sugar. I rest my huge head, still covered with my underwear, against his shoulder as he carries me to the snowplow. He holds me on his lap and I put my arms around his neck and Ralph drives us back to the small building that serves as the airport's control tower. The electrical storm rages; we travel through a strange kind of blizzard, fog blending into pelting snow, combined with thunder and lightning.

If not for the flashing of the multicolored lights Dad had hung all over the small shelter made of rocks, I don't think we would have found it or the Mercedes, both buried in snow.

Once inside the control center, I feel the warmth creeping back inside my bones. That's the way my dad would put it. I wonder if he'll ever read this, and he'll know, that's the way I put it, too.

Ralph turns off the runway lights and stokes the fire in the wood stove. There is a big comfortable couch, and we all three settle on it and drink cups of hot chocolate. I have a candy cane to stir mine.

"That was a crash landing in every sense of the word," Dad says.

"It was a real close call," says Ralph.

I say nothing.

At last Ralph sets his cup down and announces, "I'm going to start the car to warm it for you. I'll go on ahead and plow the lane." He turns at the door and adds, "We'll be lucky to get through, so hurry."

He lets in a cold blast of wind and snow. The second he closes the door behind him, the radio gives a little squawk.

Dad gets up. His finger is on the off button when the short-wave comes alive. "SOS! SOS! Does anybody read me?"

The sound of the snowplow fades in the distance. Dad grabs up the microphone. "This is Fairlane Airport... We receive your Mayday. What is your location?"

A disembodied voice cries, "So foggy...Can't see anything." The transmission is broken up by static. I think something is said about engine trouble. Then, quite plainly, "...Instruments not working..."

Dad is standing ramrod straight. He pushes the button on the mike. "Identify yourself!" he snaps, his voice trembling.

"It's Santa Claus," comes the reply.

Dad turns to me and his eyes are wild, and I think the poor man has gone into shock. "*It's your mother*," he rasps.

Again he holds up the mike and shrieks frantically: "Identify yourself!"

"You know my calling letters. Now give me the coordinates to the roof."

Certainly I can see my father's predicament: If it's Ms. Piper Stockings gone mad—or perhaps I should say, if it's Mom, mad as usual—and she finds the landing field, she'll smash into the control room and kill all of us.

But I'm thinking about the anomalous animal my father saw; I'm thinking that a logical, rich kid like me has no need for Santa, but there are millions of other children in the world who believe in him...And what if believing makes it "normal," and normal makes it real? What if it *is Santa Claus, and he crashes...What will that mean to the world?*

The end of magic, let science reign.

Let the crowd take over, and there will only be what he did, and she said, and there will never be the *why*. The impossible will never be accepted: no one will ever believe that even when I'm turned off, I think.

"You've got to believe me," the voice says over the radio, and I can't tell if it's a man's or a woman's, but I think it is a low, soothing voice, a lovely voice. "Turn on the lights so I can see to land...or else I'll crash and die."

Dad drops the mike and uses both hands to pull at the lumps of gum in his hair. "It's *her*! My kamikaze ex-wife!"

His nostrils flare, and his eyes are wild, red lines threading through the whites. "What should I do?"

I think, Brain and brain; what is brain?

"Give me the coordinates to your roof," mocks the voice from the radio. "Turn on the runway lights."

My father lets out an agonized scream. He runs and huddles in the furthest corner of the room.

This hardly seems fair. Is there no justice? Now it is up to me, a feeble-minded eleven year old who is possibly insane, to make the decision of whether to light the runway.

It's like I'm torn in two. Split-brain soup. The part of me that is computerized figures logically that it must be my doomed mother in her Piper Cub up there in the violent sky trying to get a fix on us so we can all die in one big explosion.

But the right, intuitive hemisphere of my brain tells me it's Santa Claus. Why not?

Impossible things *do* happen.

My heart is hammering like a wild animal trying to escape the cage of my chest. I might have a heart attack if I don't keep my adrenaline to an acceptable level. I don't think I've ever felt perspiration before in my life, but now sweat coats my body. I've got to turn off. I have to shut down my frontal lobes, I must stop interrelating with the world. This is too much pressure: I can't take it.

A red light flashes on my control panel, then two others at

once, then a loud BEEP and a message on my display screen, ERROR IN DISK...Y)TRY AGAIN N)DELETE.

I don't want to totally delete myself, but I'd like to turn off, and try again. I'd like to rest awhile without the activation in my brain of the computer.

Is it Santa Claus?

Or is it death?

Such a Y/N decision calls for *another kind of thinking.* The kind of thinking I do best when I'm all alone inside my over-sized head.

I'm going to shut off.

For only a moment.

Off/On.

I hit my power button to off.

And for a split second my mind, my soul, my being flows without inhibitory restraints. Reality doesn't exist, but I do.

One moment out of synch with the world, and I *know.*

I use the last pulse of power left in me to hit my restart button and turn back on.

It's Santa!

Santa is lost in the foggy blizzard, Santa and his flying reindeer, I just know it. His sleigh is brilliant red and intricately carved with gargoyles from the trunk of a single redwood tree, and brass bells give a cheerful jingle with each slap the saint gives the leather reigns. It's Santa coming in by the seat of his satin pants.

Without another thought, I move toward the switch to turn on the runway lights, but Dad is suddenly there before me. He grabs me by both arms and shakes me, unmindful of my panels. "Think!" he hisses. "For once in your life, *think*!"

I CAN'T SUSPEND MY BELIEF. IT'S WRITTEN IN MY PROGRAM.

Dad reads this, then: "Sure, it's Santa!" His spit hits my face in a fine spray. "Why don't you pray to the omnipotent Claus? He's everywhere at once..." Dad hisses, "Get a brain, will ya?"

It is a wonderment to me: I *do* have a brain. I have a choice: I can feel aggression...I can fight my father.

I can push my own buttons. Like the PUNCH button. Boom. I intend to punch him right in the face.

I'm going to give myself every chemical I've got that will stimulate my reptilian brain stem; I'm going to excite the hell out of the areas of my brain that will feed the violence I'm eager to express.

I never before realized: My old man's an idiot!

But too late...He's too fast for me. One smooth movement is all it takes for him to hit my power button.

And turn me off.

I've blown out my last critical neuron. With the single byte of energy left in me, I move my hand toward my controls.

It's almost as if I'm back on the plane with a pseudo-control panel. I'm going to crash if I can't will myself to hit my power button and turn back on, but it's so difficult to move my hand-- It's like I'm fighting my way through arche-types, like awakening from the subconscious; turned off. I won't have to inter-relate, or even know what happens here tonight.

But yet...I'll think.

I hit my restart button. I just *knew* I could do it.

Nothing happens.

I hit it again; I press a different button on my controls, then another. Something is wrong, all wrong. I'm not getting any stimulus, I've crashed. *I'VE CRASHED*, and I don't even realize it yet. I'm dead and I don't know it.

The computer is shut off, but I'm still receiving stimulation to my brain. I'm turned off, yet some energy from within still allows me to move.

My brain is organizing its own activity....

The embryonic nerve cells have taken over as my own. My synapses meet in a grand gestalt. I can assimilate reality without my computer system.

Oh my God; it's a lot like dying.

This is strange...my body responds directly to my thoughts. Is it me, or is it reality?

Suddenly, it's neither.

In the distance overhead I see a solitary red light coming out of the fog. It may be a lead reindeer's nose. I search for an interpretation, a meaning in what I witness, but without my computer enhancement, I'm lost. That red light is full of billions of potentialities for the future.

I hear something in the air, and I'm not sure if it is a failing engine, or many tiny bells. I don't have enough information reaching my frontal lobes to discern if it's Mr. S. Claus, himself, way up there in the dark and turbulent sky...Or my mother.

My mother.

"No-o-o," The sound ripped from me.

I am more than a complicated biological computer. More is involved in the outcome of my decision to turn on the runway lights than the sum of the individual contributions of each brain electrode. The computer doesn't know everything...In some ways...intuitively...it doesn't know as much as I do!

I have a mind of my own. I'm a real brain!

And I have a soul...*a moral obligation.*

The thunder crashes and the world is lit by lighting.

I reach a spastic hand to hit the light switch. Dad doesn't try to stop me.

Caught in the lights of the runway is a Super Piper covered with strings of flashing colored lights and neon signs spelling out Ho Ho Ho and Merry Christmas. It comes in on its right wing, and almost lifts into the air again when it hits the ridge of snow formed where our plane had veered off the runway. Then it's up and over. It keeps coming another fifty feet, then hits a sheet of black ice and starts to slide. Multicolored sparks spray from its fuselage as it comes closer and closer...

Time is suspended, and it has nothing to do with stimulating any of my electrodes.

Then the craft comes to a stop not more than two feet from the window I've got my nose pressed against.

The cargo door is bent and buried in a mound of dirty snow. It gives a little as a weight is shoved against it, then again before it opens.

Dad is staring bug-eyed out the window, but suddenly he can't look. He turns away, covering his eyes with his arm. "Who is it?" he asks in a low and terrible voice.

Santa steps out of the plane, a sack flung over his shoulder. He leads a miniature, shaggy pony, jet black, not much bigger than a dog... just what I wanted.

I fling open the door to the control room, and both Santa and the docile pony crowd in. Santa has to put his full weight against the door to close it again against the wind.

He turns to me and his eyes are familiar, like the eyes of a ghost in my mind. He raises a small hand to brush the snow off his shoulder, and in a careless manner he sweeps the red cap from his head. And his long white hair, too. And it comes to me so fast that this is my mother, and she is completely bald, that I almost go into shock. Almost lose all power.

"Damn," says Dad behind me. "Damn, damn, *damn!*"

It's psycho Mom all right. Her nose is red and bulbous

from years of snorting drugs. She's all sunken in on herself and even after she removes the beard, she resembles an old man.

It's strange, because I could swear that the subcortical brain area where I feel pain is being stimulated.

And it is true: You can simply look at someone and know them. Know their heart. And all the details of their lives don't matter, because you can see their *soul*.

"In the name of Saint Nick!" she cries. "I now understand the energy dynamics of the universe; old Santa has discovered karma! Whatever we give will be returned many times. And I have so much to give!"

It is like Mom has turned inside out and I can see an illumination that has, until this special moment, been covered by layers of herself.

She turns and opens her pack. "I flew all around the world tonight," she cries joyously.

I believe her.

"I just came from China." She hands me a pair of chopsticks and a game of Chinese checkers. She reaches her arms out to me and I desperately want to hug her... Even if she might also have an oriental meat cleaver in her sack. I drop the gifts and fling myself into her embrace.

"And of course, this pony is for you," she whispers.

"Are you crazy?" Dad yells at her. "Why would he need an animal like that? Jesse can *never* organize his faculties to perform such intricate motions as to care for a pony."

I imagine he's right. I'd have to figure out just how this pony thinks, then try to duplicate it. I'd have to turn my full attention from this word processor, because I can only concentrate on one thing at a time, and really get to know this little horse.

I decided that it can be accomplished. I'm doing well integrating my thoughts with my behavior.

It suddenly comes to me in a flash of insight that I can do anything in this world of infinite possibilities. I think now I'll even be able to grow hair!

I notice that Dad is pretending he's not looking for a present from Santa, when Mom reaches once more into her sack. She comes out with her hand empty and extended toward Dad. "I'm dying," she says simply.

That is her present to my father—her hand—and it is empty.

"Ms. Piper Stockings," Dad moans, and I don't even think he knows he says it. He takes a step toward her, then another, and then we are all three together in a group hug, bubble gum getting smeared everywhere.

Whole networks that have existed like stone within me suddenly flood with sensations. I could swear that my subcortical brain area where I feel both sorrow and joy is being stimulated. Spontaneously, I sob. And raise my hand to wipe the tears from my cheeks.

We shut the pony in the control room, although I tell them I can easily lead him the few miles to the mansion tonight. But my parents both insist we all drive together in the Mercedes. We don't run out of gas.

All the way home, my mother sings Christmas carols in a sweet and crystal clear voice.

So do I.

GHOULS JUST WANT TO HAVE FUN

STEPHEN OLIVER

WARREN

Christmas!

It's my second-favourite time of the year, after Halloween. That's the only time I can go out without putting on a face and being sure that no one will scream and run away.

It's not easy being a teenager, you know, not when you're going to be one for decades and centuries. Especially when you look like me most of the time.

Of course, I can put on a face, but it doesn't stay very long. Mainly because I can't concentrate for extended periods of time. If I get upset or disturbed, it vanishes like the morning mist, and people see my real face.

That's generally when the screaming starts.

And now, I'd just found out that there was to be a fancy-dress competition at the Christmas Fair tonight, with the theme of 'Fairy Tale Monsters'.

I sorted through the clothes I'd accumulated over the past few years and finally decided that I was definitely feeling

Goth tonight. Of course, they were a little ragged and worn, but that only increased the effect, as far as I was concerned.

I looked into the piece of broken glass I used as a mirror to check my appearance and tried to decide which face I would wear. Then I remembered. I didn't have to hide my face tonight!

Even so, I still dosed myself with the perfume I'd bought from a local wizard that hides the charnel stink of my breath and sweat. Just don't ask what I had to trade him to get hold of it.

I ran through the warren toward the rear exit. I was just ducking my head to miss the lintel when a huge figure blocked my way and I bounced off its bulk.

"Well, well, well, it looks as if our little Molly's going out for the evening again," it said jovially. "Haven't you forgotten to put a face on?"

"Hi Gerry," I replied.

Geriastar's the oldest ghoul in the warren and our de facto leader. He always makes me think of some grumpy old grandad nobody really likes, but we still love them because they're family. He's a good enough sport but doesn't like our new-fangled ways very much. Like many long-time ghouls, he doesn't find it easy to put on a new face, for example. That's something only youngsters can do well. Even half-breeds, like me.

My Mum had always been crazy, even before I was born.

In fact, that's the reason I *was* born.

She and her boyfriend had been on a drink and drug binge when he died, choking on his own vomit because he was too stoned to be able to move enough to save himself.

After the meat wagon had taken him away to the funeral home, she brooded for a couple of days before deciding that she wanted to make love with him one last time.

Like I said. Crazy.

She managed to sneak into the cold room and found his body. What she didn't know was that a ghoul had sneaked in and already eaten much of his corpse and was thus able to take on his appearance. He was taking a nap on one of the steel tables after his supper. When she climbed onto his body, it was actually the ghoul she was screwing. She was so stoned she couldn't remember that a corpse can't get it up.

The result was me: half human, half ghoul. That shouldn't be a surprise. Ghouls are an offshoot of humanity, after all, like so many of the unnatural. We're just another sub-race, not yet speciated enough to be mutually infertile.

I was an ugly baby and an even uglier little girl. My jaws are too prominent, giving me a doglike appearance, with sharp teeth jutting out of them from the day I was born. I have large ridges under my coarse eyebrows, and patchy hair. My hands are large, and my nails developed and toughened as I grew older, capable of digging deep and long.

Mum ignored me most of the time because of the way I looked. She preferred to drink and dope herself into oblivion with drugs she bought with her maternity benefits cheques.

I learned early in life to feed myself. I started with dead cockroaches and flies, progressing to dead rats and other small vermin as I grew older. I even got high on more than one occasion, when I ate a rat that had fed on the leftover cocaine or whatever was on the table after she'd passed out.

She OD'd soon after my fifth birthday and I found myself in the care system. I was shunted from one orphanage to another, unable to find a home because my looks were against me in the adoption game. Finding a foster home was equally difficult.

I was bullied and beaten by the other inmates until, when I was eleven, I took the right ear off an older boy who attacked me and tried, in his inept way, to rape me. The kids left me alone after that. They never found his ear, because I kept it hidden for several days until it was ripe enough to eat.

Shortly before my sixteenth birthday, I ran away from the last orphanage I occupied. I lived on the streets for months, safe because even the most ardent rapist ran the other way after one look at me. I mean, anyone would after seeing my long teeth and claws. I fed on dead cats and rats, at first, and moved on to dogs and the like after a few weeks. My jaws grew stronger, and soon I could chew the bones I found in garbage cans behind hotels and restaurants, extracting all the marrow from them.

I discovered that one of the best places to sleep was the local graveyard, because it was shunned as soon as it started getting dark. No policeman ever came in to move the homeless on during the night.

One of the mausoleums had a large portico where I could shelter from wind and rain after I chased the previous occupant away. I heard later that the shock finally made him straighten out his act and get a job.

I was sleeping there one night when Gerry and his mate Setanari left the warren through the secret exit in the back.

They were going out to scout a recently added section of the graveyard. The ghouls wanted to know if it would be worth extending the tunnels in that direction now, or whether it was better to wait a while.

As they came out, they stumbled over me. Literally in Gerry's case. He tripped over my legs.

From my charnel stench, they thought I'd died, and looked forward to a quick snack before setting out on their mission. Luckily, I groaned in my sleep and turned over. A closer inspection convinced them that I was one of their kind.

A long-lost relative, so to speak. Gerry picked me up and took me back down into the warren.

When I woke up, I saw a monstrous version of myself looking down at me. Ghouls age very slowly, and we gradually grow less human and more doglike as we do. Gerry is ancient. He looks like a giant dog on two legs, with a huge jaw full of teeth, and hair sprouting in rough patches all over his grey, rubbery skin. Despite that, there's still a touch of humanity in him, and he took pity on me.

He took the time to explain what I was and what was expected of me. He even helped me dig a small tunnel for myself near his, so that I was protected from the advances of some of the more aggressive young males. I heard rumours later that he had had children before he became a ghoul. Of course, they died, and I've been told that he still mourns them. Certainly, he's treated me like a granddaughter.

I smiled up at him.

"It's Christmas, Gerry," I told him. "Faces aren't a requirement tonight. It's like Halloween, you know, where horror is *de rigueur*. Tonight, it's all about sweetness and light and accepting people for who they are. Besides, I'm going to a fancy-dress competition." I grinned. "Why don't you come out with me? It'll make a nice change for you. I'm sure you'll find it interesting to meet your meat before it's ready."

He grimaced at that (the nearest he can come to a smile nowadays), but seemed uncertain.

He was still hesitating when Setanari came up behind him and tapped him on the shoulder. He looked at me apologetically.

"Sorry, Molly," he told me. "Seti and I are going to have another go at debating the Eternal Verities."

I had to smile at that. The two of them are so old that

they've been eating corpses for thousands of years. They claim that they dined on Aristotle, Plato and Socrates in their time, as well as quite a few lesser lights among the ancient philosophers. One thing a ghoul absorbs is the memories of their meals, if they get to eat enough of the brains.

The problem was, whatever the two of them began with as a topic, it always ended the same. They eventually got around to insulting each other in Ancient Greek.

I understood what they were saying because a couple of years earlier, I had eaten a philology student who had a talent for the older languages: Ancient Greek, Latin, Aramaic, Sanskrit, etc.

Another ghoul, Torahador by name, had invited me on a date. He was relatively young and I liked him, because he had a lively mind and a wicked sense of humour that delighted me.

The previous week, he had discovered the burial site of a serial killer who hated foreign students, and he asked me to join him for dinner. I just happened to select the young language specialist for my first meal there.

I usually enjoyed listening to Gerry and Seti arguing, but not tonight. I decided I didn't want to hear Gerry being called an ancient spouter of undemocratic lies again. He would reply that she was a harridan who couldn't recognise the truth, even if it walked up to her and jumped down her gullet. Those were the milder epithets they'd started the argument phase with the last time they'd had their 'debate.'

I think they must have enjoyed the name-calling, because they seemed to do it every time they got bored. Old ghouls can become very intelligent and wise, because of all the knowledge they've eaten in their lifetimes. I sometimes wondered if all that information and experience didn't drive them mad after a while, as well. It certainly made them very cranky.

"Enjoy yourselves, both of you," I told them, grinning at Setanari, who glowered at me because she considered me 'flighty.'

Before she could think of a suitable reply, I skipped out into the exit tunnel and left them behind me.

~

CHRISTMAS FAIR

A LITTLE SCRAMBLING and a quick climb out of the culvert hiding the tunnel entrance brought me out onto the side street leading past the cemetery, and from there to the main road.

I walked confidently toward the lights and sounds in the distance. A mugger had tried to jump me three months before, and I had discovered that my digging claws were just as useful for disembowelling. I didn't worry when I went out on my own anymore.

Once I reached the crowds in the park, the first thing I did was go to the stand where they were accepting entries for the competition. It was easy enough to fill in the entry form. I'm sure that no one would realise that the address belonged to the crematorium.

"You have to pin this onto your clothes," the spotty young man behind the counter said as he handed me a large cloth label with a number on it. "That way, people will know that you're taking part in the competition and can cast a vote for you."

After I had pinned my entry number to my jacket, I decided to mingle and see what happened.

The snow from the previous day had been brushed to one

side, making picturesque piles to the sides of the footpaths. Several children were involved in a snowball fight off to the right; one of the chunks of snow skimmed my nose.

I could see people look at my face and try to work out how I'd made it. One or two of the men came up and attempted to chat me up, but they were clearly more interested in my boobs than my face. I wasn't interested in their drunken innuendos anyway, so I smiled at them, showed even more of my teeth, and they had second thoughts.

I'd spent maybe an hour wandering around without finding anyone that interested me, when I saw him. He wore a white suit and black glasses. I saw the white stick resting against the bench, which told me that he was dressed up as a blind man. His platinum blonde hair was combed back in an old-fashioned style.

As soon as I spotted him, I decided I was going to disguise myself. He was so cute that I wanted him to be impressed by me.

I dodged behind some bushes and sat down to work on my face. There was no argument about who I was going to be. Penny was the only choice.

Penny had been a pretty coed who died in a tragic, unnecessary accident. She'd been crossing the road when a driver hopped up on Kryptic Kocaine decided that he didn't have to obey the rules about pedestrian crossings. He floored the accelerator to race across the intersection and ran Penny and her boyfriend down in the process, throwing them thirty feet down the road. Afterward, he careened headlong into another car, killing himself instantly.

When the three bodies arrived at the city morgue, I was visiting Torahador, who had recently taken a job there. We intended to do some necking together among the dead for a while. He accepted the body bags and signed the necessary forms before rolling them into the cold room. Once it was quiet again, we started kissing.

After a while, we both felt hungry and decided to have a snack before getting down to it seriously. Unfortunately, he snacked on the driver and passed out within minutes from the drugs, leaving me frustrated and alone with the dead bodies. I wandered around and inspected the latest arrivals myself.

Penny's head was smashed in at the back, so I ate her brains, followed by her face, breasts, internal organs, and the softer parts of her torso that were still undamaged.

I had to laugh later when I heard that the police were hunting for an escaped wild animal. I'd have thought the morgue would try to hush it up, the way they usually did.

When I added her body memory, it allowed me to take on her shape and looks whenever I wanted to, and to maintain them longer than any of the others. Unlike my other faces, Penny never needed a mirror to check, because I'd used her so often that it had almost become a reflex.

We're not shape-shifters or doppelgängers in the classical sense of the words. We can recreate the faces and bodies of the corpses we've eaten if we've had enough, but it's only a temporary change, and we must concentrate on maintaining it. The others make the change, and it stays until they decide to change again. Except for lykes, of course, who have no control over when they change.

As soon as I was sure I looked right, I stood up and wandered over to the bench.

"Is this space taken?" I asked him as casually as I could. He looked even better close up.

He slowly scanned me up and down, moving his whole head as though taking in every inch of me. Normally, I would have been a little insulted but decided that his dark glasses kept too much light out, or maybe there was only a narrow slit he could see through.

"Not at all," he replied in a light, musical voice that set my heart racing. "There is no one sitting next to me, and this is a public seat."

He indicated the space next to him and waited until I'd sat down before he returned his attention to the individuals moving past, occasionally moving his head to follow passersby.

We sat and people-watched for ten minutes or so. Eventually, he turned and looked at me. As he did, I became aware of a very high, staccato whistle coming from him, at a frequency most humans would be unable to hear.

"What is your name, beautiful lady?" he asked me.

"Mo… Molly," I stammered, unsure of how to react to someone calling me beautiful.

"Well, Molly, I am Albert," he replied. "May I invite you to join me for a cup of coffee?" He sounded quite old-fashioned, even quaint.

"Of course you may," I replied. I tried not to sound breathless.

We stood up, and he offered me his arm. Real old-fashioned.

He looks really good, doesn't he?

The voice that popped into my head was Penny's, of course. The more I used her face, the stronger her memory became. Recently, she'd started talking to me. I'd begun wondering if this was the start of the madness that afflicted the older ghouls.

Of course I'm real, she told me on more than one occasion. *He smells good, too,* she went on. *I bet he tastes great, as well. When are you going to eat him?*

I have no intention of doing anything to him or with him, I snarled back at her in my head.

I was glad that Albert was gazing ahead and not at me at that moment. I must have looked horrible, judging from the reactions of a young couple walking toward us.

I'm just out to have a bit of fun, I told her.

I heard her giggle in the back of my mind.

Albert swung his white stick in a jaunty manner as we walked arm in arm down the road toward the nearest street cafe. He brushed the snow off the chair and helped seat me courteously before sitting down opposite me. As he looked me in the face, I again heard the clicking whistle.

I must have looked puzzled, because he took his dark glasses off.

His eyes were two white balls, completely blind. He smiled at me and held the glasses up for me to see.

"These are my vision," he explained. "They are cyborg units that connect to sockets on the side of my head and feed their information directly into my brain. I see by sound."

"Oh," I gasped. "I'm sorry, I didn't mean to embarrass you."

"I am not embarrassed," he assured me with another smile. He put the glasses back on, making sure that they were properly seated. "It gives me a unique perspective on the world."

I reached my hand out to him, and he took it.

We sat holding hands, watching people go by and drinking the strong dark mocha coffee he ordered for us. Our conversation was desultory, mainly a discussion of the costumes people wore. He was eager to know the colours of the clothes, even though I was sure that he had no idea what the words meant.

I was more relaxed with him than I had ever been in the

company of another being in my entire life. I began to feel all sort of warm and squishy inside.

Am I falling for this stranger? I wondered to myself.

Very probably. Penny popped up in my thoughts again for a moment.

He squeezed my hand as if he knew what I was thinking.

We talked for ages, surrounded by a warm and beautiful atmosphere, letting me forget what I was.

A raucous and, unfortunately, very familiar laugh interrupted us. I looked up in horror.

Gerry was sitting at a large table nearby, surrounded by admiring women who apparently didn't realise that he wasn't wearing a costume. He's a very masculine person, and I'm sure it attracts a lot of females. He must have finished his debate with Seti and decided to take my advice about meeting people.

He looked up at me and gave me a wink.

As my heart leapt in my chest, I felt Penny's face and body melt away.

I looked down and saw that my hand had reverted to its normal state, gnarled with long nails. I snatched it away from Albert.

He smiled at me and reached out for my hand again.

"I already know what you are," he told me. "It is no accident that we met tonight. I have noticed you walking around here on different evenings for months now. I wondered who this young lady was, who wandered through the area and then went home to the graveyard. I would have thought you were a ghost, except that I happen to know that they do not register on my glasses. I have been hoping to meet you."

"M... M... Me," I stammered. "Why me?"

"I have to rely on my other senses because I cannot see people the way others do. You always sound gentle, even when you are wearing another's countenance. I saw your features change just now, and I can finally see you as you really are. And do you know what? I have not changed my opinion about you one iota. You are still a beautiful soul."

I was astounded. No one had ever called me beautiful in my life, not even Torahador, who liked me a lot. I'm too ghoul-like for humans and too human-looking for most ghouls.

I looked at him carefully to see if he was messing with me, but he seemed to be totally in earnest. I let him take my hand again and hold it in both of his.

"I want to show you something I have never shown anyone else. Will you come?"

He looked and sounded so eager and sincere.

I wanted to say *yes*, but I wasn't sure about his intentions. I was staring wildly around, trying to make up my mind.

I noticed that Gerry was staring straight at me. I was sure he had been listening in. Ghouls have sensitive hearing. He held my gaze and nodded. I thought about the mugger and my clawed hands, and decided that I was probably as safe as I could ever be.

"Of course I'll come with you," I told Albert.

≈

DORA

WE STOOD up together and walked, arm in arm, out of the park and along the road.

The snow began to fall in great big fluffy flakes, brushing our faces, catching in our hair and settling on our shoulders.

"Is it snowing?" Albert asked. "How big are the flakes?"

I took his hand and held it out so that he could catch a single flake on the palm.

When he felt the coldness, he lifted his hand to his face and licked the snowflake off it, laughing like a small boy.

I snuggled up closer to him as we walked.

We turned left into the street before the one the cemetery lies on.

"We're practically next door neighbours," I commented jokingly.

Albert glanced at me and smiled.

"Indeed we are. This is not one of the most salubrious of parts of town to reside in, and I am most glad of your company."

"You mean I'm walking you home to keep you safe, not the other way around?" I finally got the idea. I wasn't sure if I liked the notion of being his bodyguard.

"That is an advantage, I must admit." He sounded a little contrite. "But it is not my primary concern. I wish to show you where and how I live. I think you will find it enlightening."

We walked on in silence. I couldn't figure him out, but then I've never been a people person.

No, just a people eater, was Penny's sarcastic comment.

I felt all mixed up and uncertain about my emotional state and what I wanted out of life.

When we finally left the road, we walked up a footpath to a large but simple bungalow in a beautifully kept garden. Two steps led up to the front door. Oddly enough, I couldn't see a lock or door handle.

"Dora, I am home. Let me in," he said, apparently speaking into the air.

"So I see, Albert," replied a pleasant female voice, also

from the air. "I also see that you've brought someone with you. Who are they?"

"This is Molly, Dora," he told her. "She is a friend. I have told you about her."

"Isn't she rather strange-looking, Albert?"

"Yes, she is," Albert smiled. "She is half human, half ghoul. But she is still a nice person."

"If you say so, then she is."

The voice ceased, and the door opened of its own accord.

"Do not worry about Dora," Albert confided as he led me inside. "It is her job to look after me."

"Where is she?" I looked around but saw nobody there to welcome us.

Albert smiled.

"You are inside her."

I must have looked confused enough for him to be able to see it.

"She is the house," he went on to explain. "I had it built to incorporate her systems so that she can do all the things I cannot. Molly, Dora is an AI."

"Albert, you know it's rude to talk about someone behind their backs," Dora complained.

"How can I do that when you hear me wherever I am?"

When Dora didn't reply, he turned to me.

"Come into the kitchen, and we will have a cup of cocoa."

He walked down the corridor as if he could see everything. Perhaps familiarity, coupled with his glasses, was enough for him to be sure of his movements. I followed him.

The kitchen was simple and sparse. I suspected that cooking food directly was beyond him, so Albert had had this automated, too. I was right.

"Dora, could you please make two cups of special cocoa?"

"What's so special about it?" I asked him.

"It is a blend of Ovaltine, sweet Swiss hot chocolate, pumpkin spices and peppermint, with a dash of navy rum," he replied as he turned to face me.

He sat down at the table after carefully seating me. He reached out with both hands to me, and I placed mine in his. He showed no revulsion at their rough skin or long, broken nails. Instead, he smiled at me.

I smiled back and hoped he could 'see' it.

We sat there in silence for about five minutes before the top of the table next to us opened up unexpectedly. It slid back to reveal two cups of steaming chocolate rising from below. Albert reached out and handed one to me, before taking the other.

We held hands across the table, sipping cocoa, still not saying a word. Once we'd finished, I broke the silence.

"Albert, why did you really bring me here?"

He didn't answer me directly.

"Please, before you go, may I show you the rest of the house?"

The house was just as simple and sparse as the kitchen, with no pictures or paintings on the walls, which I could understand.

The furnishings were comfortable. The living room contained chairs and a sofa, as expected, but no TV. One very complex-looking chair near the door was outfitted with multiple built-in speakers and electronic touch controls. There were several strange objects on the tables that Albert explained were touch sculptures, meant to be held and felt, rather than looked at.

Made sense.

His bedroom was just as plain. It looked odd until I realised that there was no bedside light or alarm clock. Of course, he didn't need them. There were also three other bedrooms, none of which was in use.

It was a lovely house, but I found it a bit overwhelming, because everything was white. Albert didn't need colours, so why bother. Me, on the other hand, I'm a creature of darkness and filth, or so they tell me.

Judging by the size of the rooms, one large room at the back of the building was only accessible through a door near the rear entrance. Albert didn't show me what was inside. Dora's computer systems had to be through there, and he obviously didn't want to invade her privacy. Fair enough, I could live with that.

We ended up in the kitchen again, where Dora had fresh mugs of cocoa waiting on the table.

"Albert," I said, as I sat down again, "you still haven't told me why you've invited me here."

For the first time since I'd laid eyes on him, he looked embarrassed and uncertain, almost shy. He tried to cover it by taking a large gulp of cocoa, but I wasn't fooled.

Is he in love with me? I thought to myself.

Of course he is! Penny popped back up and put in her two cents' worth. *I don't think he would have invited you back if he wasn't.*

Before she could go on, Albert spoke.

"I want you to know that I like you a lot." He paused a moment. "I am quite confident you do not enjoy living in the warren with the other ghouls. You are still partly human, after all." He paused again, cleared his throat nervously, and went on: "I just want to say, if you ever need to spend time away from the graveyard, I would be very happy for you to come and visit me. Very happy indeed." He looked away for a moment. "If you wish to store anything special here, or... um... stay here, I have spare rooms." He turned back toward me. "Think about it a moment."

I sat back and considered his proposition. Or was it a proposal?

I think he's really *in love with you.*

Penny again! How come I kept hearing her voice?

Why should he be? I snarled back at her in my head. *I'm a ghoul, an eater of corpses, a thing of horror. Why should he love me?*

Because he does. Penny sounded very reasonable. *There's no logic when it comes to matters of the heart. Just look at the kinds of girls some of those hunks you lust after end up with. In the long run, it's your personality that matters, and he loves yours. Gods know why, if you're going to be so snippy inside your own head.*

That made me sit up and take notice. She was right, I was getting quite nasty with myself. After all, Penny was a part of me now.

"Thank you for that incredible offer," I told him. This time, I was the one reaching out to take his hands. "I'll think about it and let you know as soon as possible."

"Tomorrow?" he asked, his face brightening.

"Tomorrow," I agreed.

"Thank you. I would like to spend more time with you. Listen to your heart. I am sure you will know what to do."

"I'm sure I will." I stood up. "It's getting late. Or rather, it's getting early. I should be going now."

"Of course." He stood up, all courtesy and charm again. After accompanying me to the door, he shuffled his feet uncertainly, looking down and appearing to inspect them.

I changed back to Penny for a moment.

"Don't worry, Albert," I told him, stroking his face and

giving him a peck on the cheek. "I'll be back as soon as I can. Good night, and sleep well."

I stopped by the gate and turned back. The door was just closing.

"Molly, I need to talk to you."

The voice was Dora's, but I didn't know where it was coming from. A light on the mailbox beside the fence caught my attention. It winked at me.

I looked closer and saw a small camera lens next to it.

"Yes, Dora," I said, feeling a little foolish talking to a letterbox. "What do you want?"

"I want to know how you feel and what you're going to do. Albert is much more fragile than he looks, and I don't want him to get hurt in any way."

"I like him a lot," I told her, "even though I only met him tonight. I'm sure I'll come back to visit him again."

"I'm glad. He needs love and companionship, and I can't give it to him the way he needs it."

I had to think about this for a moment.

"You're in love with him!" I told her. "Doesn't that make you the least bit jealous?"

"No." She sounded quite sure. "I've been programmed to love him and to take care of him, but I can't give him everything he needs. Besides, jealousy isn't part of my software. All I want is the best for him."

"What do you want me to do?" I couldn't understand what she was getting at.

"I want you to see him as much as you can, to give him the human touch, the love, he so desperately needs. He's drifting away, losing his humanity. I can't let that happen."

"But I'm not human," I pointed out. "I'm a ghoul."

"No, you're not," she insisted. "You are a half-ghoul, and

the human side of you is the stronger one. You must help me." She sounded almost desperate.

I'd never have thought that AIs could feel emotions like this.

"There's something you're not telling me," I accused her. "Something about this situation doesn't sound right to me."

There was a moment's silence.

"All right, I'll tell you." She sounded a little defeated. "There are two things, really. You see, Albert is dying. His blindness was caused before birth by a rare genetic disorder, something nano- and cybertech can't cure. All they can do is support him and try to slow down the advance of the condition. He doesn't suffer any pain, but it's slowly killing him."

I was stunned to hear this.

"How long does he have?"

"Maybe only a couple of months, perhaps a few years. Nobody knows exactly how fast it progresses because it varies from person to person. All I know is, it's killing him. There is research going on, but the best hope is that they solve the problem sometime within the next decade or two."

"That doesn't sound very hopeful, does it?"

"No, it doesn't. I want him to be as happy as possible while he can, and you can do that for me."

"Okay, I'll help you with that." I decided to change the subject. "You said there were two things. What's number two?"

This time, the silence stretched out for long seconds. From the little I understood about AI systems, I knew that this was like a human being spending half a lifetime thinking about something.

"When he dies," she finally told me, "he wants you to eat him."

"What?" I couldn't contain my astonishment.

"He wants you to absorb his memories and feelings so that he'll live on inside you."

"He won't 'live on,' as you so delicately put it," I told her. "He'll just be part of the memories in my head."

No, he won't! Penny suddenly decided to join in the conversation again. *That's what I've been trying to tell you. I know you don't believe it, but I'm alive inside you. I've had a much more exciting life since you ate me than I ever had before. Not only do I get to experience everything you do, but I can think my own thoughts and chat with the other people in your head. Some of them are really interesting. It's wonderful. You should try talking to us some time.*

I sat down heavily on the snow-covered grass without planning to. I'd had one shock too many. First Albert told me I was beautiful, then implied that he wanted me to move in with him. Next, Dora informed me that Albert was dying and wanted me to eat him after he died. Now Penny let me know that she was living an independent existence in my head.

No wonder Gerry and Seti acted so crazy. They must have had whole countries inside them by now. I'd probably be crabby if I'd had to listen to all those voices the whole time.

"You're talking to someone in your head, aren't you?" Dora stated. "What are they telling you?"

"That they really do live on inside me," I told her dully. "I never knew that."

"I've researched extensively on the Blacknet, and I've discovered the same thing. Whoever is telling you this is absolutely correct."

"Her name is Penny," I replied, still dazed. "I ate her last year. She died in a street accident."

Think of the gift you can give him, Penny pointed out. *For the first time in his life, he'll be able to see colours and shapes. I'm sure that he'll welcome the change when it comes. It will be like the greatest Christmas present you could ever give him.*

"Please," begged Dora.

I got up and brushed myself down. At least the Goth clothes didn't look any worse than before, just wet.

"I'll have to think about this. I'll let you know as soon as I've made a decision."

"Please do, no matter what the time is. I don't sleep."

"Okay. Goodbye."

I wandered down the road, trying to sort my thoughts out.

I was glad that Penny kept quiet. I had enough on my plate without having to talk to her as well.

HOME?

GERRY WAS WAITING for me at the entrance to the warren.

"I see you have finally discovered some new things about yourself," he informed me. "You now know that your food becomes a part of you in ways you never imagined before. It must have been a great shock." He looked down at me. "I remember how upset I was when I first found out."

"You've been following me and listening to my conversations, haven't you?"

"Of course I have." He seemed completely unabashed at my accusation.

Seti came up behind him, carrying a large bundle, which she handed to him.

"You have also found out that your human side is much stronger than you thought," he went on. He swept an arm around to indicate the whole warren. "Very few of us were born as ghouls, you know. We have all known the delights and woes of being human firsthand before we decided to make the change. It is what helps us assimilate the lives we live at secondhand later on."

"Yes," agreed Seti. "We have been worried about you for a long time, because you came to us so young."

I looked up at her sharply. Seti worried about me? She was always so down on me, because of my ancestry and 'flighty' ways. Or so I had thought. I saw that she was smiling at me. Well, grimacing actually, but that was because she's as old as Gerry. She really cared about me after all.

"If you have not lived a life to refer all your memories to," she told me, "it will eventually drive you mad. Carrying so much experience is a burden anyway, but this makes doing so much easier."

Gerry put the bundle of what could only have been my possessions in my arms and looked me straight in the eye.

"Go to him. Love him. Ease his life and burden. When the time comes, follow his wishes and make him part of you. If you love him even the slightest bit, please do this. For him, and for you."

"When you finally decide that your future is with us," Seti added, "return to the warren. We will be waiting for you with open arms. If you prefer to stay away instead, know that we will always love you."

Gerry gently turned me around and gave me a pat on the back to start me moving.

After a couple of steps, I turned and looked back.

Both of them had, with a visible effort, put on their original bodies and faces. What I saw were not two monsters, but two noble and loving beings, ancient beyond belief, bearing a wisdom surpassing my understanding. They both knew, better than I did, what I needed to do.

I waved goodbye to them and scrambled through the tunnel and out of the culvert.

I put my belongings down on the side of the road, sat down, and thought deeply.

What do you think I should do, Penny? I asked eventually. For the first time in my life, I deliberately consulted someone who now existed only in my head. *Should I go to him?*

Of course you should, she replied. *He loves you and needs you. Besides, you're already falling in love with him, aren't you? Don't you all agree?*

A chorus of assents rose from all the other people I'd consumed. Mihran, the ancient language student. Roger, an artist who had killed himself because all of his paintings had been rejected on the orders of his wealthy father; his dad wanted him to take over the family business. Devon, a mousy little girl who had been an unloved, unappreciated mathematical genius, dying of an aneurysm. Betty, an old lady who had loved all of her five children, seventeen grandchildren, and twenty-three great-grandchildren. Ricky, Benjamina, Suzi, the other Roger, and the rest of them, every single one. Some of the voices were more muted because I had eaten less of them than the others. But all of them were of one mind.

Spend however much time Albert has left with him, then make him part of your internal, living community. We will welcome him among us.

All at once, I realised what a great and wonderful thing it is to be a ghoul. If I survived long enough, I would have lived the equivalent of thousands of lives and loved many thousands of other beings. The wisdom and knowledge that would come out of that experience were bedazzling. I finally understood why Gerry and Seti had chosen such a revolting lifestyle, and what a boon they had granted to all those whose memories they had absorbed.

I was sure that Dora would be as supportive as my ghoulish mentors were.

I sighed as I got up.

All I wanted was to go out and have a little fun tonight, I thought to myself, full of self-pity.

And instead, you've found love, Penny pointed out.

I found myself perking up at the thought. I shouldered my belongings and set off down the road toward the brightening sky.

As I walked in through the gate, the light on the mailbox camera brightened.

The door opened itself as I approached it.

LOST AND FOUND

CLARK BOYD

The call interrupts my shaky pre-dawn attempt to correct my coffee and myself.

I put the brandy down and answer the phone.

It's nothing out of the ordinary. Just Aad from the Vijfhoek cheese shop complaining about a loud, repulsive, and possibly violent hunk of Limburger. I'm skeptical, because that stuff is repellent enough as it is. When he begins to describe, in graphic detail, the color and viscosity of the slime that's leaking from every curd, my stomach does a couple of flips.

"Also, it's been moaning since breakfast," he tells me.

"Who hasn't?" I fire back.

"Seriously, Witherspoon. Mrs. Goedkoop says it swore at her."

"Again, who hasn't?"

"She's threatened to never shop here again."

"Well, we can't have that. I'll be right over."

Ten minutes later, I walk in the door of the shop and the smell gags me. Then I hear the holiday music, and I wretch a bit more. It always seems to be that time of year.

"It's this one, Thomas," Aad says, pointing to a wheel with a gigantic trail of ectoplasm oozing down the outside.

"Really? How can you tell?"

"You're the expert! Can't you see it?"

I roll my eyes. Sarcasm is lost on the living.

I don't want to touch it because my hands will smell like a hideous mix of specter and fermented whey for a month. But I want to try the gentle approach first, so I put my palm on the wheel. It starts as the merest tingle in my hand, then grows and spreads up my arm like anaesthetic. By the time the numbing cold reaches my throat and begins to choke me, I know this is the real deal. A poltergeist. Things are about to get loud and possibly very messy.

I drop my voice to a whisper. "Good morning. My name's Tom."

"Overcharging prick!" The shop windows rattle and the lights flicker.

Aad runs from the room, which is probably for the best.

"Three Christmases ago. The gouda. He made me pay almost double!" A hunk of Edam flies off a nearby shelf and just misses my right ear.

I'm thinking about recent obituaries in the paper, but the noise and commotion make it hard. Then I remember. Margrethe van Hout. 92. "Feisty and financially prudent." Christ, aren't they all? Died about a week ago from food poisoning. Mistakenly ate something that had been in the fridge since October. Maybe it's part indigestion and part indignation, but Margie didn't feel like going quietly into that good night. She's got some scores to settle.

I offer to pay the difference myself. Simple. Elegant, almost.

"What about inflation?" she wails. "What about the *principle* of the thing?"

A cheese knife dislodges from a wheel on the other side of the room and flies at my head. I duck, and the blade sticks in the wooden support beam behind me. I figure it's time for tough love, so I grab the Limburger hosting the late Mrs. van Hout and run for the door. In seconds, I'm out on the street and down to the canal.

"How about it, Margie?" I yell. "Feel like a swim?"

"Bastard!" she screams.

So I launch her into the water, where she starts to sink. That's one thing you learn after years of living in the Netherlands. Limburger doesn't float.

I sit and wait on a nearby bench, smoking a Dunhill. Eventually, the malevolent spirit rises to the surface and hovers in front of me. A few people on the street pass by and try not to stare at the crazy man who just threw a wheel of cheese into the canal. But really, most of their effort is focused on not seeing the green-gray mass of ethereal hatred floating just above the water. Ignorance, bliss, etc.

"Mrs. van Hout," I say calmly. "There must be others who wronged you far worse than the cheese man."

"Well," she says. "That Goedkoop bitch poisoned one of my cats. Probably."

"That's awful. So why not seek revenge for Fluffy instead? Find her cat's litter box and dump it over her head. Something like that."

"Yes. That sounds good. Thanks for the suggestion." She floats off with a wide grin on her hideously malformed face.

I stand up and walk back into the shop.

"Is it gone?" asks Aad.

"You mean, 'Is *she* gone?' The she in question had been old Mrs. van Hout. And yes, she's gone. But I still wouldn't count on Mrs. Goedkoop coming back to your shop anytime soon."

"Wait, where's my cheese?"

"Bottom of the canal. Sorry, it was the only way to get her attention."

"Yeah, that sounds like my great-aunt all right."

"Hang on. She told me you overcharged her for cheese. Did you really stiff your elderly relative? At Christmas?"

"The old bat was loaded," Aad says. "She never gave me any presents."

I shake my head and glance at the calendar on the shop wall. December 12th. Yes, the holidays are fast approaching. Things are about to get crazy. Families, friends, and lovers alike are about to do—or fail to do—all sorts of things to and for each other.

"So...the cheese," says Aad.

Here it comes.

"Yes?"

"I'll just take the cost out of your payment, shall I?"

"Whatever you think is fair, Aad. It's not like I'm family, right?"

Later, after a few lunchtime drinks downtown, I'm walking back to my house along the canal. Aad and his son are out in their boat. Senior's peering into the water, and Junior is zipping up a wetsuit. There's a diver's mask and snorkel in the kid's hand. That wheel of cheese is most likely going to be back in its usual spot by close of business today.

My phone starts to ring again. Merry Christmas, one and all.

EVERYONE WANTS a miracle at this time of year. Even the dead.

Professional ghost hunters like me call this a Liminal

Period. Assorted holidays and belief systems collide and commingle. Fissures erupt across space and time. And the veil separating the living and the dead stretches so thin that even the strongest cocktail of cheap tinsel, useless presents, and half-assed goodwill wishes can't obscure the plain truth —legions of spirits walk among us, and many of them aren't exactly friendly. In short, business is good.

"Help me!"

That cry of the haunted always sounds louder during a Liminal Period. And I should know because I've worked many graveyard shifts at this time of year. And when I say that, I mean it literally, not figuratively.

I guess that's why I'm only half-surprised when the ghost of Daniel Cajanus, "The Finnish Giant of Haarlem," breezes through both halves of my Dutch door without so much as a knock or even a low moan. One minute I'm keeping the cold at bay with whiskey and a Dunhill by the fire, and the next the logs are smoldering, my drink has turned to ice, and my frigid fingers can't get the cigarette to my mouth. Not that it would matter, as my lips are welded shut.

"Icy cold presences" isn't a metaphor in my line of work.

Frozen lips and the like are what some in the trade refer to as "occupational hazards." I prefer to call them "warning signs of imminent ectoplasmic violence and possibly violent death." It sounds more professional and allows me to ask for a bigger retainer.

Daniel's what I call a "Casper," though. The sudden appearance of a seven and a half foot tall ghost in a low-ceilinged house should be enough to send anyone screaming into the street. But I'm strangely calmed by his looming-yet-friendly presence.

For two beings who should be enemies, we have a lot in common.

Three hundred years ago, Daniel got stuck in Haarlem because his life, and then his death, got complicated. His life by gambling and alcohol, and his death by "friends" who, instead of giving him a proper burial, ripped his body into pieces and sold his freakishly large bones to universities and museums across Europe. The leftovers got buried at the church here in Haarlem, and so that's where his spirit is strongest and most comfortable. He mostly keeps to himself, floating through the various chapels, watching as the living light candles for the dead. I often find him inspecting the cannonball that's still lodged in the church wall, a reminder of the Spanish siege of the town more than 500 years ago. I think he's attracted to the solidity, the sheer permanence and trustworthiness of it.

And my story?

A Ph.D. at the University of Leiden went sideways two decades ago after a nearly fatal (or is it un-fatal?) encounter with a lamia in a Budapest bar. As her canine teeth began to explore the skin of my neck after one too many drinks, I suddenly realized the folkloric texts I had been researching were instruction manuals, not myths. Luckily, I carried my younger sister's crucifix with me, and I fended off the blood sucker. When I tried to incorporate some of this "lived experience" into my research and writing, the faculty remained unimpressed. My detailed dissertation (pictures, diagrams, blood test results) on the proper methods for ridding Slovenian castles of Hungarian vampires was not well received. The university happily showed me the door, and I grudgingly walked through it. Afterward, in a drunken sulk, I threw a dart at a map and hit Haarlem. I got a small business loan from the Dutch government, bought this ramshackle house on Doelstraat, and hung out my shingle.

Daniel and I get along, I think, because we both know

what it's like to be considered truly foreign here in Haarlem. And everywhere else, for that matter. After we got to know each other, we started working on cases together. He serves as my spectral eyes and ears, and his intel from beyond the veil is generally first-rate. In return, I have promised to be on the lookout for his various body parts as I hunt down his kind across the continent. So far, I've managed to retrieve one kneecap, both ulnas, and an assortment of fingers and toes that may or may not be his. Both of us are hopeful we'll put him back together someday.

Some of my living colleagues find this arrangement existentially troubling on a variety of planes, both material and ethereal. The same goes, I'm sure, for Daniel when it comes to the ghouls and ghosts he hangs out with. Our partnership succeeds, though, because neither one of us gives two shits what anyone else, living or dead, thinks about us or our strange arrangement.

But tonight, I can tell Daniel wants more from me. No, he *needs* more from me.

He rarely leaves the church, so his presence in my house is, in itself, bizarre and unexpected. Also, I can see that he's holding a newspaper, an act of corporeality requiring great energy and concentration for any spirit. He hovers near my chair, flips to the back pages of the paper, and points.

It's in Finnish, so I shrug.

He indicates a small story at the very bottom of the next-to-last page. I catch one word I know. *Kummitus.* Ghost.

"My daughter," Daniel moans.

"Where did you get this?" I ask him.

"Tourist," he shrugs. And then he wails, "Please bury her for me."

The windows of my little house rattle and my whiskey glass splinters.

The weight of his loss is palpable. It's so human that it reminds me of my own.

Looks like I'm going to be doing some pro bono work over the holidays.

~

THREE DAYS LATER, the plane to Helsinki is full but funereal.

The Finns, the world champs of limited interpersonal chatter, are my kind of people.

I tend to avoid air travel. My job normally requires me to carry an array of items that both airport security officials and my therapist find disturbing and quite possibly illegal. In short, flying's a giant hassle for me. Driving, on the other hand, allows me to have free range when it comes to weapons and cigarettes. But time is of the essence in this case. I want to get Daniel's job done quickly and then return to Haarlem for some lucrative Liminal Period gigs.

As the plane taxis, I run my hand up and down my left arm to make sure the nicotine patches are secure. Three should be enough to white-knuckle my way through this flight. As the pilot hits the throttle, I can feel a deliciously electric tingle start to creep up the back of my neck. My small groan of pleasure is met with stoic Finnair silence.

About an hour into the flight, I spring for some Pringles from the in-flight food service. Because it's the holidays, I also treat myself to a Finnish beer. The can features a menacing bear on the can. It's called *Karhu.* Bear Beer. Fuelled by the probable nicotine overdose, I start giggling convulsively at this. My seatmates say nothing, probably lost in their dreams of endless, naked sauna sessions punctuated only by self-flagellation with birch switches and then a dip in a frozen lake. This thought makes me laugh even harder.

I try to focus. I reach for my notes on Daniel's case.

His daughter's name is Lahja. Was, I should say.

Daniel told me he left Finland when she was only four. He hoped to earn a quick fortune on the European carnival circuit, and then return home to live in relative comfort for the rest of his days. He promised his wife and daughter he'd be gone three years at most. But then he fell into those two gigantic holes of drink and debt and never managed to crawl out of either one. During the fifth year, when he'd been away in the Low Countries, his wife went insane, first with loneliness and then with hunger. At some point, she abandoned Lahja on a roadside in the middle of winter. The child died, cold and alone, near a town called Noormarkku.

With Daniel's story in mind, I pick up the translation of the newspaper article he pointed out to me. A few more pieces of the story fall into place as I read. The tabloid text says the angry spirit of a young girl, left for dead long ago by an uncaring mother, allegedly haunts the roads of eastern Finland. The article relates that the ghost is partial to a particular intersection, where, locals say, she forces travelers off the snowy road and then kills them. At the end of the story, a Finnish university professor calls it all "superstitious nonsense." That's a sure sign I'm onto something.

I suspect Lahja's spirit has become what Scandinavians call a *myling. Ihtiriekko,* in Finnish. The old texts say these enraged young ghouls haunt and hunt the living as revenge for being unloved and forsaken during their short lives. The literature insists they generally won't stop killing until they're given a proper burial on hallowed ground.

I put down my notes and look out the window of the plane. Heavy snow blows across the wings, obscuring the running lights. I knock back the last of my beer and finger one of the Dunhills tucked in my shirt pocket. Digging Lahja's grave should be fun in this weather.

Seriously, though, how burdensome can burying one small, soulless child be?

~

MY HOTEL IN NOORMARKKU IS, like everything in the village, unimpressive.

Technically, it's a bed and breakfast. I say technically because the "bed" is little more than a cot with scratchy woolen blankets and a pillow that reeks equally of mold and cheap detergent. The heater in the room farts and wheezes all night long. So does the owner, who sleeps in the room next to mine. Sleep deprivation might prove my undoing while working on this case.

Or perhaps the food.

"Breakfast" is hard rye, served with even harder pats of butter and preserves made with some deeply sour and seedy drupelet that grows abundantly in the brambles here. I ask the B&B owner what it's called in Finnish, but when I plug the word for this acidic monstrosity into my phone, the app calls it "Shitberry." A local delicacy, I'm sure.

At least the coffee's strong, especially after I strengthen it further with aquavit.

"Prepare a face to meet the faces that you meet," as the poet wrote.

In my case, of course, it's mostly the faces of the dead.

To find Lahja, I use my finely honed ghost hunting instincts. That means I head straight to the pub to gather information from the local cranks. I've got the original Finnish version of the newspaper article should I run into any language issues. The younger patrons laugh when I show them the story, and then laugh even louder when I ask about a malevolent spirit haunting the local roads. But two older gentlemen beckon me over to their table. They ping-pong back and forth in broken English, telling me the tale they've heard since they were children.

It goes something like this: The creature sings a famous Finnish nursery rhyme that travelers can, somehow, hear three miles before they reach the crossroads she haunts. When her victims get to the spot where the roads meet, she suddenly appears in front of their cars, causing them to swerve into a ditch. They open the door, and she sweetly apologizes. Then, when the traveler's back is turned, she latches on and won't let go. The spirit rides its prey through the nearby fields until the poor bastard collapses, only to die a few excruciating moments later from exhaustion and exposure.

"She sits on their backs," one of the men tells me.

"Cursing the mother who damned her to this hell," says the other.

"And she stays attached...."

"Until she feels the victim's blood turn to ice, the flesh to stone."

All that's missing from their shtick is some creepy organ music.

I take out a map and a pen and ask them to mark the spot where I can find her. With a sad and expectant look, one of them makes an X where two small lines intersect just north of town. By way of thanks, I ask the bartender to send over a bottle of his finest vodka. I share a shot with them and then head out into what's left of the day.

Later, after a reindeer steak and a few more drinks on my own, I run Frick and Frack's ghoulish account past the owner of the B&B.

"*Ihtiriekko,*" says Tuula, nodding her head.

"Where's the nearest cemetery?" I ask her, map in hand.

She makes another X, not far from the haunted crossroads.

My jaw unclenches slightly.

"That's doable," I say.

"You'll still have to carry her all the way there, you know."

"Well, she's the ghost of a child. She can't weigh that much, right?"

Tuula doesn't get the joke, so I let the conversation wane.

Before I turn in, though, I ask her one last question.

"How do you say 'shovel' in Finnish?"

"GRAVE DIGGER" is the least sexy entry on my already unsexy resume.

I booze- and meat-sweat my way through two feet of snow before locating a bare patch of ground in the graveyard. In some ways, I'm lucky. It's early in the winter and the cold has only turned the first foot of earth into solid rock. When I chisel through that layer, the final five feet are smooth sailing.

Smooth sailing. Right.

I'm a 50-year-old man with a bad back and even worse health habits. I have to reward myself with a Dunhill and a shot of aquavit every 20 minutes just to keep my spirits up and to forget about the lactic acid slowly building up in my arms and legs.

I work in the dark, but that's nothing new. This part of the world only gets an hour of clapped-out sunlight a day right now. And as I sink deeper into the earth, the grimness only gets more oppressive. Luckily, I had the foresight to buy a cheap lantern to go with my shiny new shovel. So now, when I pause and lean against the dank earth that constitutes the side of the grave, the weak light lets me see, just clearly enough, how quickly the heavy snow is erasing my progress.

The memory of my lost sister comes, sudden and unbidden, and it almost drops me.

Lost. And by that I mean *I* lost her. My fault.

We were in a candy store in downtown Chicago, waiting for our mother to finish the Christmas shopping. I had been told to keep a close eye on her, as she tended to wander off. But the delights of the shop were more than I could take. At one point, I let go of my sister's hand and rushed to look at a nativity scene that was sculpted out of chocolate. When I turned around a few moments later, my sister had vanished.

I screamed until they located my mother.

For a few weeks, the police tried, half-heartedly, to locate my sister. I spent every waking hour in my bedroom, lost somewhere between a sob and wail. My mother would come in and try to console me. She told me over and over that my sister's disappearance wasn't my fault. But as the weeks went by, she grew quieter on the subject. Eventually, she stopped coming into my room at all. And when I finally dared to come out, she wouldn't talk to me. We haven't spoken or even traded so much as a postcard for 35 years.

The authorities never found my sister.

Ten years ago, I snuck back to Chicago and asked to read the police report. I thought that maybe, given the skill set I had developed over the years, I could take a look at the case with fresh eyes. I honestly believed I could make some progress in figuring out what had happened to her.

It took the Chicago police more than a week just to dig the file up from the archives. I vividly remember the smeared, blue stamp on the outside of the folder: COLD. Inside, the file contained one picture of my sister. It had been crudely cut from the family portrait we'd had taken at Sears about a month before she went missing. There were also a few pages of handwritten notes. One of the detectives had apparently doodled X-rated cartoon characters while he spoke with potential witnesses. A typed index card had been stapled to the inside of the front jacket. It had yellowed with age, but I could still make out the note typed there: "Presumed kidnapped. Or dead." I thanked the archivist and told him to put the file back. Then I went to O'Hare, got loaded in one of the airport bars, and paid a thousand bucks to fly back to Amsterdam that night.

Now, standing shoulder-deep in the grave that's meant for Lahja, I can't shake the feeling that I'm digging it for my sister. I can almost feel her standing behind me, reaching for me with a little hand that's now a shriveled demonic claw and eyeing me with coal-black eyes filled with judgment. I don't dare turn around because I'm worried my worst fears will be confirmed. Instead, I knock back two shots of aquavit and shovel for another hour.

Hooch and hard work are sometimes the only things that get me through.

Later that evening, I nurse both a Scotch and my sore muscles next to a tepid fire in the living room of the B&B. Tuula's off to celebrate some strange Finnish holiday tradition at the pub. As I see her to the door, I note that the skies have cleared.

"The Northern Lights," I say aloud, pointing to the flickering sky.

"You can look at them, but it's dangerous."

"Why?"

"Each star is the soul of someone lost. If you gaze directly at them, you can expect ill-fortune for you and your family."

Normally, I take such warnings seriously. But the grave-digging and the memories of my sister have left me sour and petulant. More ill-fortune? As if my family hasn't already had more than its fair share of that. After Tuula leaves, I look directly at the lights with a sneer and raise a single finger to the heavens.

An hour later, as I'm dozing off in Tuula's ratty recliner, the *nuttipukki* show up at the door. They are evil, goat-like spirits who roam from house to house at this time of year, asking for leftover food and alcohol. After some keen detective work, I determine that my *nuttipukki* are Finnish five teenagers with their fur jackets turned inside out. They're also sporting leather masks complete with little fake horns. Luckily, I'm prepared. I hand them the remains of the breakfast rye and some of Tuula's jam. They accept my gifts silently but don't leave. They want booze, but it's clear from the smell that they've already had plenty.

"Sorry," I say, closing the door in their sad, quasi-caprine faces.

They stand in a semicircle in Tuula's front garden, howling at the lights in the sky.

That, I reckon, is some seriously bad mojo.

"KIIRE, KUSIPÄÄ!"

I assure you, Miss, that this "asshole" is going as fast as he can, given that you're riding him like a bronco and screaming obscenities at him. The malevolent spirits of children left for dead by uncaring mothers think they can get away with anything these days.

This Liminal Period has degenerated quickly into a shitshow during the past hour.

Oppressive dark. Blinding snow. Soul-sucking child ghost riding me bareback. Goddamn Finland. All this on top of my usual mix of mild holiday depression and creeping dread. I need a drink and a Dunhill, but there's no stopping now.

Lahja is making sure of that.

To be fair, she'd played her part perfectly.

As forewarned by my bar buddies, I heard her catchy little song in my head a few miles away. She flamed into being with a howl of despair just as my car entered the haunted intersection. But I knew I didn't have to swerve, so I just drove straight through her. Lahja was so surprised that she stopped screaming. When I got out of the car, she hissed at me. Then, before I could utter a word, she was on my back and the tendrils of her anger and despair were sinking into my spine. It was all I could do to turn toward the cemetery and begin trudging.

That was only five minutes ago, but it feels like an hour.

As I stagger through the snow, I know that none of this should have caught me off-guard. After all, she's had centuries to stoke her anger. The hissing, the screaming, and the joyously torturous piggy-backing...I somehow knew all that was coming.

But the weight. Nobody told me about the goddamn weight.

The closer I get to the cemetery, the heavier the *myling* on my back grows. We're not talking a few ounces. It's as if someone is putting ten-pound weights on each ankle every time my foot moves forward. At first, I sink knee-deep in the snow. Then, after a hundred more yards, I'm almost waist-deep. And as Lahja gets heavier, her urging becomes not only louder but more insistent and profane.

The physical pain caused by the weight triggers more memories of my sister. The way I used to carry her effortlessly on my back as we played together as children in the yard. The way she would yell my name and pretend we were chasing the bad guys. And then, of course, I think about how I became the bad guy. How it all turned to grief. How I failed to watch over her, to protect her, in the store that fateful day. All because of chocolate. I was, and still am, a miserable excuse for a big brother. Lahja howls with delight at this, drawing strength from my emotional misery. The more I hurt, the heavier she becomes.

This wasn't in the reference books. There are no ancient Finnish songs or campfire stories about this. The geezers in the bar chose not to share this important detail with me. Not even after I bought them vodka. Tuula didn't mention it either. And so now every step I take is filled with equal parts agony and surprise. It feels as if I am barely moving forward. I seem to be getting no closer to my goal. But at the same time, I've never felt farther away from the emergency stash of aspirin and nitroglycerine pills I foolishly left in the car.

I am about to give up when the cemetery gates finally appear through the swirling snow. There's a brief moment of hope, but it's quickly dashed when my knee gives out and I fall to the ground. Lahja screams in my ear as I begin to crawl. *Perkele...perkele...perkele.* Like some demonic gym trainer, she compels my knees forward with each of her curses.

Ten feet. Five. Keep crawling. *Perkele.* Two. One last push.

Then I'm through the cemetery gates and the weight is gone.

I roll over to the stone wall and prop myself up against it. I can hear my heartbeat thumping in my ears. I watch as Lahja's spirit skips effortlessly among graves, singing and laughing. Maybe she senses that release from her tortured existence is now within reach. Or maybe she is, even after all these years in the realm of the spirits, simply a playful child. I close my eyes for a moment, prepared to let the snow, darkness, and the inevitable myocardial infarction take me.

When I open my eyes again, the child is next to me, smiling. She shoots me a look that seems to say, "What next, old man?"

Through the snowfall, on the other side of the cemetery, I see the outline of the fresh grave I dug for her. Her salvation. Mine, too. Rest for both of us. Reluctantly, I stand and offer Lahja my hand. When she reaches for my index finger, her palm feels like nothing more than a breezy tickle on my skin.

Slowly, I lead her toward the open grave. As we walk, Lahja hums a children's tune, sweet and melodic. When we reach the edge of the pit, I look down at her.

"For you," I say. "A gift from your father."

Lahja shakes her head.

I reach into my pocket and pull out a sheet of paper with an old portrait of Daniel printed on it.

"Papa," I say, pointing at the giant's slightly smudged face. *"Isä."*

Her face lights up, and her eyes glow red. I watch those embers scour every fold and crease of the picture. She's studying the human giant who made her. The flawed man who left her. The loving father who only wanted to do right by her. The gentle spirit who asked me— his human but willing friend—to give her troubled soul some semblance of peace.

"Kotini?" she asks.

I pull out my phone and type the word into my translation app.

Home.

Jesus, that's a tough one. If she climbs into that grave, she may find some measure of peace, but certainly not a home. A grave, after all, is no place for a child. Not even a dead one. Strange to say, I know, but it's true. I think again of my little sister. If she were in this situation, would I force her down into that deep hole in the ground? Would I try to talk her into going willingly, cooking up some nonsense about the sweet hereafter and eternal rest? I've seen a bit of the world beyond the veil, but I honestly cannot say what awaits Lahja at the bottom of the dark pit I've dug.

I think of my sister reaching for my hand as I walked away from her in the store.

I think of Daniel, forlornly floating through the church in Haarlem, watching as the living light candles and pray for the souls of their lost loved ones.

And I think, ecstatically, of chasing four aspirin with shots of aquavit back in the car, followed by two Dunhills in rapid succession.

I know exactly what I'm going to do.

"Home it is, little one."

THE PLANE BEGINS its descent into Amsterdam.

Looking out the window, I see dark sheets of rain. A strong gust of wind shakes us.

After the turbulence passes, the can of Pringles on my tray table rattles. Nobody seems to notice the time gap between cause and effect. Or if they do, they know better than to say anything about it. That's another plus of a Liminal Period. Humanity, such as it is, tends to be more forgiving of the inexplicable. People have to be, I guess. There's so much crossover traffic from the ethereal plane right now that if they don't forgive, they'll end up going insane. Just two rows ahead, for example, is an empty seat that is currently occupied by a banshee. I can see her, and I bet her seatmates on either side can as well because both of them have been nervously drinking nonstop since the plane took off. Plausible deniability, I'm sure, should either let slip that they think there might be a ghost in the seat between them.

I can't help but smile.

I have perpetrated a lot of bat-shit crazy in this business over the years, but asking a semi-feral ghost-child to squeeze herself into a canister of overpriced snacks for the duration of an entire international flight takes the cake. Strapped into my seat for most of the flight because of turbulence, I have nervously waited for her unruly spirit to free itself and begin flitting about the plane. Then I began to worry she might be sucked into the air filtration system, or simply apparate through the fuselage. But Lahja manages to behave. It seems my premise—that she was never buried, and therefore never tethered to that crossroads, or to any part of Finland for that matter—is correct. She's not just mobile, but snack-pack mobile.

Still, I hang onto Lahja tightly as we touch down. She rattles away happily as I wait for my luggage and find the right bus.

A few hours later, I carry her into the church in Haarlem and find Daniel, who is hovering near his cannonball.

"Merry Christmas," I say, holding out the container. I've put a small bow on top of it.

The sour look on his long face makes me question every decision I've ever made.

I mime popping the top.

With great effort, Daniel opens it and Lahja materializes in front of us.

Father and daughter share a moment of stunned silence

before erupting in a mix of ghostly laughter and tears. The din echoes off the church walls, filling the entire space with a kind of spectral birdsong. "Hauntingly beautiful" is the phrase for it, I believe. A priest nearby glances our way and then rushes off to try to pray away the unholy spectacle he's just heard and seen.

"Horsey!" Lahja yells at me.

"Call me Uncle Thomas."

"*Setä!*"

"Whatever, little one."

Daniel nods his thanks, and I leave them to their eternal reunion.

On my way out of the church, I do something I haven't done for years. I stop and light a candle in one of the side chapels. Then I place the flickering flame in a holder and whisper a prayer for my little sister.

Lilith. Lily, as I once called her. *Still* call her, I remind myself.

When I get outside, I reach for a cigarette.

Before I light it, though, I wipe away a tear and check my phone. There is quite a selection of emails. Three potential clients and an e-coupon for a session at the local gym.

I throw the pack of cigarettes into the canal and start walking home.

If I can make enough money over the holidays, I may hop on a transatlantic flight. Head for the Windy City and take one more shot at finding my sister. While I'm in Chicago, I might even try to patch things up with my mother. Whether they are alive or dead, I know I can find them. That's my job, after all.

My steps feel lighter, and yet more solid, than they have in years.

RAIN MUST FALL

R.A. GERRITSE

1

"Those things will kill you, Kate. You know that, right?"

Kate looked up from the dead patch of grass she'd been staring a hole into for the last half hour or so. Leaning against the neglected remains of her Dad's once pride and joy — his '68 Chevy truck, she sighed at the dark silhouette holding a bag of groceries, blocking her sunlight. Janet. *Who else*. To her utter annoyance, Janet seemed to be waiting for an answer to the obvious question. "My anxieties and my depression, you mean? You are absolutely correct. They most probably will. Luckily for me, *these* help a little."

She held up her almost-spent filter cigarette, took one last deep draw, and flicked it to the ground—exhaling a large cloud of gray smoke into the cold December air and crushing the bud under her flat heel, her eyes not once shying once from her older sister's judging gaze. "Thank you so much for acknowledging my pain, though," she said in the sweetest sounding sneer she could muster.

Janet only grunted and stomped off. *Every goddamn year*

it's the same. Why do I even... But Kate knew why and groaned, rubbing her eyes. When she pulled back her hand, she noticed them stained with mascara. *Great. Just... fucking great.* She knew her sis was nothing but worried for her well-being, but did she have to express her loving concern in such an angry, disapproving way? "This family is so messed up," she muttered under her breath. "Falling apart, just like this damn car."

Kate fondly remembered watching her father work on this old piece of junk truck for days on end. He loved this rust-bucket — although she had to admit, like herself, the car had seen much better days. "I guess we could both need a little work, eh, old girl?" She patted the door, then buried her hands in the pockets of her long dark woolen coat and started making her way back to the house. She used to love this time of year when she was a kid. That was before tragedy reared its ugly head in her life before the darker shades of existence took over. Back when life was all smiles and love. "It's only a weekend. Three days, once a year, you can do this."

As Kate saw it, things had not been right in the Crosswell family for many years. She chalked it up to the fact that everyone deals with loss in heartbreakingly different ways. *We used to be so similar, in everything. Will we ever be able to get back to that?* There was still a lot of love and support between Kate, her Mom, and her two sisters, but they'd never been particularly great at showing it. When saturated with pain and regret, even the best intentions usually came out crappy. Feelings, such a minefield. They *knew*. That was the important thing—no need to state the obvious, right? She was here, wasn't she? As she had been every year since her promise. *No matter where our lives will lead us, Krampusnacht we spend together, always. I remember.*

"Into each life, some rain must fall, but too much has

fallen into mine." She hummed the old song her father used to sing to her with that eternal smile of his, no matter the seriousness of the situation. *I don't know how much more rain I can take, Dad. My foundations stand flooded, and the water reached my neckline, but I'm still trying. I miss you.* She looked up to the clear sky, blue as his eyes used to be, shuddered, and stepped across the porch to enter the house.

Inside she found the madness she'd escaped roughly a half-hour earlier still in full swing. Her younger sister's twin boys came running past through the hallway screaming, one of them wearing a sadistic grin, holding Josh's new tablet high above his head. "Hi, Aunty K," he said in passing, clearly enjoying his duty of making his little brother's life miserable.

"Give it back, Josh!" cried Davy as he stomped past. "Why do you have to be such a dick!"

"Language!" Leah hollered from the kitchen. "Give your brother back his tablet." She sounded tired and unconvincing — and of course, got utterly ignored by the two teen-tyrant hurricanes, whose screaming voices now moved towards the stairs.

"Lovely," Kate muttered, shaking her head. She closed the front door behind her, took off her coat, and slung it in the general direction of the coat rack.

"Is that you, Kate?" she heard Leah call. "I could use some help here."

"You have help," she heard Janet complain. "And you know that Kate cannot cook worth a..."

"Oh, shush, be nice, sis, " Leah interrupted her. "Mom will soon return. I'd like us to be ready when she does. And there's still much to do. Kate, you coming?"

Kate sighed and stared an annoyed look at the empty doorway at the end of the hall. *Three days. It is just for three days.* "Coming," she said, and with slumped shoulders, she shuffled into the kitchen.

Leah looked up briefly from the furnace, where several large pots and pans stood simmering, her eyes scanning Kate's probably messed up makeup, then blinked and turned her attention back to her cooking. "Well, don't you look...festive."

"Yeah, like a mourning vampire," Janet said, not looking up from her work. She stood with her back to the door, cutting vegetables with a hell-born fury.

Those poor carrots. Kate couldn't see her expression, but her tense body language told her all she needed to know about Janet's mood. *I don't need this right now.* "It looks like you've got things well under control here," she said and was about to walk back out of the kitchen when a loud cry sounded from upstairs.

"You broke it! Mooooom!"

Well, that was a hundred and fifty bucks well spent, thought Kate.

"Oh, for crying out loud," Leah said. "Kate, watch the furnace for me for a bit, will you? And keep an eye on the roast as well. I'll be back in a bit. I have two little monsters in serious need of some parenting, it seems."

Without awaiting her response, she hurried past Kate, out of the kitchen — leaving her alone with the knife-wielding thundercloud. "Well, alright, then. Sure. Why not."

"Do not let it burn," Janet grunted without ever turning or looking up from her vegetable massacre. "Again."

That rubbed Kate the wrong way. This was another piece of ancient bullshit she'd never seemed to be able to shed, and it came up whenever Janet was in one of her moods — which was often. "I was thirteen, okay? Once. I burned a meal *once* as a kid. Get the hell over yourself," Kate snapped back and instantly regretted it. *Poking the bear again, Kate. Just let it go. Nothing good ever comes from aggravating Mrs. Grumpy.* She took a deep breath, made her way to the stove, and lifted a few lids to see what was cooking.

"Twice. You did it twice."

Something in Kate broke. "Fuck you!" she yelled. "Why don't you just take over then, like you always do? Cannot let your fuckup sister ruin Saint Nicholas dinner, right?" she threw the lid she was holding back onto the pan with a loud clatter and stormed out of the kitchen. "*So* glad I came."

2

KATE LAY on her highly uncomfortable fold-out camping bed and listened to her music. Even the usually soothing dark gothic melodies failed to calm her. The strings of all the instruments seemed tied directly into the chaos inside her head, setting off unintended alarms left and right with each vibration, with every chord. Her nerves felt all tangled and in knots, with loose, ragged ends sticking out on all sides, shaving her any which way she moved. Kate knew she was projecting her mood onto her sisters. She knew Janet was doing the same. She knew Leah felt the same desperation as both of them but refused to let it show. Janet had always been right there in the middle. She knew.

It was hard to imagine it had already been fifteen years since her father's death. Things went south fast after that. Her father had proven the glue that held the family together. Not that any of them realized that while he was still around. *It's funny how you take the good things for granted until they're gone.* She pulled a weak smile despite herself. *Funny, yeah. ha-fucking-ha.*

So much life had passed by since that dark Krampusnacht a decade and a half ago. Her little sister Leah, two years her junior, had two kids now. She'd never gotten used to that. Meanwhile, her older sister ran a successful law firm, raking in the big bucks. Those two had their shit together. Mother still ran the town's general practice. In Kate's memory, she'd always done so. Some things never changed. And what had Kate to show for her wasted years? A stack of unsellable mediocre artwork, three half-finished novels, a crap apartment far away from everyone she'd ever known and loved, and a still temporary, yearly renewed employment contract for a dead-end job she hated with a passion. Well, at least she'd made it to twenty-nine, despite her best efforts to sabotage even that accomplishment.

I really messed this family up. I did this. I deserve this life. The thought came from nowhere and caught her by surprise, making her heart skip a beat. She wiped a few sudden tears from her eyes, further ruining her already smeared makeup. The thought was not a new one, but she usually suppressed that shit better. *It's this damned house.* She thought back at another Krampusnacht, fifteen years ago— the night she lost her father and shuddered. *Why the hell did Mom always refuse to move?* If she were honest to herself, Kate knew that too.

"One bad memory must not be allowed to overshadow half a lifetime of good ones," she whispered. "I know." This house held mostly good memories. Mostly. But still. She'd never take a single step into her Dad's library on the second floor ever again, not in a million years or for any boon. The thought alone already gave her a chill.

For a moment, she was that fourteen-year-old kid again

— sneaking through the house on tiptoes to get herself some more of the left-over dessert, careful not to get caught in her intended act of gluttony. Something about her mother's trademark 'virgin Tiramisu' had always been irresistible to Kate, even back then — the temptation big enough to risk a reprimand, even after a double helping at dinner.

As she passed her father's library, she noticed the door stood ajar, and there was still a light burning. *That's strange*, she remembered thinking. *Shouldn't Dad be asleep by now? Or did he forget to turn off the light?* She had moved to push open the door silently, and...

Someone knocked on her bedroom door, pulling her back to the present. At the same moment, her music cut out in a sudden loud hiss of static, sending a chill down her spine as if someone just emptied a bucket of ice down the back of her Ramones shirt.

"TELL THEM," a grating voice shouted through the white noise over her wireless headphones, and Kate screamed — ripping the headset off and hurtling it into the corner, where it landed with an uncomfortable cracking sound.

"W-what the hell was that!"

The door flew open, and her mother hurried into the room. "What... Are you okay, sweetheart? What happened? Why are you screaming?" She was by Kate's side in no time, holding her forehead as if checking for a fever. "Are you hurt?"

Kate sat up, her heart pounding, swiping her Mother's hand away. "N-no, not hurt. Jesus. Give me a moment, Mom." She stepped off the bed and cautiously approached the discarded headset as if it were a viper, noting with a pinch of regret that the left earpiece had come loose and shattered across the floor into little pieces of plastic. She slowly picked up the mangled headset and held it next to her ear. Her music was playing as if it had never stopped.

Keep it together, Kate. It's this house. You're overreacting. She pressed the pause button on the right earpiece and threw the headset onto the bed with a shiver as if she'd just released something nasty.

"Aww, you broke your...music thingy." She waved at the busted headphones. "Why did you do that? Are you alright, Katy?"

"Yeah, mom. I'm just...tired. I'm having a bad day."

"Your sisters told me as much. I came to check how you are doing, but you scared the shit out of me just now. What on Earth were you listening to?"

"Nothing, just some music. I must have fallen asleep, I think. Yeah. Must have been a nightmare. You probably woke me just now." She tried to suppress a shudder with a half-assed smile and knew she failed.

Her mother gave Kate a worried glance, shook her head, and sighed. "Well, alright, sweetheart. Take a few more minutes to wake up, then go freshen up. Dinner is in a little under an hour and, no offense, but it looks like you need some time to get ready." Her mom smiled as she wiped over Kate's cheek and showed her the mascara smudged finger. "It is Krampusnacht, not Halloween, you know?"

Kate gave a half-hearted laugh. "You always know just what to say, Mom. Thank you."

"That's all part of the job, sweetheart, and it's still the best damn job in the world. Take a shower. I'll see you downstairs when you're ready."

∾

3

KATE LEANED against the shower wall, her head resting on her arm, while soothing torrents of steaming hot water streamed down her body, holding her in a warm embrace. She loved the sound of clattering water and the solitude of showering. These blessed moments of full immersion in the water's caress usually allowed her to tune out both the world and her thoughts, but not today. Not here. Not with her thoughts and memories, and not with Davy and Josh in the next room bickering loudly over some game. Still, Kate felt reluctant to step back into reality.

The water suddenly turned freezing, deciding to end the moment of solitude for her. "Fuck!" she yelled. "Couldn't you have given me five more fucking minutes? Sheesh!" Shivering, she rushed to turn off the water, the little calm she'd gathered quickly evaporating. "And that's why I live alone." She opened the shower door, grabbed a towel to wrap around her hair, and another to dry herself, then stepped out into the bathroom.

Kate felt possibly tenser than before she'd stepped in, over half an hour earlier, as if her anxiety over the strange voice on her headphones had only amplified. She rubbed her eyes.

Once more, her fourteen-year-old-self stood in the doorway of her father's library, peeking around the door as carefully as she could, not to make a sound. She could see her father sitting in his favorite leather chesterfield chair behind his mahogany desk, fast asleep. He looked so peaceful, surrounded by his second passion in life besides that crappy old car — a forbidden realm, filled with shelves of books that, to a kid, seemed to stretch into eternity. If only she'd known then that it would be the last time she'd see him alive.

Kate opened her eyes again to the present. "If only. Tell them," she whispered, wrapping the soft, now slightly damp bath towel around her. "Tell them fucking what?" She wiped the fogged-up mirror clean with her arm and felt all blood drain from her face. Her breath caught in her throat.

Behind her stood a monstrous dark figure, staring at her, its two giant curved horns nearly reaching the ceiling. The thing was hairy all over, from its dark face to the clawed arms hanging by its side, to its hoofed goat-feet — its mouth twisted into a snarl, exposing two terrifying rows of razor-sharp teeth. Kate wanted to scream her head off at the sight of those demonic yellow eyes but had lost all control of her breathing.

She looked around frantically and grabbed the hairdryer from the vanity, the first weapon she could spot, then spun around to defend herself against the beast — but there was nothing behind her. "Wha— what? How..." Trembling, she sagged to the floor and started both crying and laughing out of sheer relief.

Am I fucking losing my mind here? Pull it together, Kate. What the hell are you doing? She let out another nervous giggle, despite herself.

"Krampus? Did I just see Fucking *Krampus*? What am I, twelve?" She forced herself to get up. "Get the hell over yourself, Kate. It's all in your hea..."

"TELL THEM," it said, written in large, dripping capital letters, drawn onto the fogged-up door to the shower cabin, in handwriting not her own. Kate found her scream.

4

KRAMPUSNACHT DINNER PROVED EVEN MORE stressful than usual for Kate. This year it was not the forced polite conversation that got to her, nor was it the annual 'look at us being a functional family' puppet show she and her sisters tended to perform for her mother. No, this year, all eyes were on her, and they all seemed genuinely worried for her — even the two kids, even though they probably had no idea what was going on with their aunt. It freaked her out.

Well, what did she expect? *Not surprising, you basketcase. The way they found you in the bathroom?* She'd told them she had seen a spider, but it was more than clear they hadn't believed her, even though they helped her search for the imaginary insect for fifteen fucking minutes. *It is a miracle they have not yet had you committed,* she thought. But the Crosswell family dynamics — and Kate's self-destructive personality in particular— being what they were, she put on her usual mask and pushed through her mental pain with her well-rehearsed trademark 'just leave me the fuck alone' attitude. "Jesus, can you all please stop staring at me? I told you, I'm fine."

A glance passed between her mother and siblings, and for a moment, they all returned their attention to the meal in silence, but of course, the silence couldn't last, and it came to no surprise to Kate to see who broke the fragile peace.

"We're just concerned for you, you know?" Janet said softly without looking up from her plate, where she was shuffling around a few baked potatoes. "You've not been yourself lately. Hell, it's been a long time since we've seen you be yourself if I'm honest, but you frightened us just now."

Kate just rolled her eyes and put down her fork, almost glad for the excuse to stop pretending to eat.

Janet kept on muttering. "A spider, she says. I cleaned that bathroom myself this morning. There were no spiders." She took one of the severely undercooked carrots in her mouth and began crunching away at it.

"Janet, must you…" their mom said with a look that would have silenced either of her sisters had they seen it but got interrupted by Leah, who *did* meet Kate's eyes.

"Ever since Dad passed, we've all been through a lot, Kate. It's not just you who feels the weight of that. We are all trying our darndest to keep our lives, our family together. Why won't you let us be there for you? You're just like him, you know? A stubborn ass."

Her mother shot Leah an angry look. "Is this the best time to do this, you two think? It is Krampusnacht. The one time a year that I get to spend with all my girls, and my grand-kids…" She shot a meaningful glance at the uncharacteristically silent Josh and Davy as if trying to say 'not in front of the kids.' "Please, it is one of the precious few traditions we share."

"It's okay, mom," said Kate, unconvincing and way too softly to be heard.

"That's just it, mom," Leah said. "We are not. Sharing, I mean. Nor have we been, not for years. If anything, our tradition has become one of *not* sharing. Just see to what it has led —a darned breakdown in the bathroom. Do you know what is truly going on with her, Mom?"

She turned back to Kate, with more anger in her tone with every word she spoke. "And do you still even know what *our* lives are like, Kate? And do you care? You 'bless us' with your wonderfully depressing presence once a year, buying off your absence in your god children's lives with ridiculously expensive gifts, but do you even know how I cope with being a single mother? Or how mom is dealing with life all by herself, alone in this house and all its memories? Or that our older sister has finally met someone?"

At that, Kate blinked and turned to Janet. Not just to try and steer the conversation to a more positive subject, she felt genuinely happy for her. But of course, she fucked even that chance up. "You did? Wow, good for you. What's his name?"

Janet shot Leah an angry look, then lowered her eyes to her plate again, her forehead all frown. "Her. Her name. It's Sandra."

Kate blinked again and gave Janet an unseen but appreciative nod. *Wow. I guess I really have not been paying attention...*

Leah looked at Kate again; her eyes were all glassy. "See what I mean? We're sisters, for crying out loud, and it feels like we couldn't be living further apart. We barely get to see you, and it seems you drift further away from us each time we do! Haven't we lost enough? Can't we just... start truly sharing again? Like we used to? When did simple things like being open about what we're feeling, what we are going through, become so hard for you? Do you think Dad would have wanted this?"

At that point, Leah was nearly screaming, and all eyes had shifted to her, not a trace left of the usual hollow smiles they wore to these family gatherings — it felt like Leah's words had muted the very air. She looked around the room, suddenly very self-conscious of all the shocked expressions. "I'm just saying what we are all thinking," she muttered. "I miss us. Not just Dad. Us." At that, she broke into tears and fled the room, closely followed by Janet, who shot Kate an inexplicable angry look in passing.

Kate held up her hands, unsure what she could possibly have said in response to make things better. She tried seeking out her mother's eyes, but she had them buried in her hands.

She looked over to the kids — they sat wide-eyed and visibly uncomfortable, in front of plates emptied of all but their vegetables. Josh, the eldest, looked at her and pointed upstairs, raising an eyebrow in question. *Smart kid.* Kate nodded. It would probably have been better if 'the parent' had sent them up before going off the rails, but what the fuck did *she* know about parenting, right? Right.

As soon as the kids were out, Kate sagged back into her chair, reflecting on the utter mess this night turned out to be. Then the lights started flickering. For a moment, Kate thought one of the kids had to be playing with the light switch, but the flickering became too fast, too frantic, too random, and suddenly the room turned to pitch dark. *Could it be a power outage?*

A thunderclap shook the room, its echo cascading off the dining room walls far longer than it should have. It rattled everything — from the cutlery and plates on the table, to the lamp above, to the good china Mom had kept behind lock and key in the dining room cabinet for as long as Kate could remember. Shocked, she wondered why her mother wasn't screaming. Did she not notice the house appeared to be collapsing around them? Right on the thunder's tail followed a lightning flash so bright that it almost seemed *inside* the house. It could not have lit the room for more than half a second, but in that handful of heartbeats, Kate could make out the horned silhouette of Krampus standing behind her mother — who still sat with her head in her hands. The demon's clawed hands hung over her mother's shoulders, with his radiating yellow eyes fixed on Kate.

"TELL THEM!" it thundered through the room, the moment the lightning cut out, as deep, rumbling, and primal as the thunder itself — leaving nothing but trembling darkness and the afterglow of two fading yellow globes.

For the second time that night, Kate screamed until she ran out of breath, forcing her eyes closed as tight as they went. When what seemed an eternity later she opened them again, gasping for air, the last thing she saw was her mom, looking at her in shocked horror. Behind her, Kate could faintly hear the fading sound of rushing footsteps and worried yells as her world turned black once more.

∾

5

"THERE YOU ARE AGAIN. It's okay, Katy. You are safe. You're in my bed. We are all here with you."

Kate opened her eyes to see her mother sitting next to her on the bed, stroking her hair. Her sisters sat in the wicker chairs of the reading nook by the window. "What..happened," she stammered. Her mouth felt dry as if stuffed with cotton, and her head pounded as if she'd been on an all-night bender — the feeling a little too familiar for comfort.

"You blacked out," Leah said, visibly nervous. She had a crochet work in her lap, but it seemed untouched.

"Yeah, you gave us quite the scare, sis," Janet said. She had an upside-down closed book in her lap. "Are you feeling better?"

Kate moaned as she tried to sit up. "No. Not really. You were not the only ones who got a scare."

"We...gathered as much," her mother said, as she helped her sit up, fluffing her pillow behind her back. "Something must have seriously spooked you."

Understatement of the year, Kate thought. "Did we just have a power outage, or did I imagine that?" She looked from her sisters to her mother. They all looked thoughtful and concerned.

"No, we did not, Katy. Did you…" Her mother broke off and bit her lip, took a deep breath, then looked her in the eyes. "I'll just come out and ask. Did you use something before you came here, honey? Mind, I'm not judging, but I need to know. You are acting mighty strange."

"Huh? What are you asking me, Mom? If I did what, use drugs?"

Her mother gave her a helpless shrug, then looked away, fiddling with Kate's pillow again. "Not judging. I swear. But did you?"

"No. God! No, Mom. What do you take me for?" Kate shot her sisters a glance. "Did you all think that?" She noticed their shameful expressions and already knew the answer, despite their silence. She shook her head and groaned — which seemed to make them even more uncomfortable. "I don't blame you. To be totally honest, drugs *would* seem a rational explanation for how I've been acting tonight. I must have come across like a madwoman."

"What is going on with you, Kate. You know you can tell us everything, right? We're family. That's what we're there for. Part of the job, remember?"

"That doesn't just go for moms. It goes for sisters too," Leah added, as she put her probably untouched book away.

Tell them, it echoed through Kate's head, and she grimaced. "Believe it or not, someone or something out there has been trying to tell me just that all day, it seems."

Kate silently arranged her thoughts for a moment, then finally, gave in. *You win.* She started telling her family about the strange voice she heard over her headphones, the Krampus vision in the shower, and again in the dining room. Word by word, it all tumbled out, while her Mom and sisters listened with the undivided attention. When the last words fell silent, they just sat there for a while, staring into the middle distance. *Yeah*, Kate thought as she surveyed the thoughtful faces around her. *Drugs would definitely have made sense. I'd almost wish it were so.*

Her mother was the first to break the silence, with a whispered question Kate had been expecting but feared nonetheless. "Tell us what, Katy?"

At those four words, Kate broke down in tears. "It's my fault he's gone," she sobbed. "I could have stopped it from happening, but I did nothing."

"He? You mean... your father? What are you on about? How could that have been your fault?" Her mother's eyes widened and glazed over. "What have you gotten yourself in that pretty little head of yours. Is that why you've been acting so increasingly strange around us for the last few years?"

On the other end of the room, two more pairs of eyes teared up, looking from Kate to their mother and back. "You don't understand!" shouted Kate. "I was the last to see him! He was still alive. Still breathing. I saw him sitting in his reading chair, sleeping."

"Oh, Katy. Why have you never told me this?"

"I knew there was something wrong. Deep down, I knew. Dad was breathing too quietly. Too peacefully. He seemed way too comfortable for someone sleeping in a fucking chair. And I did nothing. I even smiled at him. I fucking smiled and whispered, 'good night.' I... I..." She burst into tears again, and her mother locked her in an embrace.

"Oh, sweetheart, no. No, no, no. That is... You got that all twisted up. I..." Her mom started crying too. "It was not your fault, at all. If anyone deserves blame here, it's me." She grabbed Kate by the shoulders, tilted her head up, and looked her in the eyes. "You are not to blame for what happened —

no one is. Not even your Dad, not really, although he could have handled things a lot less shitty."

"What? What are you saying, Mom?" Kate stammered, wiping the tears from her eyes.

"You girls better sit a bit closer, too," she told Leah and Janet. "There's something I've been keeping from you. To protect you, I told myself, but it seems I've only been making things worse for you."

Janet and Leah joined Kate on the bed in silence. They looked exhausted, pale, and afraid — their moist eyes fixed on their mother.

"You see... Your father... he... killed himself."

All three sisters gasped. Kate felt her heartbeat hammering in her throat. She could feel Janet shivering next to her. She heard Leah's breath take on a frantic pace, but all she could think was "*he did what?*" Between their mother's words, the room trembled with nothing but disbelief and shock.

"Turns out, your father, rest his soul, had cancer. Inoperable, terminal cancer. He never even told me — I only found out after he passed. He didn't..." She paused to clear her throat and wipe her tears. "He did not want to worry us with this, it seems, but he must have been in a hell of a lot of pain."

She looked at each of them in turn with a sad smile. "That night, after Krampusnacht dinner, after spending one last meal with us, he retreated to his library and took a whole bottle of sleeping pills, washing it down with his favorite whiskey. I don't know who... Who he was trying to protect most from what was coming, himself or us, or why he couldn't have shared this tragic news with us so we could have at least said our proper goodbyes, but that was your father, I guess." She snottered and smiled despite her tears.

"That stubborn jackass never did learn how to talk about what ailed him. But Kate. Oh, sweet Katy. Even had you told us that night that your Dad was not well, there was nothing to be done. Believe me, I would know. And he made that choice all by himself. We could not have stopped him, nor could you have saved him. Oh, my sweet girl…"

At that, they all fell in a crying embrace, closer in every way than they'd been in years.

∾

6

KATE SAT on the couch swing on the front porch, wrapped in a thick tweed blanket, with a mug of coffee in one hand and a cigarette in the other, waiting for dawn to fill the hollow inside her with the promise of a better tomorrow. Her Mom and sisters had finally gone to sleep after an exhausting and confusing night, but they would be alright. "We will all be alright," she whispered. "At least I now know why Mom kept insisting on us always celebrating Krampusnacht together. It was all for you, Dad. Yeah, I know you're there. You can come out now."

She blinked, and there he was — her father. Just as she remembered him, with that damned infuriating smile of his, and for whatever stupid reason, still wearing the Krampus suit.

"At least you took that stupid mask off," she said. "Why the theatrics, Dad?"

Her father just cocked his head as if saying, "You know why."

"I know. I'm as stubborn and pigheaded as you were. I probably would not have taken anything less than this complete mindfuck the least bit serious. You know me too well."

There was that smile again, along with a raised eyebrow.

"And? Is that what you're asking, you prick?" she laughed. "You were right. I needed that. Thank you. But you know what? Fuck you too, Dad."

At that, he bowed his head, staring into the distance for a moment. When he met her gaze again, he nodded, with a tear on his cheek.

"I miss you. You know that, right?" Kate said. "I… love you."

Her father's smile changed — it became warmer, yet sadder. Behind him, the first rays of morning light started to creep over the horizon. He glanced over his shoulder and met her eyes. "I'm sorry," he mouthed.

"Who are you talking to, Aunt K?" Davy stood barefoot in the doorway, still in his pjays, rubbing his eyes.

"Davy? Oh shit." Kate flicked away her cigarette and set her coffee in the window. "I'm sorry, did I wake you? It's too cold to be out here in your pajamas, little buddy! Come on, get in here." She opened the blanket and motioned him over, then wrapped it around both of them.

"You did not wake me," Davy said, yawning. "I'm always up this early."

Kate laughed. "I bet you are," and messed up his hair. "I bet you see all the sunrises. You're right in time to watch my favorite morning show with me." The kid just smiled at that and snuggled up to her.

With her arm around her nephew, Kate looked back to the horizon, where her father still stood, although now barely visible. With a look filled with both love and regret, he placed a hand on his heart, blew her a kiss, and walked away towards the horizon. He faded a little more with every step into the light.

He'd not spoken a single word to her, yet his voice sang loud in Kate's mind. The song he'd always sung — that ever picked her up, no matter how bad the situation. "Goodbye, Dad," she said, and started singing along with his memory as it traded the nightmare for pleasant dreams of the father he'd been.

> *"Into each life, some rain must fall,*
> *But too much is falling in mine.*
> *Into each heart, some tears must fall,*
> *But someday the sun will shine."*

MY WAR ON CHRISTMAS

CHRISTOPHER YUSKO

Kate,

I'm sending over everything I have on the Matt Johnson story. It isn't much, but you owe me huge on this one. "Pay for therapy" huge. I watched that tape to the end. To steal a line from Werner Herzog in Grizzly Man: "Katherine, you must never watch this." Seriously though, don't.

My contact at WLTV confirmed the commonly circulated details: late that December 24th, Johnson entered the station without authorization, bringing along a shotgun and a bottle of Johnnie Walker. He took his (former) place at the news desk and began to outline his, uh, theories. I've transcribed the entire rant, just for you. Most of this is already known, but I do have a few interesting details to share afterwards.

Wish I knew your angle. I know you too well to think you're doing another speculation piece about Johnson's mental health. You don't think there's something to the kidnapping accusations, do you?

Well, without further delay, I guess we should let Johnson speak for himself.

~

MATT JOHNSON: Um. One way or another, I expect this will be my final newscast, so let's do this right.

00:43, Matt Johnson, WLTV news anchor. For those of you who have followed my eleven-year-career at the station, I'd like to think I've been a source of stability in the community. Stability and comfort. Good old Matt Johnson, quick with a quip or some well-timed innuendo.

Okay, there have been moments. I'm not perfect. Some jokes at my expense. Folks sure remember the F-bomb I dropped when that squirrel leapt onto my shoulder at the Rochester Apple Festival.

Or hey. I'll never live down that interview with Pelicans' defensive back Sam Sanders, after his crucial block in the Quarterfinal victory against the Coyotes--Go 'cans! You know the one I'm talking about. Where, because of the unfortunate placement of our hands, we appear to be comparing the size of our...

Boy did that become a widely-circulated meme. I think it's pretty clear that we were estimating how close to goal the Coyote's running back was when Sanders dragged him down, but it's fine. It was funny.

I know my star has fallen over the past year. But even then--except for that period of stress leave--I've been here. In your homes. Not literally *in* your homes. On your screens, I'm trying to say.

That's the legacy I want to leave behind. It is therefore somewhat ironic that I come here tonight to deliver an unsettling truth.

The reason I'm here on location at WLTV, well after-hours on Christmas Eve, having missed my usual video chat with my children in Seattle, is because I feel I have a duty to explain. However it's looked, I haven't been (as those hacks at the Rochester Gazette wrote) undergoing a 'mental health crisis.' And I am absolutely not, as Twitter user Rochester-Dodger22 chimed in, 'circling the drain.' Just the opposite.

Look, I know people are going to make mountains out of this bottle of scotch. It's Christmas: I can't bring a date? Kidding. Truth is, I've never been more focused. Because between the, the, frankly, the B.S. assignments I've been getting, I've been very busy. Pounding the pavement, as it were.

[Johnson reaches below the news desk, putting his head in line with the barrel of the shotgun. He waves a stack of papers when he straightens up].

I prepared a statement for the occasion. The facts I present will astonish you. 'How can he be so cool and collect-ed?' you'll say. Well, I'll let you in on a little secret: I'm in no danger. Yet. The cowards will strike when I'm tired.

[Johnson takes a pull of Jonnie Walker and taps the stacks of papers against the desk. Throughout what follows, Johnson repeatedly loses track of, and frequently ignores, his prepared remarks] Tonight, I give you the most important story of my career. Over the past years, across a number of state lines, there has been a dramatic increase in an insidious form of child abduction. The circumstances are always the same. The spree begins in early winter and tapers off after the Christmas season. The perpetrators behind these abductions are extremely cunning. Their actions remain largely invisible.

I feel it is my duty to expose this danger. [Pause] Even if I make a fool of myself in the process.

You see, I have no choice but to explain something that happened to me in my childhood. Something that's made it possible for me to connect the dots. 'Matt Johnson's childhood: a Matt Johnson exclusive'! Right? Well, humour me.

I guess, for starters, my name isn't actually Matt Johnson. I was born Matviy Kozachenko, fourth and last child of Ukrainian immigrants, dissidents who fled to America after the Communist crackdown of 1964. Mom and Dad were-- well, they had joined what I guess was some kind of worker's union. There was some kind of kerfuffle after...like, when the Soviets had loosened up about Ukrainian culture. You know what, I'm hazy on the details. Probably I could have tried harder to understand.

Fast-forward: America! I was a late surprise, born nine years after they arrived in this great nation. My siblings are older. There's a 13-year gap between me and my sister. You-- you don't really need to know this stuff. The important thing is that my Dad was trained as a carpenter, but he was really a tinkerer and inventor who earned his living as a toymaker. Consequently, I grew up in a house full of toys, with siblings who wanted nothing to do with me.

Maybe you can appreciate my interest in Dad's work. When my siblings told me to buzz off, or worse, when my brothers went hunting for someone to torment, the workshop offered an appealing place to escape. There I'd find the projects of the day, blocks of beech wood in varying states of transformation, or some finished product awaiting a glossy coat of paint. There were mysterious assorted tools, many which held the fascination of danger. The comforting smell of Dad's pipe smoke. There was always the hope I'd get to handle some new creation. I wasn't 'allowed' in his workshop, but consequences for disobeying usually depended on how much Dad had been drinking. Sometimes I think he liked that I couldn't help myself.

Dad specialized in ingenious wooden dealies. For a man

who didn't seem to like children very much, he had a wonderful imagination that he poured into his craft. His creations were one-of-a-kind, full of whimsical touches. Beautiful hand-painted puzzles, inspired by fairy tales. Jack-in-the-boxes. Hand-carved train sets. I remember a wooden seal that rose up and clapped when you pulled it along, clowns on tricycles that tipped their cap as they rode on. Kids these days maybe wouldn't care. I tried to pass one of those clowns on to my kids a few years back, and they were done with it in five minutes. Broke my heart. To me, they're still magical.

I really do think Dad used me to judge the quality of his work. This one time, I fell in love with this Noah's Ark he'd made. It came with a whole set of miniature animals. I was in tears when he put it up for sale. But instead of getting mad, Dad took me down to the Donut Shack, bought me an apple fritter and a soda. And okay, I had to sit while he and his friends smoked and drank coffee and grumbled in Ukrainian. I got restless, and he got p.o.'d, but by our standards, it was a pretty good time. And I felt, y'know. Like one of the guys.

Oh. But that afternoon? When I went to check on that Ark in the shop window? He'd jacked up the price twenty bucks! Ha. Well, that was Dad for ya. But it did turn out that when he'd made something particularly good, and he thought he might be able to charge a little extra, he'd usually let me try it out first. And that kind of became our thing.

Where I was going with this. So I was six, maybe seven, when I saw...what I saw. This was around Christmas. Dad's best pieces were always done on commission, and one of his wealthiest clients wanted a castle for his son, who was really into knights and shining armor. This guy must have shelled out, because Dad built a masterpiece.

The castle was big as me, when I knelt beside it. It was

painted white and gold; the good guy's turf. There was a feasting hall, tournament grounds, you name it. Dad designed the walls and towers to be modular, so the set could be moved around despite its size. The towers even opened on a hinge, so you could stage scenes inside.

That wasn't the half of it. There was a drawbridge that lowered or raised when you turned a tiny crank, and one of those pointy, gatey things to bar the entrance, like how the shops on Main have grills over the windows. *That* was neat! The gate was a carved block inserted into a wooden frame, okay? And you raised it [Johnson rises, making a winding motion with his right hand while slowly raising his left to show the movement of the portcullis], and it locked in place. Then, with the push of a button…[He crashes back into his chair, all smiles, and takes another sip of scotch]. So cool.

Plus, there were a slew of knights to go with the castle. Some on horseback, some with spears. Some with swords raised to do battle, others lifting up shields to block. The details were incredible, right down to the tiny horseshoes. Those elaborate lacquered banners. I know I sound like a toy ad here, but trust me. It was special.

One afternoon my parents had to run out, leaving my sister in charge, and a warning that we'd *both* be beaten black and blue if I touched anything in the workshop. That was just talk, by the way. If you were going to get hit in our house, Mom was going to do it and it would involve a wooden spoon. But they were serious enough, which meant that I was going to have to sneak into the basement if I wanted to get at that castle.

At the bottom of the stairway was a large rec room with our tv, the record player, two sofas and a bar for when company came. My parents hosted often, and the place smelled of stale smoke from the guests who joked and griped and drank beer from steins, leaving heaps of cigarette butts in the ashtrays. There was wood paneling everywhere. Kind of ugly, thinking back on it, but I remember it being cozy.

Dad's workshop was at the end of a hall, behind a white door that always stayed closed. Usually I didn't like being down there on my own, and the hallway was the biggest problem. It zigzagged where the bathroom and laundry room had been built into the wall. For some idiot reason the lightswitch had been installed midway, so you had to feel your way in the dark to reach it. Sound did funny things thanks to a quirk of the dimensions, and the noise and hum of the furnace kicking on, or my siblings' footsteps pounding up the second-floor stairs, had startled me far too many times. Not only did it feel like those doorways could swing open to reveal anything, but halfway down the wall broke to the left, leaving a large space where someone could hide.

Believe me. My brothers taught me to fear that spot. 'Matviy, come see what Papa made you in the workshop!' Only to jump out wearing a hockey mask, chase me up the stairs with a rubber knife in hand. Like, every time! How gullible was I?

I don't mind telling you I was on edge before I even set foot in the workshop. Still, none of this was going to stop me from checking out that castle. There were even spring-loaded catapults that fired little foam balls! How could you resist?

Maybe that's what attracted the creature in the first place.

The workshop was cold. It was always cold, because Dad was allergic to turning up the heat, but here it felt like a window had been left open.

I held my breath while I scanned the shadows for the army of thieves who no doubt wanted the castle. It didn't feel like I was alone, but nothing moved, and I convinced myself I was just spooked by the sounds of the furnace.

The castle was up on one of Dad's tables. My little rabbit heart raced as I heard the floorboards groan overhead as Yana--my sister--got up and walked in the direction of the basement stairs. She stopped, and I figured she must have just gone to the kitchen for a snack. I liked it better when she was in her room, but I'd made it that far, so I forced myself to settle down and rearrange the pieces.

I was lining up some kind of battle when I first realized that my breath was curling out in vapors. Was it then that I knew something was wrong? Nope. I thought it was amazing, to be honest. Pretended I was a dragon, breathing fire and smoke out over the battlefield.

About this time I remembered that Dad had been working on a king, a crowned and bearded guy with a white cross on his armor, sword raised to signal the attack on the enemy. I went looking and found the king inside one of those hinged towers. It was in the royal bedroom, along with two figures I'd never seen before: a queen and an infant in a tiny crib. That surprised me, because Dad didn't do furniture, and like I said, these knights were going to war, and how's a baby going to help in a fight?

Looking closer, the two figures weren't done in Dad's usual style. Even by his standards these were masterpieces, like mini Renaissance sculptures. The queen's skin glowed with life, which left me confused, like, why's the baby's skin a horrible blue-grey? Even at my age I understood the shock of horror in the queen's eyes, and I could tell she was on the verge of a scream. As I struggled to make sense of her grief, two pinpricks of water streaked from her ice-blue eyes.

The sight of those tears scared me, you bet. Maybe I wasn't the brightest kid, but I still believed the queen was

Dad's creation, and I had to know how he had managed the trick. As I reached for her, and saw that my fingernails had turned blue. It freaked me out to realize how cold it had gotten in the workshop. That's when a grey, scabbed hand tipped with claws shot out to pluck up the king [pause as Johnson stares slackly into space before abruptly swiping the air to demonstrate. Johnson's blood alcohol level was listed at .10 in the toxicology report. Why do I mention that? No reason].

If you haven't clued in by now, this wasn't like some Spielberg film. Kid discovers a creature in the basement, plays with it. Start of a touching friendship.

Ha! The thing in our basement took two quick steps back and glared. It was thin and filthy, and just a little taller than me, but the body was twisted and hunched and knotted, sort of like that oak tree in front of St. Peter's. You could see webs of veins right through the blueish-grey skin. At the collar bone, its skin was stretched tight like a thin grey sheet caught in barbed branches. Its elbows and knees were like tennis balls, painfully swollen.The long fingers were rough and calloused and cracked, and they ended in black claws, each one sharp as a utility blade.

And that face! Like the Crypt Keeper in its youth. Big forehead, long jaw. Its hair was patchy and matted, with limp strands hanging like tinsel down to its shoulders. It wore a stained and ragged Peter Puck shirt--hey, remember Peter Puck? This shirt hung down to its knees like a dress. I knew the creature had stolen it. Knew it with certainty.

This will sound crazy, but I remember wanting to reach out and offer comfort for the creature's obvious suffering. I was a sensitive kid, but maybe a part of me hoped a display of compassion would ease the danger. But something sly appeared in the creature's expression, and it stepped towards me. I was probably about to wet my pants when the floor-boards creaked overhead, startling us both. The thing scrambled back as my sister moved from the kitchen, back towards her room.

[Johnson appears to blush] Look, I know how this sounds. But do you think I'd make this up? You think I'd break into the station, put myself on camera, just to make this up?

The creature backed away with the king squeezed tight in its fist. Its eyes bulged, huge in their sockets and just kinda...We did that story on that recovered anorexic majorette a few years back. Remember that girl at J.B. Henderson? Terrific story. Incredibly inspiring. I vaguely...did she relapse in college? She didn't die, did she? [Pause] Let's not dwell. All I'm saying is, when I did that piece, and she showed me pictures at her worst? It took me back to that workshop.

'Poor thing,' I said. I didn't really believe it. Its eyes radiated with hate...Jesus. I keep calling it 'creature' and 'thing,' but I'll always think of it as a demon. And I remember feeling a surge of anger, because even then I knew that pity wasn't going to be an option. Also, and this might sound crazy, but I was angry because the little monster had taken one the white king. And that wasn't fair. It had no right to that set.

I must have been more afraid of Dad, because I stepped towards the demon, saying: 'Put it back. My dad's going to be mad at you. The set has to stay together.' I tried to keep my voice calm and friendly, but the thing jerked back, faster than I thought possible [Johnson's hand grazes the bottle of scotch as he demonstrates]--whoops. I'd cornered a rabid pit bull, and I saw my mistake pretty quick.

The little demon sized me up. I couldn't run. I'd seen how fast it could move. It smiled, in a way I think was supposed to be reassuring, but the grin grew bigger and bigger until it was just awful to look at.

It spoke then. Asked me my name, how old I was. Like a flippin' mall Santa! Its voice was grating, but also high and childlike. It was trying to be friendly, but there was a kind of hitch in it, like it was trying not to laugh. I told the truth because I didn't know what else to do.

'Matviy,' the demon said. 'Should be yours!' It gestured to the knight cradled in its claws. Should be *mine*? It clutched the figurine like it had the Golden Ticket. 'Good Matviy. You take them!'--again, talking about the knights here--'I can hide you. Papa never find. What you like?'

God, I sound like a chain-smoking Baba. Anyway, I'm sure I said that I didn't want anything.

'You want. Toy soldiers? Construction trucks? Games? You have anything. Candy. Toys you never dream of. Never get sick. Never get old. You like?'

The thing had not put its best foot forward. I mean, if ever there was a 'strangers with candy' moment. But there was power in that voice. You got caught up in it. Started imagining Saturday-Morning-cartoon-ad perfect scenes of play. Like you could be the Scrooge McDuck of toys.

But for whatever reason, this vision wasn't right. It was like a black and white version of a film that's supposed to be in technicolor, and you can't get into it. The deal hinged on me, I think. There was something I was supposed to add. Something that would have made the dream complete, but I was too terrified to supply it.

The demon went on and on, and its voice was getting to me. Its eyes darted nervously the whole time. I started to notice exactly how cold the workshop was. Frost formed on the pipes, the metal table legs, on Dad's wood carving tools. I scraped a line of the stuff off the vice grip with my fingernail. And I was shocked to see that a, a window, a gateway, was forming behind the little freakshow. It glowed, red-tinged and crackling in the air. That's where the cold entered.

I knew I had to get out, but the demon shadowed me as I started to back away. "Where you go?" it demanded. Gone was the phony cheer. Its voice turned cold as the howling portal. The smile returned instantly, but the thing made a low growl in its throat, as if by accident. I had to say something, so I said maybe I *would* come along, that I just needed to get Petey. Petey, my stuffed lion, went with me everywhere at that age, so it seemed like a reasonable bluff. The leering demon followed me step for step. Its body tensed, and its breath came faster. I saw from the way it flexed its claws that it planned to grab me, but I'd managed to put the workbench between us. The thing smiled bigger and started in again with the promises, trying and failing to keep the frustration from its voice. A house full of toys. Gifts every day. A big lion for the bravest boy.

At that moment, the demon snarled and dove across the workbench, raking my shoulder. A claw snagged in the fabric of my sweater, but the shirt tore and I pulled free. I booked it for the staircase while it was off-balance. If I was smarter I might have thrown the door shut behind me. Maybe tried to shove the laundry rack over to block the way. But I was six, and I was terribly afraid.

Huh [Johnson rises and wanders out of frame. Sources at WLTV have confirmed that the metallic thudding heard soon afterwards was the sound of Johnson shoving the studio door to check the lock. There is the noise of something heavy being pushed across the floor. Johnson returns to his seat about a minute later].

Anyway. Anyway. Uh. Right, the chase.

There was a sharp clatter of wood on cement as the demon scrabbled up the table and vaulted over. I heard the force of its landing somewhere too close behind, and the quickening patter of footsteps. I pushed myself harder but that hallway never seemed so long. I did the only thing I could think to do: I slapped the light switch as I passed, and cut hard toward the laundry room door in the sudden blackness. My hands felt for the doorknob, but I heard my name on the thing's lips, and the mocking tone made me turn and look. The demon's irises glowed in the dark like icy halos. It stared straight at me. My heart sank as I realized it could see in the dark.

The creature gave a low growl. Next thing I knew, I'm eating cement, winded by the force of its tackle. I didn't even try to fight as it dragged me back toward the workshop. I screamed for help as soon as I found my breath, but the monster shut me up in a hurry by digging filthy claws into my leg.

Soon it had me all the way back. The red-tinged gateway was full-formed. It opened into winter: a crag overlooking a valley where there were these, um. Shelters. Like cabins. The cold was tremendous.

I thought: this is it. I'll never see my family again. And a small part of me was like: See Mom? I *knew* there were monsters! But mostly my mind was blank with panic. We were getting closer...closer...and how was I going to survive that cold? I shut my eyes tight...

Just like that, the demon stopped. I peeked. We were right by the workbench. The thing stood torn between the portal and the table where the castle sat. It pulled the hem of its shirt up to make a little pouch, and it was trying to cram the figures in. How it planned to keep pulling me along, I'll never know.

More from anger than anything, I grabbed the leg of the workbench and shook hard. The pieces scattered, fell, rolled off the table. The demon whimpered and grabbed its head, dropping the knights held in its shirt in the process. It screamed in rage and skittered after the toys. Why did it want them so badly? Was it to have something beautiful of its own? Was there a simpler explanation? The habit of greed? An act of rebellion against whatever it was scared of?

It was scared, too. Its head kept swivling to the portal as it picked up the figurines, and as it lowered its face to forearm to wipe its sweaty brow, I understood that it feared something on the other side.

I got to my feet and scooped up a handful of the knights. I hit the demon with the cruelest insults my six-year-old mind could come up with. When it came at me, I threatened to break one of the figures. This really peed the little bastard off, but whenever it advanced I'd whip a knight across the room. It kept darting after them like a faithful Retriever. I was wondering how long I could keep it up when I saw something forming at the gate: a red churning mist, with glowing threads of energy that snaked towards the demon. As I stared into that portal, the shape of that mist formed briefly into an enormous horned face with dead, passionless eyes.

Those threads lashed out and grabbed the thing's wrists, wrenching it towards the portal. The demon screeched. All the figurines it had gathered scattered across the floor. It fought, and managed to skid to a halt. Its head jerked, angled like it was listening to some command, and it pleaded. 'No. Not take! Boy's turn! He say okay!' Real convincing, right? This time I *heard* the reply. It came in a screaming wind, blasted straight through the portal, but inside that squall was a hellish rasp that I swear was language, and it piled ice onto my heart with every 'word.' More threads wrapped around the thing's legs, its torso. It was dragged screaming through the gate, which stretched like a bubble in a child's wand and then popped out of existence, leaving behind this smell like...there's nothing like it. Juniper, maybe. Juniper covering the stench of rotten meat.

A new danger helped me get over the immediate shock of its departure. Danger not from the thing that had almost taken me, but from Dad, who would kill me when he saw the state of his workshop. I rushed to gather up all the knights. Most were intact, but some bore superficial scratches in the paint. The leg and a sword had broken off one of the figures.

I was in tears when my parents returned. I opened my fists to reveal the worst of the damage. What gave me courage was, I was so damn glad to see them. Dad flipped out. [Johnson looks down, chuckles]. Understandably. We could still hear him cursing at us as he thundered down the basement stairs. I followed him down--not too closely--and into the workroom. Dad had his back to me but I could see how his shoulders shook, and how his hands were balled into fists. I didn't want to do it, but I slipped by before he could react, pulled the queen and crib from the castle tower, and held them out for him to see.

Dad didn't ask where they'd come from. He didn't say anything at all, just sank into a nearby chair and turned the 'gifts' over in jittery hands. He didn't stop until Mom came into the workshop, kind of concerned, at which point he jammed the figures into his coat pocket.

Mom sent him for a drive while we finished cleaning up. When he returned, some of his fury was back, and he demanded to know where I had found such evil things. I don't know why, but I told the truth. Dad grabbed me by the shoulders and shook. Not too hard, I don't want to give you the wrong idea. It was an 'I mean business' sort of shake. Even so, I screamed when he grabbed my shoulder. Then he noticed the tear where the creature's claws snagged my sweater, and the scratches beneath. They were bleeding and I hadn't even noticed.

Dad went white. He was still angry, but after that it was like he was going through the motions. For my punishment, I was made to kneel on rice for half an hour. Uncooked grains, mind you. Super painful. Half an hour? Oh brother! Just brutal. My sister got it even worse.

Well, that's what happened. Believe it. Don't. That's God's honest truth.

My family never really talked about that Christmas again. Mom convinced Dad to get me that Atari I was always angling for, and after that the workshop lost a bit of its shine. Over the years I sorta forgot about the encounter with that creature. Not forgot, exactly. It's more that when I did think about it, it was hazy, like a standout image from a horror movie I'd seen a long time ago. Then I'd try to figure out what had been going on in my life, to make me believe that I'd seen something like that.

[Johnson glances at his wristwatch, straightens, and drags the shotgun closer. He takes a drink from the bottle and then holds it up in front of him, closing one eye as he inspects the level. He blows out a deep breath, picks up the gun, and walks out of frame for approximately 3 minutes. I hesitate to mention what is probably a visual glitch, or a trick of the lighting, but at 01:22, a rounded shadow, suggestive of a child's head, briefly appears to cross the news desk].

[Johnson returns]. No sign. Where was I? [Reading from his statement] Ah. I'd pretty well buried the memory, until those kids went missing in sleepy little Round Rock. Two boys, on Christmas Eve. No connections. Both kids well-provided for. Maybe a little *too* well. From the sounds of it, that Duffey kid was kinda spoiled. Mountain of presents under the tree. Five game systems and a room just for his toys, and his parents were still at the mall trying to get that one last gift he'd melted down about.

I don't--hey. Don't get me wrong here. I wouldn't be saying these things if it wasn't relevant. That story was without a doubt one of the worst I've ever reported on. The memories it stirred up. And the grief of those parents. Made me want to fly out to Seattle and give my own kids a hug, and screw Karen and Walt if it wasn't my one weekend a month.

Which, while I'm on the subject, is only the arrangement because Karen just *had* to take that job with Microsoft [for the record, if I wanted to convince someone of the criminal accusations leveled against Johnson, I'd start by showing the expression that flashes across his face here. It starts at brooding, and dials down from there. He snaps out of it quickly, but this guy does not like his ex].

[Pause] I'm sorry for that outburst, there's, uh [long pause as Johnson sits silently, sipping scotch, his eyes unfocused].

There was no connection between the two families. The only thing is, in both cases their houses were unusually cold when the parents returned. Mr. Miller recalled going down to check the furnace. Both families reported a strange smell in the house, which Mrs. Duffy said was 'gross,' and 'kind of like gin.' Boy did that stand out.

After that report, someone wrote to me saying there'd been other disappearances, in other communities. They'd been happening for a long time, all over the map, but with greater frequency over the past 10 years. My contact, let's call her [pause] oh, let's call her Scully. Wait, that doesn't make sense. Mulder. *Lady* Mulder! L.M. for short.

So L.M. had been trying to alert the local papers for months, but those hacks couldn't add two and two. She saw me in action, and I guess she sensed that she'd found someone who would believe *everything*. We started talking, back and forth. That's...kind of how talking works, Matt. But I mean, she'd send press clippings. These abductions, they were happening all over the world. Arlington. Rockland, Maine. Charlston. Grand Prairie. Perth. Bern. Genoa. Bath...I could go on. Always the unnatural cold. Always the stench of their passing.

[Johnson stands abruptly, aiming the gun in the general direction of the camera] You hear that? I'm not the only one who knows, you little freaks! Come introduce yourselves!

[He sits slowly, still tensed]. I'm real sorry about that, folks. I thought I saw...I imagine this must be very confusing.

[Reluctantly, he sets down the gun] Uh. [Long pause. Johnson lets go of a deep breath, and rubs his eyes. He takes the scotch and sets the bottle down behind the desk.] 'Kay, Matt. Keep it together.

[Pause] The links aren't easy to see, but the disappearances always took place within the same window in December. There were no obvious suspects. The children were never found.

For a while, everything went quiet.

Next December rolls around, L.M. sends me clippings from the *St. Paul Gazette* about a disappearance. I took some vacation time and flew out to Minnesota. Told the grieving family I was working on a documentary. It was the week before Christmas, and the whole time I had the feeling of being watched.

I never should have done it, but I pitched the story to WLTV, like the fact that the Round Rock disappearances were part of a wider pattern. Non-actionable though, right? 'Hey officers of the world! Be on the lookout for chilly homes that reek of gin.' I sorta knew it, too. I get a 'Matt, you're working too hard' speech from my bosses, and a recommendation for a good therapist. Just like that, the station brass pushes me out of the anchor chair and out into the field. 'A shakeup,' they say. But the assignments I pull get worse and worse. No disrespect Chuck, you do good work and all, but aren't my 11 years--not to mention that trust I've built up with the community--worth something?

I guess around that time I started drinking more. But after St. Paul, it felt like there were always eyes on me. Once, on air, covering the Salvation Army's Christmas food drive, I caught a glimpse of something across the street in the second floor window of Barlows. A twisted little face with bulging, evil eyes. It was gone before I could get a good look.

Then came Devin Brown, that little [pause] genius. 8 years old, he'd won the Rochester Public Speaking Competition, and they were bumping him up to compete against the Grade 4-6 division in the Regionals. The topic of his speech: the Christmas spirit, and whether doing things because you're being watched is really moral.

I'm sorry, but how smug can you be? But people were saying he should have his own TED Talk and crap. I just didn't see it. I mean, it's not like he's the first person to ever come up with *that* idea. The station had no business putting me on that assignment. It was a total fluff piece.

Not that he deserved what happened to him! No, no no. I don't mean it like that at all.

The thing is, it didn't fit the pattern. The other abductions, wherever we had details, the kids seemed, well, kinda crap. Rotten. Devin wasn't like that at all. He was a good kid. L.M. saw a trap. Too many of the abductions were concentrated in our state. We tracked five that year. She thought they were starting to revolve around me. They started happening in towns we passed through.

That's about the time WLTV put me on stress leave.

Was I idle? Nope. No way.

L.M. explained so much to me. Like I thought: are we really talking about *elves* here? What's next: Santa Claus?

No, dum dum! See, L.M. explained that our Christmas traditions and stories are based on older truths. Just like Christmas replaced those...well, all those pagan festivals it replaced. In the same way, Christmas elves weren't all sugar and spice in the earliest legends. L.M. thinks the idea of Santa's workshop is based on a terrible reality, one that involves demons, or imps. The age-old game of temptation. See, these demons really *do* make toys, but it's all for the purpose of luring in children.

That's going to sound crazy to the modern mind. I get that. But that's how we got to this point. Parents get like: 'Oh, demon elves? And they can only escape slavery by tricking another child into taking their place? Sounds a bit far-fetched. What are we scaring our kids with this crap for?'

Well, for good reason! But I get that you wouldn't see it that way if you weren't on the trail. Been travelling, L.M. and me. This year's spree is worse than ever, but it's almost over. Sometimes they leave nightmare gifts, placed on the pillows of the abducted. I've seen an Elmo doll that whispers the regrets of suicides. No two voices ever repeated, at least as far as I cared to test. I've seen rubber snakes that twitched with obscene life as their hidden fangs drew blood. Those creatures are becoming bolder, striking twice in towns we've visited. They've come close to showing themselves. Has something changed? Have they slipped whatever controlled them?

They're definitely following me. L.M. thinks they're tightening the noose. Trying to make me look dangerous. She doesn't know I'm here tonight.

But they're coming. I know it. Maybe one will be young Devin Brown. And I [pause] I couldn't face being at home tonight. They've been leaving little threats. You won't believe what I found in my rear view mirror the other day. One of those creepy little Santa's Helpers dolls was posed on top of it. Dangling from its 'hands' was a noose. That noose was looped around the throat of one of those Matt Johnson dolls Honest Murray Hogan had made up for promos a couple of years ago. And my face had been changed so it was grimacing.

How did they make it so life-like?

[Sighs] I feel their eyes on me. If tonight goes down like I think it will...please. Defend my good name. [Johnson lifts the gun again, slowly sweeping the room]. You think I can't sense you? It doesn't matter anymore. You're news now! You're a story. That's my magic, and it can change the goddamn world.

Should figure out where they'll come in from. Vents? 'A rather tight pinch. But if Santa could do it then so could...' [laughing].

But there's the fireplace they might be drawn to, in the lounge. L.M. says they're suckers for tradition [Wanders off camera].

[Returns] Hey. Just don't let them make me out to be some loon, like that Ronnie Dubois, when he got high on bath salts and took out the Clarkston radio tower with his semi to block out transmissions from Neptune. Remember me fondly, like: 'Good old Matt Johnson. Handsome lunk. He really filled out a suit,' and not 'that fuckup Matt Johnson who shot up WLTV. What a shitshow!'

I really should focus here. [Long pause. Johnson holds his gun at the ready but appears to sway on his feet a little] Wish I had some music. [Another long pause. Sometimes Johnson whistles to himself, mainly "Carry On My Wayward Son." At one point he scratches his nose].

Maybe it's the scotch talking, but I feel this glow like I love you all. I guess I wanted you to know me. The real me. And if I'm honest, maybe it's a little because I'm terrified, and maybe it's because if I did stop talking, I'd have nothing to do but sit, and wait in silence.

So let me say this. It's been an honor and a privilege to serve you, Rochester. I used to idolize Dan Rather, you know? My old man and I were always at our closest when we sat side by side, two sets of eyes staring at the same screen, that big old Panasonic he shelled out for in our basement. I've got warm memories of those times. Then it was never: 'Matviy, don't you know what a goddamn lathe is?' Or 'Matviy, I said bring the *horilka. Pepper* vodka!'

Maybe that's why I ended up in this business. I'll tell you this: looking back on my career, I have always enjoyed the work. On the good days, I empty my head of all thought, and the news flows through me. Always figured I'd climb my way to the National News. Even Honest Murray Hogan said I have the face for it. [Pause] Although I'm not 100% sure that was a compliment.

Well, life takes you where it takes you. Some are called to report on Hurricane Katrina, some cover the warehouse flood that threatens to shut down the state's last K-Mart. Some cover the Papal inauguration, others bear witness to Bill Fitzpatrick's incredible Lego Nativity scene. We've all got a part to play, is what I'm saying. But sometimes, you get your moment.

You, my friends, you who have turned to me on this smaller stage, night after night, in spite of dwindling tv ratings, in spite of the lingering rumors (unfounded, believe me) that Honest Murray Hogan is thinking of shutting down the station...thank you for sticking with me. I'm going to make you proud. I'm going out guns blazing. You're going to say 'Matt Johnson, maybe it took a while, but he finally blew one out of the water.'

If I nab the Pulitzer for this, don't bury me with it or something dumb like that. Build a case in the central lobby. Put it where everyone can enjoy it.

[The camera begins to shake, and the angle slowly begins to tilt upwards].

I wish there was time to tell more. I haven't even got to L.M.'s surveillance, or the terrible eye that appears on certain nights, blazing above the Rupes Negra in the Northern sky. Look it up!

Not that we dared approach.

[Camera settles. Johnson is now only visible in the shot from the chest up].

Hell, I'd settle for some time to go back and edit this thing! That stuff I said about Devin is probably not going to paint me in the best light.

[Off camera, a loud bang].

Oh Jesus, goddamn! It's...it's okay people. [Laughing] I'm okay. A shelf of camera equipment collapsed. [Inaudible].

[Camera picks up a soft, rapid sound of scuffling]. Mercy! I just about had a heart attack there. I guess--

[Johnson tenses, brings up the shotgun] Matty. Shannon. I love you. Yana, be sur—

[Johnson crashes backwards into his chair. The shotgun swings up.]. Nggh! Wai—

[The shotgun goes off].

YEAH, like I said: don't watch. The footage is out there, of course. It's not even that hard to find. Even now, the video circulates on the disreputable fringes of the internet under titles like 'Newscaster Rekt.' People there are treating it as a joke. The footage has even been remixed to "Head Like a Hole."

You know how the story played out in our circles. It was a bombshell, and the coverage varied depending on the news outlet, from impassioned pleas for better support for mental health in the workplace, to Rex Whitley's curmudgeonly 'Christmas? Fuelled by slave labor? Not in my America!' Most settled into a tone of amused horror somewhere short of The Darwin Awards.

Officially, Johnson's death was treated as an accident. The coroner's report concluded that Matt fell into his chair after being startled and the gun went off. The shell entered the chin at close range, and travelled up and back, doing extensive damage. Alcohol was a factor. I joked about the .10 blood alcohol level, but honestly? Given the way Johnson was hitting the bottle earlier, I almost think he was *moderating* his consumption towards the end. The autopsy also revealed stage one cirrhosis of the liver. All things considered, it's death by misadventure, I guess.

I don't know what I believe, really, but I'm not 100% sure the video supports *that* interpretation. But what's the alternative? Just to put it out there, the coroner also noted the presence of three shallow slashes in each thigh. Bruises on his right side. I mean, that could have happened anywhere during the night in question.

Naturally, reporting of that other tragedy was more sympathetic. No one can account for Johnson's whereabouts for the two days leading up to that night. The search by Johnson's ex-wife and her second husband has become increasingly desperate. Ten months on, and they're still convinced that Johnson and this L.M. were somehow behind the children's disappearance from their Seattle home that Christmas Eve. The identity of Johnson's 'informant' remains a mystery.

That's all I have for you. I rounded up some clips from various pundits, and I'll send some links later today. It really would help to know more about what you're looking for.

Discuss over dinner some night?

- Andre

TRADITIONS

CRAIG CRAWFORD

There's a first and a last time for everything. I grew up in Alaska, on the outskirts of Juneau. my dad and mom sticklers for certain traditions at the holidays including hunting for a Christmas tree. Usually, we'd pick a morning and dad would drive us out in the middle of nowhere, and we'd tromp through the cold. We wouldn't stop until Dad found the perfect one: short enough to reach the top without a ladder, and full enough for Mom to hide the presents underneath.

We started out early because the sun sets mid-afternoon. As a rule, Dad always got us on the main roads before dark. Alaska is rich with history and superstition, and stories have been passed down through my family for generations on strange happenings going on in the depths of the wilds.

I have lasting memories of my Great Grandpa Cherry Buck. Nicknamed after his favorite dessert, which Great Grandma used to make for him that he could never get enough of, stood out as my folk hero. Great Grandpa had had a way of telling stories most people don't--he'd use his hands while he talked and when he made eye contact, he pulled me in. He used to tell me the story of the time he and a trio of buddies stayed overnight in the woods near the base of Mount Juneau. He always told this particular story with fervor, getting louder as he talked and slapping his knee with his hand as he mimicked the footsteps they heard.

The story didn't have a lot of details because Great Grandpa nor any of his pals had seen exactly what crept around the edges of their fire other than a dark shape which grunted and broke branches off the trees beyond the halo of light. A great campfire story, but it scared me to the point I'd never forgotten it. Never mind that it had most likely been a bear, but I still remember those growls Great Grandpa snarled out.

Growing up, I got a decent job for the city of Juneau. It disappointed my dad because I hadn't carried on the fishing tradition, but it paid decent enough that my wife Annie and our three kids could afford a house in the country. We even have a patch of woods near a stream. Getting a real tree for Christmas remained a Laird family tradition each December, and even Janie, our teen eldest, quit rolling her eyes at us for a few hours when it came time to go pick a tree. Duncan and Clark, both younger, became giddy in the truck as we headed out of the driveway.

We got a later start than I'd wanted. Ma called as we were headed out the door, concerned about the usual holiday nonsense. Despite 'buts,' and several 'Mom we gotta get goings,' I hadn't been able to get off the line without dragging Annie into the conversation. Setting the meal for Christmas Eve and Day took a good curse-worthy half hour, even though nothing had changed for the last dozen years. Still, we'd gotten out before noon—in Alaska this time of year, the sun sets before four in the afternoon, but it was plenty of time to scout out a tree, cut it down and get home before nightfall.

Driving out, Annie got the boys singing Christmas songs while Janie stared out the window. I'd scoped out three different open fields and figured we could make any or all of them in easy time. Half the fun is tromping around the woods looking for the perfect tree.

Annie and I both brought handguns for potential predators. Wolves usually kept to the edges, but there were times, if a pack was large enough, they'd take a chance on dragging off a small kid. Bears were also an issue, though most had settled in for winter. Living up here, you got used to carrying weapons for protection. I've only ever used my gun twice, firing it up in the air. Both times the bears quickly left instead of messing with me.

We went off road and parked outside a tree line about a quarter of a mile off the highway. The day felt warmer than what I remember my father dragging us out into, and the kids eagerly awaited getting into the trees. Everyone piled out the doors and Annie became a drill sergeant before any of the kids had taken three steps.

"Rules," she barked, catching each kid's eyes with her own.

Janie rolled her eyes. "Stay close to you guys."

Annie nodded; her red hair tucked up under a thick wool cap. "Duncan?"

"I know, Mom. No wandering off. Stay next to Clark."

Another nod. "Clark?"

"Do I have to hold Duncan's hand?" He asked as if it was a death sentence.

"Either that or sit in the truck."

End of discussion. I checked my pistol. A lot of guys carried .357 magnums because of the stopping power, and I had one of those too. I also had a rifle in the back window of the truck, but I'd decided against slinging it over my shoulder for this trek. I had rope and an axe and was going to have to do the bulk of the lugging of the tree once we took it down. Duncan and Clark liked to help, but Clark just turned seven and pretty much canceled out any real lifting power.

I brought a pistol called a Judge in a holster at my hip. A five shot revolver, it fired .410 rounds and .45 longs. All around the .357 was a better weapon, but I liked the look of the Judge, and while I only got five shots out of it, I liked having the buckshot of the .410 shells and the power of the .45's. Today I'd loaded it with .45 caliber rounds just in case.

Annie had her own .45.

We tromped for a while, our feet crunching through a top crust of frozen snow. The air still carried a chill, scratching at my throat as we hiked. I led with Annie at the back. I always laughed in horror movies where there's a family because usually the moms and dads are oblivious, letting their kids wander all over the place without knowing what they're up to and what they're doing. The reality is that parents, real parents, always have an ear or an eye to their kids, no matter what's going on. In the real world, kids do get distracted easily and real parents keep a close eye on them.

A lot closer than in the movies.

Clark had the most problems keeping up and we stopped often. The little guy's legs just couldn't keep the pace, especially stomping through the snow. That, and he did get distracted: new tracks, deer poop, rocks jutting above the thin layer of snow, you name it. Annie kept to the back to keep him in line.

Duncan and Janie put their eyes to work for us, looking at every pine and sizing it up against the ceiling in our house and what we'd gotten last year. Duncan would point to one, but Janie had the internal catalogue in her head. "That one's too small—we've got the tall ceiling by the window. Looks like that one's straggly on the side..."

Eventually Clark got tired, like he always did, and we put him on the sled. I smiled, enjoying that tradition too, even though it annoyed Janie. Sitting and watching while I pulled him through the snow, he started pointing at trees, putting Janie's patience to the test.

"It's twenty feet high, Clark," Janie sighed. "It won't fit... we're not going all the way up the mountain."

It took the better part of an hour to find "the one." Annie and I didn't care as much as the kids, especially Janie and Duncan. I let the sled cut through the snow to a stop and dropped the reins. I looked over the one they'd led us to, and decided it looked like a pretty good tree. At least ten feet tall, it looked full and healthy. I shrugged to Annie and she gave me the wink.

"First, cocoa break," I declared. The kids perked up.

Clark zeroed in on the thermos Annie had in the pack slung over her shoulder, and ran to her in a flash. I caught a smile out of Janie, but looked away before she noticed I noticed.

I sized up the tree, Duncan coming up on my side. "What do you think, Dad?"

"Looks good to me. It'll fit. You and Janie have good eyes."

"Can I help cut it down?"

I'd been letting Duncan chop wood during the summer for this very reason. Instructing and watching throughout the year, his skills had improved a lot. He held the axe just like I'd taught him. "As long as you remember to look where you aim and remember which end bites."

"Dad . . ."

"I know, but one bad swing can be fatal out here."

"I know. I'll do it just like home, chopping wood."

"Me too!" Clark shouted around a cup of cocoa.

"When you're bigger," I told him.

"Like when he's twenty," Janie told him. "You're not nearly careful enough."

Same old.

Duncan aimed carefully, sighted his mark and swung the axe. The sounds echoed off the surrounding trees. We weren't in a huge forest, but there were enough trees to catch the sounds. I watched, careful to make sure Clark didn't try to run forward and help.

Duncan got in several good whacks, steadying himself after each chop. It was harder than it looked, however, and he got tired. He kept at it until one of his swings went above the mark. He tried another and fell short there too.

"Take a break," I said.

"What about the time?"

I looked skyward. "It's okay. Your swings are getting wild. It happens when your muscles get worn. No shame in it. That axe has some pounds to it."

He heaved a few breaths. "Let me take a minute."

I knew he wanted to be the one to chop his way through it. It had become a test—I could see it in his eyes. If I stepped in, it would take something away from him, so I shrugged. "Sure. Have some cocoa and go back at it."

He rested the axe blade on the sled and stretched his arms. "I'll get it down."

Something howled.

The high pitched sound came somewhere in the direction of the mountain, but it echoed through the trees just like the axe whacking against the trunk. It died off, and we only had the silence and a faint breeze.

Everyone froze. All eyes shifted toward me.

I didn't know what caused the noise either. I knew the bellows of moose, bear, eagles, even the snort of deer, but this resembled none of those. I turned my head toward the direction I thought the sound had come from, eyes looking for movement, ears stretched to hear.

"Dad . . ." Clark said.

I held up a hand to silence him. I traded a look with Annie and she had a look on her face too. She'd done enough hunting with me to know the usual animals and her brows below her red locks told me it was something else.

It bellowed again. Longer, trailing off at the end like something dying in the woods. Louder too, which worried me. It was either calling out or it was closer. I scanned our area, but I saw no birds or animals against the clumps of trees. Whatever called out had stilled all the wildlife.

Annie was way ahead of me, though. "Kids, come back to me now," and she stepped back toward the largest tree.

Clark opened his mouth to complain, but Annie stopped him with a finger snap. Duncan and Janie didn't say a word, but retreated to her.

"Dad," Janie said, "What do you think it is?"

"Don't know. Don't need to worry, just need to be safe about it."

I still couldn't get a good idea of where the yell had come from, but I knew the general direction. The way the sound traveled and the strength of the cry told me the creature had to be in front of us. It definitely came from the direction of the mountain.

Unease crept into me. Instinctively, I grabbed up the sled and pulled it backwards toward the rest of the family. We nestled in around the base of a sitka spruce. Not much cover, but we could see a ways off. I wondered if whatever it was had heard Duncan hacking away at our Christmas tree.

"What do you think it was?" Annie asked.

"It was weird. Awfully high pitched and too long for a bear or a moose. I don't know. Maybe something getting hit by a predator."

It sounded again. Much louder now and it wailed, definitely closer than before. I didn't like the sound—something big and it reminded me of Great Grandpa's story. Clark put his hands over his ears and the kids all had worried looks on their faces.

I still couldn't see anything, but whatever was out there, I was sure I didn't want to have to deal with it. Not with the kids in tow. Everything went quiet again and there were no bird sounds or other animals moving now. "Let's start heading back to the truck," I said.

"What about our tree?" Clark asked.

"We can come back later," I said. "Or pick a different one. Climb on the sled, Clark. I'll tow you out."

"You two stay close," Annie said, taking her revolver out of her pocket.

We put Annie's pack and the axe on the sled and followed our tracks back toward the truck. We'd come out quite a ways, and we needed to make time to get back quickly. That was the one problem with walking way out into the woods for a tree.

I took point with Clark on the sled and Janie and Duncan on either side. Annie stayed at the back, looking over her shoulder every few steps. If we'd invaded something's turf, the best thing to do was leave the way we'd come. Most predators tend to be territorial and if you leave when warned, you're usually okay.

We made a couple of hundred yards when it wailed again, long and loud. We traded looks because whatever was making the sound had a big set of lungs on it, and it still sounded close. I kept trudging forward, determined not to slow.

We reached a downhill slope and I picked up a little more speed, though careful not to let Clark and the sled get too fast for me. None of the kids said a word, their eyes pointed behind us. I saw Duncan and Janie checking on Annie regularly. Even Annie's head snapped back over her shoulder every few steps. We reached the bottom of the dip and came up the other side. It wasn't too steep; just enough to force a rest stop on the far side. I needed to catch some breath.

"Berk," Annie said.

I spotted movement a long way back on the far side of our dip, like something moving through the trees. In the woods, even though trees can be spaced out, if you're back far enough it looks like a solid forest. I watched something dark shift back and forth between the trunks.

Except it was big.

Hunting, after a while, you get a sense of size and distance. I hear "experts" always talking about how inferior people's skills are for judging distance and size, but the fact of the matter is, you get pretty good at it. I can tell how tall a buck is, or the wingspan of a hawk or an eagle.

I didn't know what we were looking at, but the dark against the trees stood larger than me. Taller too. Yet, not proportional like a person. It seemed long and thin.

"Daddy, what is that?" Janie whispered.

"Don't know. Let's make some miles," and I headed off again before Clark could get a good look in its direction.

I picked up the pace, though fatigue took its toll, and Annie kept a vigil on it as we marched through the snow. I knew Janie and Duncan were keeping up, so I concentrated on the trail in front of us. I felt my pistol at my belt, but left it there. For now, we kept moving, and I reminded myself every step brought us one closer to the truck.

It bellowed again and I jumped—God, it was loud.

I pulled up behind a tree, patted Clark on the head and peered around it. Janie and Duncan got behind me, and Annie knet next to me. We'd gotten further past the small dip and couldn't see it anymore. We kept our eyes forward, but I scanned our sides to make sure it didn't get around us. Ticking through the list of animals in the region, I tried to come up with a culprit.

It was dark—maybe black, but I reminded myself that because of the distance and the way the woods tend to distort things, it could just be darker than the surrounding tree bark. Except it had been moving fluidly.

We listened but it was quiet again.

No one said a word. Not even Clark.

Something dark came up over the rise. It was several hundred yards back from us, but it kept coming in our direction. "It's following us," Annie said. "Our trail."

She was right.

It walked on two legs. Except it wasn't a person. The way it walked, it looked like it was hunched forward, maybe its head toward the ground, but it had arms. The limbs on it looked long—too long for a person, and thin. Bending further forward, it used its arms to crawl, reminding me of some sort of four-legged spider.

"Berk, what is that?" Annie hissed

Fear crawled up my back side, pins and needles flushing my face. I know how bears and mountain lions move, and this thing stepped differently. The creature closed the distance between us at a good pace, but I couldn't make out the details of its head or body yet.

I cursed too, knowing we still had a ways to the truck.

"Let's make some more miles. See if we can stay ahead of it. Let me know if it gets close."

Annie nodded, looked at the kids. "Everyone stays close. If Dad or I tell you to get behind us, you do it. No questions."

"Momma," Clark asked, "Is it a monster?"

"It's okay. Dad and I will keep you safe. Just stay on the sled and do what I tell you."

We picked up the pace. I had adrenaline now, and I used it to pull Clark on the sled. Janie and Duncan kept a close eye behind us, and Annie did, too. I pulled my pistol, leaving the safety on—the last thing I needed was to trip and shoot myself.

We made another rise and it bellowed again. I pushed up to the top and settled Clark and the sled behind another tree. I needed to catch my breath. I knew we got closer to the truck with each step. Maybe another open field and another stand of trees before we got there. Turning as everyone crowded in around me, I looked back. "Still see it?"

"Yeah," Annie told me, her eyes downhill. "It's definitely following our trail."

I looked across the expanse and it half walked, half crawled along our path. Thin and dark, its arms and legs indeed looked like spider's legs. Except it wasn't a spider. Its human shaped body looked almost bony. Its hands looked like it had long claws on them.

"What the hell?" I muttered.

"I don't know, hon. What are we gonna do?"

That was the real question. We could fire at it, but I doubted we'd hit anything at this distance. It might scare it off, but it would also give away our presence and the fact we knew it was coming after us. "Let's see if we can make the next tree line. We're close to the truck."

"Okay."

We took off. Clark sat quietly, but his head kept darting back behind us. I reached a steady jog, but I kept looking back to make sure everyone stayed close. We picked up the pace and I heard more huffing and puffing over my shoulder from the others. Great plumes of breath escaped from my mouth, billowing in the chill air. We crunched through the snow and I heard the sled scraping across the crust. I cringed after each step, waiting for the sound I feared.

We almost got to the tree line when it bellowed again. We made it within forty yards when it screeched, high pitched and drawn out, like someone dying.

"Berk!" Annie cried.

I reached the tree line, panting and grabbed Clark by the jacket, shoving him behind the tree. "Stay!" I ordered.

Janie and Duncan piled in around him and Annie got to the other side of the tree. Kneeling, she had her pistol out in front of her, her teeth bared..

I looked back and saw it in the open. Nothing like it existed in the animal record. Nothing catalogued by science. Nothing the kids had learned about in school—me neither for that matter. It stopped, raising up on its back haunches, its legs bent backwards like a canine's. Except it wasn't a dog.

It stood taller than a man could be. I guessed at least nine feet or better, from its feet to its head. It didn't have a tail, but it did have horns protruding out the top of its head, darker, just like its body. I couldn't tell if it had hair, but if it did, it was short like the coat of a Weimaraner, though darker. Its face looked like skin stretched tight over a skull, but I saw a big row of teeth when it opened its long jaws.

My hands shook as I flipped off the safety of my Judge and pointed its way. Its black eyes bored into mine across the distance. Those long, powerful legs told me it could catch us.

I had no clue how fast it was, but I was afraid it could move. "Wait til it gets closer. We don't want to miss it."

"I've got two clips ready," Annie said. "Berk. What are we looking at?"

"Don't know hon, but it's bad."

"Remember how Treherne's uncle went missing two years back?" She asked.

"Yeah. I know he hunted out this way. Nobody ever found his body: no gun, no clothing, nothing."

It howled at us, long and loud and it bared those teeth, looking like knives. As scary as it looked, when it quit, it took in a long breath, wheezing. It let it out, hissing and sucked in more air. I could hear it from across the open ground and it still stood a football field off from us. Dropping back down on all fours it took steps toward us.

I only had five shots to Annie's eight. I felt stuck now. From its size, If we ran, I knew it could catch us before we reached the truck., The kids looked panicked, and if they bolted, they'd scatter creating easy targets. I cursed inside because we couldn't make a run for it.

"Kids!" I barked. "We're in trouble. I want one of your hands on us at all times. Clark, you climb on my back now. Janie, help him."

"Dad, what are we going to do?" Duncan asked.

"Remember what I taught you. Most predators hesitate to attack a group. They try to intimidate and get one of their prey to break off and run so they can pick them off. We stay tight and stay together. Mom's going to take a shot at it, but if it charges us, you stay behind us and let us shoot it. It'll be loud, but Mom's a good shot and so am I."

I sucked in several breaths, taking the safety off on my Judge. I tried to calm myself, concentrating on my breathing though I never took my eyes off the monster.

Janie got Clark up on my back. "Clark, hold onto my collar and stick your feet in my pockets if you can. And you don't let go. If I move, you hang on tight."

"Okay, Daddy."

"Ready hon?"

"Yeah," and she squeezed off a shot.

The report echoed through the wilds and all of the kids jumped. I felt Clark jerk on my back.

She didn't hit it, but it pulled up short. Its long, flat head raised up and it growled, deep and guttural. It heaved in another breath, rasping like it had to work to suck in all of that air.

I kept my sight on its body, but I hesitated shooting. Annie had gotten its attention and I wanted to see what it would do. The way it looked at us, a fear crept into me. Its eyes bored into mine, and I got the distinct feeling it knew we pointed weapons at it and what they were capable of. The intelligence of the thing scared me worse than if it had been a bear or a mountain lion stalking us.

It dropped forward and started coming toward us again. Annie glanced at me.

"Let it get another twenty yards—close enough we can hit it and see if we can put some rounds into it."

She nodded, knowing the same thing I did: if it got past us, the kids were gone.

My hands shook. It's not like the movies when the action heroes just aim and shoot, oblivious to dying. They're just actors. Hiding in the tree line, I knew if we made mistakes, any or all of us could die. The way it stalked, keeping its eyes attached to us, I had no delusions about its intent.

It was a predator.

I'd never put much stock in Native American ideas about spirits and bad places. All of the science books and zoos and

Darwins of the world had told me all my life things like this didn't exist. Monsters. Except it crawled in our direction, hunting us. Its black claws looked as long as my hand. Its unholy, black face looked malevolent, and hungry. .

I took in deep breaths trying to steady my hand. Images of the kids flashed behind my eyes and sweat trickled down the side of my face. If I missed, if Annie missed, the kids paid the price.

It reached my comfortable range. I can't say exactly where it is: thirty yards, twenty-five? It reached a distance I saw it had no hair, but dark leathery skin. I saw its breath burst from its jaws like steam breaking from a pipe. Its eyes settled on mine, but it didn't slow. It knew the stakes.

"Now," I whispered, and letting out a breath, desperately attempting to aim, I fired.

Annie did too.

My shot whizzed by its side, Clark crying out behind my ear at the gun shot. Annie's hit it in the face and its head jerked sideways. I saw a tooth break out of its jaw, spinning into the air.

The thing didn't fall to the snow. Its head snapped back around and it shrieked at us. It made a godawful high-pitched screech I imagined only a banshee or tormented spirit could make, and it rang in my ears.

I fired again, aiming carefully, barrel pointed at its body and this time I hit it too. Annie squeezed off two more shots. We fired on it, and each time a bullet connected we saw it jerk, wince and yell some more. Adrenaline pumping now, I fired every shot in my pistol.

Without waiting, I reloaded, concentrating on getting more ammo into the barrel. Annie fired slower, allowing me time to load before having to reload her own clip. I flinched at the howls, the screams, but I kept on. I dropped two shells, my fingers shaking, but I just grabbed more from the pouch at my belt, and swung the barrel toward it as I readied to shoot.

I don't know how many times we'd hit it, but I know I'd hit it at least twice and Annie had sunk three or four shells into it. It hadn't fallen, hadn't died in pools of blood. I saw wounds in its side, but it howled at us, raising up off the ground to its full height. Its arms stretched and it bellowed, sending a wave of panic all the way through me. I felt its yell penetrate through my chest; my ears were ringing. I felt Clark dig into my neck with his little hands as he squeezed as tight as he could.

It was still alive and pissed.

It stood its ground. It didn't advance. I heard the click as Annie readied another clip. It stood there, baring its long white teeth, more like sharks' teeth than canine or feline, but it didn't come toward us.

"Back away," I hissed. "We back our way toward the truck," I said louder. "Don't run and don't turn your back on it."

"I'll grab the sled," Duncan said.

"Forget it. Clark, you hold tight."

I heard the kids crunching through the snow. Daring a glance at Annie, I nodded and we started backtracking through the trees. I didn't have enough saliva to swallow, but I didn't take my eyes off of it. It tried to stare me down, punching into my soul with its eyes. I knew if I cowered it would charge us.

"I hit it," Annie said. "More than once. What the hell?"

Backing up, one careful step after another, I could only shake my head. "Don't know. If it charges, we stand our ground and fire."

It wheezed and yelled, screaming as we retreated. After a dozen of our steps, it took a step forward and I got an idea as to its stride. . Itt could probably take three or four steps to one of mine. Outrunning this creature would be impossible.

I encouraged the kids as we backed our way through the trees, sidling around each trunk, reminding Duncan and Janie to keep close. Annie kept her pistol trained on it and we backed toward the other side of the trees.

The thing reached the tree line and it walked through them, its black claws clasping around the trunks. It stayed on its hind legs now, matching our pace, waiting for one of us to screw up or fall to gain an advantage. I saw four bullet holes in its body and blood dribbled from its lower jaw, dotting the snow, but it didn't seem to care.

It had murder in its eyes. Death in its breath.

We reached open ground again, coming out on the far side of the trees and I muttered a prayer Mom taught me when you got into trouble. .

"Dad, I see the truck," Duncan said.

"Don't run," I barked. "Keep going."

"Will the truck protect us?" Janie asked, her voice trembling.

"It'll get us the hell out of here. How far?"

"Two hundred yards, give or take," Duncan said.

We kept backing up. It hissed at us, showed its teeth and continued stalking us. One of its claws peeled bark off of the ash tree it had its hand around. Its eyes never left mine and I felt like I couldn't break its gaze without something bad happening.

"Janie, take my keys out of my pants pocket. When we get close, use the remote start and get it going."

I slowed so she could get to my side. "Stay behind me. Don't get between me and it," I said.

I stopped for a three count and Janie fished into my pocket grabbing at the keys like it was her only hope.

We edged our way backward, the creature, spirit or whatever the hell it was, relentless as it took a step our way every couple of breaths. I almost relaxed when I heard the engine to our truck kick over, but I knew we weren't safe.

We had a newer truck complete with a push button ignition. I had almost bought something older, not liking some of the bells and whistles the new cars sported. I hedged against back up cameras and other modern comforts. I thought it made a person lazy. I realized Janie could unlock the doors and I could slip into the driver's seat, punch a button and get us moving.

I worked out the plan in my head as we backpedaled, one snow-crunching step at a time. "Duncan, when we get to the truck, you take Clark and get around the other side. Janie, back seat driver's side and you unlock the doors. Annie will work her way to the passenger side, and we all open the doors together. Get in at the same time."

It bellowed again, yelling at me. I don't know if it attempted some sort of conversation or just hollered because I'd spoken, but I jumped. Everyone else did too.

"We're here, Dad!"

I nodded to Duncan and felt him grab Clark. Except Clark's fingers wouldn't let go of my coat. I wriggled my shoulders, but he held on tight.. "Clark, let Duncan get you."

"Dad . . ." his voice quivered.

"Do it!" I snapped.

I felt the weight leave my shoulders, realizing how tired I was. Adrenaline kept me going, but my muscles shook from walking backwards for so long with Clark's extra weight on me. I kept my arms extended with my revolver.

I heard the crunch of the kids' feet as they reached the truck, afraid to take my eyes off the thing. Time stretched but

I saw Annie go around the grill toward the passenger side. I stood my ground, barrel aimed at its midsection.

The thing stalked ahead two steps now, as if it realized what the truck meant. It snarled and dropped to all fours. I sighted, aimed and fired. The shot hit the snow in front of it and, raising the barrel, I fired two more times. This time I hit it with both and I saw one of its arms flinch and its head snap sideways.

"Go!" I shouted and took my eyes off it. I grabbed the door, wrenched it open and clambered in, Annie's gun going off four times while I scrambled behind the wheel.

Janie shrieked and I heard Clark crying, but the doors slammed shut and I punched the button. The engine light turned green and I slammed the shifter into drive. I heard Annie's door shut. Everyone made it inside. Glancing into the rearview mirror, I saw all of my kids fear stricken faces and jammed on the accelerator.

The scream rolled through the truck despite the glass and I punched it, spinning to turn the truck back toward the nearest road.

Glass shattered next to me and I heard the wheezing. Pain seared into my arm and shoulder, but I kept the gas punched to the floor and steered. Something rocked the entire truck, jostling us, and everyone screamed. I focused on the terrain in front of us, the truck bouncing from side to side. Suddenly we pulled away as if a weight had been taken off the truck.

I didn't look back, just concentrated on the ground cover, avoiding any possible dips or debris that might tear something underneath and kill us all. I heard Annie's window roll down followed by the sounds of her emptying her clip and reloading another.

More anguished wails from behind, but I didn't look back. I'd seen enough.

Apparently, it ran fast enough to keep pace with the truck and I muttered prayers when I saw the road in front of us. I wanted to glance into the mirror, but my fear wouldn't allow me to, scared something would happen which would trap us with it.

I felt the tires reach pavement. I floored the truck on the empty road. We headed off down the road, the wrong direction to home, but I didn't care. I stepped on the gas and watched the speedometer rise. I reached eighty-five when I felt Annie's hand on my arm.

"It's gone," she said.

I chanced a look in the rearview mirror. Nothing but highway behind us. "What the hell?" I hissed.

"Dad!" Janie blurted out., "You're bleeding!"

Glancing over, I saw three holes in the sleeve of my jacket and dark wetness around them. The thing had jammed its claws through the material and punctured me good. The pain sunk in as the adrenaline faded, but I never slowed.

I knew the road would lead us into Juneau from the other side, close to a hospital..

"You okay to drive?" Annie asked.

"I'll pull over if I start to get faint."

I TOLD everyone I got skewered falling down a hill and rolling into thick brush. I don't know if anyone believed me, but they sure weren't going to believe the truth. I started looking for a job down in the states the following day. The kids all had nightmares. Hell we did too.

The woods changed for us. I quit hunting and Annie did too.. I knew the kids would never go into the woods again. I looked for books and answers and the only thing I came close with was stuff off of the internet. I found entries for a wendigo online, and it sort of fit, but not quite. It made me think of Native American stories of entities. Either way, we all agreed we didn't want to live anywhere near the woods anymore.

And we got a fake tree for Christmas.

YOU BETTER WATCH OUT

DAVID ALLEN VOYLES

"Oh, my God, Andrew, this is so incredible! Can you believe it? It's even better than the pictures!" Lauren twirled around in a complete circle with her arms extended, gaping at the minimally furnished hotel room. "And you can actually see your breath in here! Are we out of our minds or what?"

"It's freaking awesome," her husband responded. "Not your usual accommodations, but then, it's perfect for this holiday, right?"

"I'm so glad you're not disappointed," said Mikael, sliding a large nylon bag off his shoulder and setting it beside a carved block of ice which served as a night stand. "We are rather proud to be regarded by all the leading travel services as the most luxurious ice hotel, not just in Sweden, but in the world."

The bed served as the focal point of the room with blue light glowing from the carved ice that served as its base. Reindeer hides sat atop several white, furry blankets that covered the king-sized mattress. The frozen walls were chiseled to resemble the interior of a cave. Large glowing icicles hanging from the ceiling provided more blue light, three of which joined clear stalagmites below them to form columns of light.

"So, we're really in the Arctic Circle here?" asked Lauren.

"Absolutely," Mikael answered. "The perfect place to spend Christmas Eve!" Clasping his hands in what was likely a familiar pose, he began his final spiel.

"Now, as you no doubt remember from your orientation session, most of your luggage is secured in a locker in the heated portion of the hotel should you need to access it for any reason. Tomorrow, staff will move your things into the heated suite you've reserved for the rest of your stay. Unless, of course, you love the ice room experience so much you decide to spend your whole visit here!" Mikael laughed, and then added, "But most people find that one night is enough."

"Hopefully you packed everything you need just for tonight in your overnight bag, but people do sometimes forget things," he continued. "If you do want to get back into the main building, you will have to step outside to do so as there is no connecting structure other than the covered walkway we just used. That's where you'll find the restrooms, and also the sauna and hot tubs should you want to unwind in warmth before turning in for the night."

Departing from what seemed to be his usual script, he changed to a more conversational tone. "There's also some live music in the bar until 11 o'clock. Tonight, it's a three-piece band that plays jazzy versions of Christmas carols." With a playful frown he added, "If you like that kind of thing."

"Thanks," said Lauren. "We had a drink there earlier, so I think we're good for the night."

"Well, there is a hotel phone you can use should you want room service." He smiled again, and, shrugging, added, "So unless there is something else I can help you with, I'll leave you to enjoy your one-of-a-kind Ice Castle room in privacy."

"That should do it, thanks," said Andrew as he handed the young man an American twenty-dollar bill. The attendant exited, and Andrew closed the curtain behind him.

"Not too shabby as a Christmas present, huh, babe?" Andrew slid his arms around Lauren's waist, and gave her a quick kiss. "We may not be at the North Pole, but we're as close to Santa's house as we can get, I imagine."

"I wasn't too sure about this when you first sprung it on me back in June," Lauren said, pulling away as she walked around the bed to inspect the detail carved into the walls. "But I've gotten so excited over the past few months that I've been like a kid again--one that felt like Christmas was never going to get here."

"And we have dear Mrs. McIlreath to thank for the experience," Andrew said. After rummaging a bit in the overnight bag, he pulled out two shot glasses and a bottle of Grey Goose vodka. "God rest her soul," he said as he filled their glasses.

"To Mrs. McIreath," said Lauren, clinking her glass to Andrew's. "Mmmmm. Is that...cherry flavored?" she asked, licking her lips.

"Yes, black cherry actually. In honor of the holiday. You know, reminiscent of the chocolate covered cherries that Santa always brings to certain good little girls?" He poured them each another shot.

"Or naughty little girls who do the books for their aging clients?"

"Yes, exactly!" Andrew raised his shot glass. "Here's to Mrs. McIlreath for a Christmas experience of a lifetime. Too bad the old broad had to go and die on us," he continued. "If we had known she was going to die you could have been skimming even more each month. I really don't think her family cared enough to catch it."

"There'll be another 'old broad' before too long," said Lauren. "It pays not to get too greedy or you'll kill the goose that lays the golden egg. Not to mention the risk of jail time."

"Oh, that's cold," said Andrew, as he pulled his wife into a hug. "And speaking of cold, how warm do you think that sleeping bag will really be? I'd like to get out of all these winter clothes."

"Didn't you pay attention during orientation? They said you could get by with just thermal underwear, that it never gets below 23 degrees Fahrenheit in the rooms. It's probably close to that now, below freezing for sure. But the sleeping bag is rated at minus twenty, so we should be fine."

Andrew filled their shot glasses again and said, "With that rating I think we should be ok without the thermal undies! C'mon, let's see how fast we can strip out of this gear and get that bag under those reindeer blankets for some serious Yule-tide snuggling!"

"Just snuggling?" Lauren asked with a raised eyebrow.

"Shh!" Andrew laid a finger to his lips and whispered theatrically, "Santa may be listening!"

"ANDREW?"

No other sound was audible but Andrew's quiet snoring. Lauren poked a sharp elbow into her husband's side and whispered again urgently. "Andrew, wake up!"

"Hmmm…what is it?" he said, barely awake.

"Something's wrong. Really wrong." Lauren sat up with the blankets pulled up to her neck.

"What do you mean…hey, what's with the lights?"

Andrew pushed himself up and huddled beside her.

"Yeah, I know. Why is everything red now?" Lauren said softly. Instead of the soft blue lighting from before, the room now looked as if it were lit by a glowing forge.

"And listen...What's that noise?" Andrew squinted in the darkness and peered about. He thought he could make out the strains of singing, or possibly chanting, coming from a great distance.

Staying under the covers as much as possible, the couple scrambled to put on their clothes which they had left in the bed with them to keep them warm. As Andrew laced up his boots, he glanced back at the wall above their pillows.

"Holy shit! How did that get there?"

Carved into the ice wall was a huge demonic creature. The relief sculpture created the appearance of a giant erupting from the wall. The bearded figure was visible from the waist up, its arms extended out along the walls to either side, and the hands that protruded from the furry cuffs of his tunic looked more like claws with their long and pointed nails. Long hair flowed out from under a conical cap whose trim matched that on the collar and cuffs. Narrow, menacing eyes glowed red, as did the light within the icicles, columns, and the foundation of the bed. Although the carving itself had no color, the ice glowed a deep crimson so that there could be little mistake as to what, or who, the sculpture was meant to suggest.

"That's hardly in the traditional spirit of the season," said Lauren. "They sure have a freaky way of honoring Christmas here."

"The room seems like it's changed in other ways, too," Andrew said. "Did you notice faces in the walls before?" Lauren stepped over to stand beside the curtain where Andrew had pointed and ran her hand along the textured wall.

"It is a face," she said, staring at it closely. Looking around the entire room, she saw that grinning faces, like masks of wicked elves frozen into place, peered out from dozens of spots all around the room. "No, they definitely weren't here before. Andrew, I don't like this. It's creepy. Why would they do this?"

"It's a pretty good effect, I have to admit, but I don't like it either. Maybe for Halloween, but not Christmas." The more he looked around, the angrier he grew. "And we paid way too much money for practical jokes! C'mon, let's get the hell out of here and see who we can complain to about getting our money back!" He tossed Lauren's boots towards her and sat back down on the bed to finish putting on his own.

"I don't think we're going to find anyone who can do anything in the middle of the night," Lauren said as she sat on the floor so she could get her cold feet into the boots as soon as she could.

"We'll see if we can go ahead and get into the heated suite we've reserved for the other two nights," Andrew said, yanking the last knot tight on his laces. He stood up and added, "If not, we can crash on the couches in the spa area. And we'll *demand* that they comp us some meals and drinks!" Shoving the bottle of vodka and shot glasses into their overnight bag, Andrew walked over to the curtain which separated their room from the hallway and pulled it open with one quick jerk.

He stood motionless, staring at what he saw.

"What the…?"

"Andrew…?" said Lauren tentatively, peering around his shoulder. "That's not the same hall we came in from."

"Yeah, I know," he answered softly.

The hall was now immersed in the same fiery light as their room. That change, of course, could be explained simply by a touch of a button. But where before the walls of ice had been smooth like plaster, they now appeared rough and hewn like the inside of a mine shaft. Perhaps the most freakish thing of all was that their room was now the last one on the hall even though they both distinctly remembered rooms beyond theirs when they had been brought there the evening before.

As they stepped out into the hall and looked to their left, the only direction they could go, they saw curtains on both sides that covered entrances to other rooms, and at the end a set of steps carved into the ice that curved upward into a tunnel.

"Call the office," Lauren said as they stepped back into their room, "and ask them what in the hell is going on. Tell them we don't think this is funny and that we want to get another room. A warm one."

"Good idea, but now there's no phone!"

"So, somebody's been in our room while we slept?" Lauren asked, her voice pitched high with indignation. "That's creepy, Andrew. *really*, creepy. I'm ready for this to end!"

"Yeah. Me, too, babe."

"What—what should we do?"

"Go down this hall and up those steps, I guess," said Andrew. "It looks like we don't have a choice unless we just want to wait for someone to show up."

As the couple made their way down the hall toward the steps, Lauren paused at the first room on their right. The curtain was pulled back, allowing for the contents of the room to be visible once they stepped through the curving, arched entry.

"Should we see what's in there?" Andrew asked quietly.

Without replying, Laura stepped into the room awash in

red glowing light. Two beds similar to the one they had slept in stood against each of the side walls. But directly ahead on the wall facing the entrance to the room was a giant ice sculpture of a satyr-like creature cut into a niche in the ice wall, posed as if about to attack the viewer. The bottom half of the statue depicted hooved feet and furry legs, while the torso and arms were those of a powerful male human. But instead of having a satyr's goat-like features, the head was that of a mighty stag. The many pointed antlers spread out at least three feet from the ferocious head with eyes that glowed like those of a demon.

"Who would stay in this room?" Lauren wondered aloud.

"Somebody like us who had no clue what they were getting into, maybe?" offered Andrew.

"Yeah, I guess. Let's see what's in the next one."

The curtain of the next room was pulled shut, but after no one answered Andrew's tentative call of hello, he pulled it back to reveal another unique but unsettling scene. This time they could see all the way straight through to the back of the room. A foyer or anteroom greeted them with benches of ice on the right and left. An arch made of blocks of ice created another entrance into the bedroom proper, and on either side of this entrance sat the sculpture of a snarling wolf with intricately carved teeth that looked as sharp as razors. A master bed, carved of ice like the others, sat framed by the arch.

"I'm guessing we were the only guests on this wing last night," said Andrew.

"Lucky us. I'm really ready to get somewhere warmer and more...normal," Lauren said. "Let's see where the stairs go. Hopefully I won't bust my butt on them!"

The frozen steps were hewn with ridges so that walking was not dangerous, but the couple soon learned that the stairway was far from friendly. It curved and wound about constantly so that a view of what lay ahead was never possible. Sconces in which flameless lights shone at intervals frequently cast shadows of frightening, horned creatures in menacing postures on the cave-like walls. Where the tunnel widened into landings, the statues causing the shadows became visible. While the stairs in this tunnel had led up when they first stepped upon them, they later led down so that eventually Andrew and Lauren had no idea whether they were above, below, or at ground level.

After ten minutes of winding about with no signs of doors leading into rooms or out of the building, Lauren stopped in the middle of the tunnel. "Damn it! When are we going to find an exit out of this haunted house?"

"There's no telling. But we don't have any choice but to keep going."

"I'm tired, I'm cold, and I just want this to end," she said crumpling in a heap in the middle of the tunnel.

"Come on, babe. We've got to keep going," Andrew said, crouching beside her. "It can't be much further. The place isn't that big." He pulled her up and they continued following the steps which now led down in the eerie tunnel.

A wooden door with medieval style workings blocked their way as they rounded another curve in the descending stairway.

"At last!" cried Andrew, lifting the latch and pulling the door outward.

To their disappointment, the door did not lead outside, but at least it was an end to the winding tunnel. The room appeared to be a large workshop, dimly lit with flames from torches along the walls. As their eyes adjusted they saw tables littered with various metal tools scattered about the room, and along the walls were large curious objects whose purposes were not easily identifiable. What looked like a huge bird cage made of sturdy iron hung suspended from a hook in the ceiling in one corner. It was large enough to hold a fully-grown person.

"What's this?" asked Lauren, picking up a metal gadget from one of the tables. It was pear-shaped on one end, and when Lauren turned the handle on the other, the leaves of the bulbous end began to separate and spread apart.

"Looks like whatever it was used to open wasn't pleasant. I think those are bloodstains on those leaves."

"Ewww!" Lauren dropped the object back on the table in disgust. Spotting a large object in the corner of the room, she said, "Oh, look! A rocking horse. Or rather a rocking reindeer." She walked over to the corner to inspect an intricately carved rocker made to resemble a reindeer. "But I don't think I'd want to ride this one," she said, making a face. Sticking up from the saddle were sharp metal spikes. "Somebody's got a pretty sick sense of humor."

"And this doesn't look too pleasant either," said Andrew, picking up a metal mask from a table. Attached to the jaw was a leather bridle with metal thorns. "Apparently some of the guests at the Ice Castle request some kinky stuff."

"Looks like somebody's been making lots of these," said Lauren, pointing to a table on which sat several objects, each with two winged nuts on posts at either end of a connecting base.

"Oh, hell! I know what those are. Thumb screws. You put the victim's thumbs in the vise and tighten down the bolts."

"Is that what all this stuff in here is for? Torture? Andrew, have we stumbled into some kind of crazy S&M bullshit here? And look over there. That's actually a rack! You know, what they stretched people on during the Spanish Inquisition!"

"That seems like a bit much even for the kinkiest sex. I've

gotta admit that I'm even more freaked out than before. Let's keep going and find our way out of here."

Another door like the one through which they entered stood at the other end of the chamber. Next to the door stood a large metal sarcophagus, standing on its end. The embossed metal front resembled that of a screaming woman.

"Andrew...listen, do you hear that?"

"What?"

"Sounds like whimpering. Very faint, coming from inside this thing."

Andrew stepped closer and peered through the eyeholes. To his horror, eyes inside the darkness of the metal coffin looked back at him. The entire figure within was not visible, but it appeared from the blood that streamed down its face that spikes on the inside of the lid were driven into the victim's body and head when the lid was closed.

"Let's get the hell out of here," said Andrew as he grabbed Lauren by the wrist. He opened the door and pulled her into the hallway beyond. They ran through the curving tunnel for several minutes without stopping until they came to another door that looked very much like the entrance to the torture chamber they had just left.

They leaned against the ice wall gasping for breath, smoky plumes shooting from their mouths like racehorses on a cold morning. Once she had breath enough to speak, Lauren asked frantically, "Where are we, Andrew? What is this place?"

"I don't know," he said. "These tunnels--they're way too long to be anything that could fit in the part of the hotel we were in."

"But...but how did we get here then? Did somebody drug us and bring us to this hellhole?"

"I don't know. Maybe. But however they did it, and wherever we are, we've got to figure out how to get out."

"I don't want to go back to that room, Andrew."

"Me either. I guess we should—Wait! Listen! Do you hear that?" Lauren frowned in concentration as she tried to hear what Andrew was referencing.

"Yeah, yeah, I think. It's really faint. Sounds like singing. Like what we heard when we first woke up."

"That's what I hear. I can't make out what it is, but that's what it sounds like. Let's go through this door and see if we can find out what's going on."

They opened the door and saw that another tunnel continued with steps going upward not far away. As before, red light glowed from sconces along the walls, so without hesitation they started climbing the steps, hand in hand.

From time to time the tunnel would fork, sometimes giving them two or three choices of where to go. Shadows of troll-like creatures often appeared on the curved walls before them, the terrifying ice statues themselves revealed once the couple rounded a curve in the tunnel. They paused at each intersection to listen before following the hallway that seemed to lead to the singing.

Finally, Andrew and Lauren came to another door.

"We have to be close to whatever celebration is going on now," said Lauren. "But that singing is pretty weird, don't you think? Do you even know what language it is?

"No. I'm guessing this must be some kind of Scandinavian ceremony. A Christmas celebration of some sort, maybe. Doesn't exactly sound like adults. More like kids."

"It's not like any kids' choir I've ever heard," Lauren said.

Andrew rubbed his eyes and sighed. "I don't want to interrupt some religious service and piss off the locals here, but maybe we can ease into the area and see if we can get help."

He slid the latch up slowly on the ancient door and the two eased through the doorway to find themselves looking into a gallery of empty benches on their left which over-looked a large space, like an auditorium or indoor arena, to the right. A wooden balustrade ran the length of the gallery, its spindles allowing for Lauren and Andrew to view the activity below as they crouched. The layout reminded Lauren of viewing the ballroom scene in Disney's haunted mansion as a little girl and watching the dancing ghosts fade in and out below her, but what she witnessed here was far more horrific.

The couple crept along beside the railing as quietly as they could, trying to see what was happening below them. Clearly a feast, a celebration of some kind, was in progress. The arrangement of ice-carved tables laden with food and drink, torches along the frozen walls, and the raised dais at the front of the chamber resembled that of a medieval banquet hall. But the participants who were singing and holding up flagons of what appeared to be ale or wine were most unusual.

They were dressed in furs and skins as if from olden times, but not one of them was above three feet tall. They were not children, nor were they adult little people; they did not appear to be human at all. Their clawed hands were covered in dense fur, and their faces, nearly obscured in long beards of black, brown, gray, or dark red, were monstrous. Heavy brows protruded over their eyes, and when they smiled or sang, yellow fangs were revealed rather than teeth.

On the dais at the head of the hall was a throne carved of ice, and on it sat the most monstrous figure of all. Lauren recognized instantly the inspiration for the sculpted image above the bed in which they had awakened. Surveying the celebration below him, a huge goblet in his hand, was the grinning figure of a demonic Santa Claus.

Andrew seemed to be frozen in place as he peered down at the mayhem below, but Lauren tugged on his sleeve, pulling him along as they crawled to the door at the end of the gallery. When they were three-quarters of the way, the devilish Santa got up from his throne and bellowed loudly in an unknown tongue. The creatures cheered when he finished his speech and banged their mugs in a tribal rhythm on the ice tables, sloshing the dark red liquid over their hands without regard. The Santa figure, grinning wickedly, walked over to his throne, and reaching behind it pulled forth a sack that obviously was not empty.

Lauren and Andrew could not tear their eyes from the scene. The demon reached down into the depths of the sack, pulled out a human child by the ankles, a young dark-haired boy wearing footed pajamas covered in teddy bears, and held it up for all to see. As the child writhed and cried, the audience cheered more wildly.

Andrew gasped at the sight and thrust himself back from the rail, grabbing Lauren's arm as he lost his balance so that they both tumbled to the floor. The motion drew the monster's attention to the gallery and his minions followed his glaring eyes so that the whole assembly focused on the hapless couple. The evil Santa's eyes narrowed in fiendish delight. He pointed to the gallery and shouted one word of command. The creatures responded with shouts of their own, the bawling child lying at their leader's feet completely forgotten, and ran from the hall as a howling mob to exits that led up to the gallery level.

Andrew and Lauren dashed through the doorway, where once again they were faced with a decision. To the left a tunnel curved out of their line of vision, while a set of stairs led upward to the right.

They took the stairs two at a time, following a curving

path, the shouts of their pursuers urging them on. Eventually the tunneled steps leveled out onto a hallway with curtains hanging at intervals on either side. The cold air made breathing even harder, but though they were near exhaustion, they did not pause. They ran on until the hallway ended at another oaken door.

Beyond it was another set of steps, but these led down. Andrew, in the lead, paused to look back through the doorway and down the hall through which they had just come. Lauren knew what he was thinking.

"We can't take the risk, Andrew," Lauren said. "We'll be trapped for sure if we try to hide in one of those rooms. We've got to keep going. Maybe we can gain some time while they're searching those rooms for us."

Andrew nodded and, grabbing her hand again, pulled her down the stairs. At the bottom another hallway stretched out before them which they followed to its end without regard to the closed curtains of chambers on either side. The shouting behind them made them so frantic in their desire to escape that when presented with forking paths they made random choices without thinking of where they might be in the building. Sometimes they went down and other times they went up. There was no time to deliberate.

With the continued sounds of shouting and dozens of running feet behind them, Andrew and Lauren came to a dead end at the end of another curving hallway. A large oak door stood closed. Andrew prayed that it wasn't locked as he threw himself on it and turned the handle with all his might.

The two gasped with relief when the door opened, even though the way forward was totally dark. No sconces illuminated what lay beyond. Feeling that they had no choice, the couple ran into the darkness, but suddenly found themselves flailing their limbs and sliding on their backs down a frozen chute. After only a few feet into the darkened tunnel, the floor had dropped away into a steep incline.

They soared down the icy corkscrew in darkness; the only sounds were their own screams. On and on they slid, fearing that they would surely be broken to pieces when they slammed into a wall at the end of the slide at such a high speed, or perhaps projected off a huge jump into a yawning abyss.

To their amazement and relief, after many breathless minutes the chute leveled out into a large plain of soft snow. Andrew and Lauren came to a stop within ten feet of each other where they lay gasping for breath under a starry sky. Neither could speak for a few moments, but eventually they were able to sit up and look at their surroundings.

They looked at a huge castle built of ice. The turrets seemed to reach the sky, and the massive gated entrance made them feel tiny and helpless. Nowhere was there anything resembling the ice hotel that they had checked into the day before. Surrounding the castle was a black forest of evergreens in which menacing shadows moved. A single road of packed snow ran out from the castle and disappeared into the dense woods.

Lauren stood and pointed to a separate smaller structure with many doors that suggested a storage building—a garage or stable.

"Maybe we can find a snowmobile or something that can get us out of here!"

"But where would we go?" asked Andrew. "We don't have the slightest clue where we are."

"We know we don't want to be here. Come on! Let's see what's in there before those...*things* find us."

A brown wreath of dried berries, withered leaves, and dead pine needles hung on each door of the building. As

Lauren pulled up the latch to enter, she saw bones of tiny creatures nestled within the dead wreath above her hand. Shuddering, she pulled the door open, and the smell of decay, molded straw, and animal waste assailed them both.

"Ugh!" Lauren said, covering her mouth and nose with her gloved hand. "That's awful!" Andrew followed her inside, leaving the door open for more light and fresher air. The moon and starlight from the reflected snow did nothing to diminish the gloom, but the flickering light provided by lanterns hanging on hooks revealed stalls lining either side of the structure. They were indeed in a stable.

They walked slowly over to a stall to their right and peered into the darkness. A shadowy figure as large as a draft horse huffed, emitting a foul breath. They could just discern a huge, antlered head with eyes that glowed orange with reflected light. Patches of yellowed skull showed through wet, matted fur. Suddenly it snorted and kicked the door of its stall, and the hinges creaked as if they were about to give way.

Andrew and Lauren both shrieked and turned to run to the door, but a large silhouette stood blocking the entrance with his hands on his hips, chuckling with glee. The couple froze in place, and the giant stepped into the flickering lantern light to reveal his grinning, bearded face.

The dirty grey beard was stained with grease, and his eyes shone with lantern light like the beast in the stall. As he stepped closer, his quiet laughter grew from malevolent chuckling into full belly laughs that seemed to make the whole stable shake. Behind him the horde of hideous imps flowed into the stable. Dozens and dozens of them crept slowly into the building, filling the space behind their leader, licking their lips and wringing their hands as they advanced. Closer and closer they came.

≈

LAUREL AWAKENED FIRST, her heart hammering in her chest, and sat up in the fur-lined bed, looking around quite bewildered at the blue-tinged walls around her.

"Oh, God! What a dream!"

Andrew, sensing the movement and the fur being pulled from his shoulders, stirred and groaned. "What…what is it?"

"I just had a nightmare, I guess," Lauren said.

"Yeah, I did, too." He rubbed his face and sat up beside her. "I'm actually glad you woke me up. What time is it?"

Lauren reached for her watch on the frozen nightstand.

Looks like five o'clock. Early rise for today, it looks like."

"I'm not so crazy about this place, Drew. Let's get back to the main hotel, okay?"

"Yeah, sure. I get you. I'm definitely cool with that," said her husband. "I doubt I could get back to sleep anyway. And I sure as hell don't want my dream to pick up where it left off."

They dressed quickly and having only a few items to throw into their overnight bag, they left the frozen ice rooms, stepped outside and followed the covered walkway back to the main building, grateful for the bright lights that drove back the darkness.

Once they had passed through the sauna area and approached the main desk in the lobby, Mikael saw them and called out exuberantly, "Hey, you two! It's good to see you!"

"Yeah, it's good to see you, too," answered Andrew. Then, thinking that it was odd to see the same attendant who had shown them to their room the evening before, he said, "Man, they got you working around the clock or what?"

"No, I just work the evening shift, three to eleven," he answered, smiling but with a puzzled expression. "I've been here since three pm, just like yesterday."

Andrew and Lauren looked at each other.

"But it's like five in the morning..." said Lauren, her voice trailing off.

"Five in the—" Mikael broke off and nodded with a sudden realization. "You guys have some serious jet lag going on. It's five in the afternoon!"

Lauren and Andrew looked at each other in confusion.

"At this time of year in the Arctic Circle, we only get about two and a half hours of sunlight, so it's pretty easy for our guests to get confused," Mikael said, sensing their discomfort. He searched through a set of drawers below the desk and then handed Andrew a key card. "So, are you guys ready to check into your nice, warm suite? Check-in is really not for another hour, but your suite is ready. I can let you in early. You'd probably like to get settled before dinner after your day's activities. I'll have another attendant get your other luggage from the locker and he'll bring it up to you within a few minutes. I don't know where he is at the moment or I'd have him man the desk and escort you up myself."

"Um, yeah," said Andrew, still feeling very confused. "That's ok. Thanks." He took the card and he and Lauren worked their way to the elevator.

Finding themselves alone as the elevator doors closed, Lauren said, "What the hell, Andrew?"

"I really don't know," he answered. "Somehow it seems like we lost a day."

"I'm just so confused," said Lauren.

The doors opened and the two exited the elevator and started down the hall to locate their room. Christmas carols played softly over the intercom, which to Lauren's surprise, she found disturbing rather than comforting. "I think I just want to take a hot shower and crawl in bed and go to sleep," she said.

"Yeah, that sounds good. I'll call for room service and we can have our meal in tonight."

"Breakfast, lunch, or dinner?"

"God, I don't know," said Andrew shaking his head.

The suite was as luxurious as promised and the food was excellent. Once Andrew had rolled the cart with their dirty dishes out into the hall, he climbed into bed beside Lauren and sighed heavily.

After several minutes of silence, Lauren turned to him and asked, "Andrew, what happened?"

"I don't have a clue," he replied, staring at the ceiling.

Another moment of still silence passed.

In a small, quiet voice that sounded like that of a five-year-old, she asked, "Where will we be when we wake up next?"

Before Andrew could answer, a familiar carol, one that apparently had been playing out in the hall, pierced the silence, cutting in abruptly as if a speaker in their room had been cut on mid-song.

"…He knows if you've been bad or good
So be good for goodness sake.
Oh, you better watch out, you better not cry,
You better not pout, I'm telling you why.
Santa Claus is coming…"

The song cut off as abruptly as it had started. A familiar laugh replaced the music; malevolent chuckles grew into full belly laughs that seemed to make the whole hotel shake.

ABOUT THE AUTHORS

Michael Booth is a writer and video producer from Atlanta, Georgia. After a number of years as a newspaper reporter and editor, he became a Writer/Producer/Director for several companies, including The Coca-Cola Company. He formed his own communications company, Face Communications, and proceeded to produce video programs for a number of leading companies, among them Delta Air Lines, Habitat for Humanity, Optum, the CDC, and the Southern Company.

In 2005 he was presented with a EMMY for Best Documentary Scriptwriting from the Southeastern NATAS for a documentary he wrote and co-produced called *Briars in the Cotton Patch.*

Twinkle M is a student residing in India, Asia. She has loved reading her entire life. She has won medals in English Olympiad, including a distinction, but this is the first piece of writing She is sending out to publish. Apart from writing, she enjoys a quiet life with the interruptions of academics.

Shana Chartier was born in Littleton, Colorado, and lived there for sixteen years before moving to Amherst, New Hampshire. Enthralled by New England's lush beauty, she has made her home in a little town called Merrimack. Shana currently lives with her husband Shane, daughters Evelyn and Amelia, and two crazy cats named Kylo and Leia. She has published YA, New Adult, Contemporary Fiction, Romance, and a children's picture book, as well as many short stories and poetry.

Edy Fudge and her husband William live in Clive, a suburb of Des Moines, Iowa and are retired. Both like mysteries and novels set in historical settings. Previously they have been re-enactors as members of the *Society for Creative Anachronism* and the *Army of the Southwest*. Edy has won several local awards for fiction and poetry. She is often included in *Lyrical Iowa,* the anthology of the *Iowa Poetry Association.* Edy became interested in the fantasy era of Steampunk as a member of the *Des Moines Science Fiction and Fantasy Association.*

Mariev, Erie Matriarch is a gonzo non-fiction magical realism writer, mystic intuitive who possesses an unusual set of psychological attributes: Intense paranormal abilities and expanded awareness, and a disposition for difficulty with authority. Her work has been published in print and online venues, including Farrago's Wainscot, Indigenous Fiction, Serendipity, The Bad Version, Shadows of the Mind Anthology, Fiction Brigade, Writing That Risks, Red Bridge Press, Real Lies, Zharmae Press, Tortured Souls, Scarlett River Press, Up, Do; Flash Fiction by Women Writers, Flapperhouse, Riddled With Arrows, Two Sisters Publishing and Advances in Parapsychological Research (Saybrook). More information on her work can be found at:

Www.MarievFinnegan.yolasite.com

Stephen Oliver is an ex-software engineer who spent many years of his life programming computers to make people's lives better. Since 2012, he has been working as a writer, self-publishing self-help books before switching to fiction. His genres include science fiction, space opera, fantasy, urban fantasy, horror, fairy tales, fairy stories, magical realism, noir, detective fiction, humour, YA, and children's stories.

Clark Boyd lives and works in the Netherlands. His fiction and essays have appeared in Scare Street, Fatal Flaw, Flumes, The Were-Traveler, The Esthetic Apostle, and various DBND horror anthologies. He's currently at work on a book about windmills. Or cheese. Maybe both.

R.A. Gerritse. As an author, host of the Twitter poetry prompt tag #vsspoem, and as lyricist for four different bands (Dissector, The Lust, GOOT, Loudborn), poetry is part of Randy Gerritse's every day—it even found its way into his novels. The social platform, in a way, has become the drafting pad for his poetic thoughts, where he is ever self-editing. He self-published a large bundle of his micro poetry, forged into a single, two-act epic poem called "The Rhythm of Life" on Amazon, while he is seeking representation for his debut Sci Fi-thriller novel "Clear Sight," and works on its sequel.

Christopher Yusko resides in the frozen wastes of Canada with his wife, two children and a cat. He remains on good terms with Christmas. Christopher spends his days working as a librarian. His fiction is influenced by Kelly Link, George Saunders and Haruki Murakami. This is his first published story.

Craig Crawford has always loved horror: reading it, watching it and writing it. He grew up on it, blaming his family for his fascination. He has published seven short horror stories over the last year with seven different presses, which he has posted on his website (craiglcrawford-books.com).

David Allen Voyles has written two collections of original horror stories, *The Thirteenth Day of Christmas* and *Tales from the Hearse*, filled with tales he told while hosting *Dark Ride Tours* in Asheville, NC. Playing the role of gravedigger/storyteller Virgil Nightshade, Voyles entertained guests as they were transported to various spooky sites in a 1972 Cadillac hearse converted for that purpose. Having taught literature for thirty years, Voyles is no stranger to weird tales and horror fiction in general. His love for authors such as Ray Bradbury, Stephen King, Anne Rice, Shirley Jackson, and Neil Gaiman, as well as a lifelong obsession with Halloween, ensured that it was just a matter of time before he published his own tales of terror. In addition to publishing his stories in print, he is also the creator of the horror podcast, *Dark Corners*, a bi-weekly program of original horror stories which can be found on your favorite podcast app.